BELOVED

SEQUEL TO BEHOLDEN

FRANCESCA CRISPO

IBSN: 979-8-9885719-9-5

Cover illustration by Melissa Hudson - www.mhudson-illustration.com

Editing and proofreading by Three Fates Editing - www.threefatesediting.com

Formatting by Nezhda Seyfulova - www.nezhformatting.org

CONTENTS

CONTENT WARNING

This book contains harsh/vulgar/explicit language; explicit descriptions of sexual acts including those which may be considered taboo; alcohol consumption and overuse; death and dead bodies; mention of kidnapping, abuse, and neglect; mention of harm/injury to a child; death of animal-like characters; blood and violence; use of weapons; indirect commentary on cults/religion.

To those of us looking for a place to belong.

The Invisible Cliffs
The Last Straw
KINGDOM OF BARRIEN
Grimmaker Woods
Beast's Breath Tavern
Dalcester Street Market
DALCESTER
Tuck'd I
GARDENS OF WYSTERUM
Moondew Tavern
Wyrmhole

THE WILD OPEN
KINGDOM OF EMYNOR
End of the Road Inn
Max's House
Isle of Wyrms
Wyrmhole

OPEN WIDE

MAX

"Max, seriously, you have to open up!"

I scowled. I did that a lot around people, not least of all August, and since he was accompanied by a dentist who happened to be trying to shove my tooth back in my mouth, I scowled at him, too. "It's really not that important," I argued through my lips, which I'd pressed into a thin line to fend off my attackers. "It's not even near the front of my mouth. Who cares? It's just one too—" I must've opened my mouth a little too wide at one point because the dentist managed to shove a finger in there as if to keep it open, immediately putting him at the top of my shit list. I bit down on his finger, the rest of my teeth perfectly capable of doing their job even without their missing friend, and the older man yowled like a wounded cat. All I could think was that dentists should probably be more familiar with being bitten. I was more than happy to be the person to give him a reality check; don't shove your fingers in someone's mouth and expect not to get chomped.

Some time later, when he'd scolded both myself and August about manners (I didn't have any) and the value of his time (way more valuable than the likes of me could imagine), Dr. Shuyler took off from the castle with his bag in tow. The last few scraggly wisps of hair on his balding head fluttered with his angry shuffling. My tooth remained on the floor where it had flown after I bit the man. August stood there with his arms across his chest, leaning heavily on his uninjured leg. "That's the third dentist, Max."

"And that's the millionth time I've told you that it's just a tooth. I don't need you paying some grand fee to have it put back in my mouth." How much was having a tooth in your head really worth? Definitely not as much as the dentists were quoting August. The idea that I'd be indebted to him for that much made me uneasy.

"If it's so unimportant," August said with a long sigh, picking up the white bud off of the floor, "why are you still holding on to it?" He didn't acknowledge the cost. He never did. "Why not just toss it?"

I snatched my tooth from his hand and tucked it back into a pouch on my hip, still frustrated. When the tooth hit the bottom of the leather pouch with a satisfying "plunk," I felt a little more in control. "I don't know," I muttered. It was true; I wasn't sure why I had held on to this detached piece of my body for so long, but I couldn't bring myself to chuck it. "Maybe I'll make you a necklace with it, to remember me by." That was the first time I had acknowledged the potential provisional nature of our relationship out loud, and I was as shocked as he was when it slipped from my mouth.

August's tone changed suddenly, the hurt in his eyes clear. He was, and always had been, so expressive… the opposite of me. "To remember you by? And where are you going that I'd need something to remember you by, Nightshade?"

August called me that a lot, ever since our moment on the hill, which we could see clearly from our bedroom window. He'd called me Maxine once before, but our disagreement following that event had ruined my full name in our relationship; I wouldn't let him use it anymore. He called me Max here and there, but Nightshade was his go-to. It was cute. He was cute when he said it, even if he was scolding me playfully… or when he panted "oh god, Nightshade" on the verge of exploding—that was even nicer. Before I could even formulate a clever response to cover the truth, we were interrupted. Just in time because I really didn't know how to explain what I'd said, but the thoughts had been bubbling up a lot lately…

"Yeah, Max, where're we going?" My kid brother, Danny, stood in the doorway. He looked just like me, or at least that's what everyone kept telling us, and I frequently had to remind people that he was my brother, not my son. It had been so long since I'd seen my parents that I couldn't remember which of them he looked like. He held a small dagger, one of my hand-me-downs, and was chipping away at a branch, whittling something or just doing it to be destructive. Chips of wooden shrapnel clung to the front of his shirt. I'd told him a million times that he didn't need weapons here in Barrien. That he was safe now, and that he could busy himself with normal kid things. But he almost always argued with me. He wanted to climb and explore and make and break things, not play games with other kids. Wonder where he got that from. "And how come that old man just ran out of here swearin' under his breath, huh? You know, he even said the 'fuck' word, Max, and you always said that decent people don't use that word."

I groaned internally. The "fuck" word? The way I would've slapped this child upside the head if it hadn't been frowned upon. No matter how many times I talked to him about manners, it was still very clear that I had raised him in a cabin in the middle of the Wild Open. I guess that's what happens when you don't have anyone to talk to but yourself for weeks on end; who do you really need manners for? "You," I told Danny, approaching him with a playful look of accusation on my face, "are going to school." I glanced up at the wall clock in our chambers. "You're late again."

My little brother was whining before the words even left his mouth. For all of his skills and independence, he was still a ten-year-old. "What, like they're gonna tell the king's... friend that her brother can't be late to school? Besides, I still don't get why I have to—"

I had a hand on his shoulder and was steering him out of the room before he could finish his sentence. The last thing I needed was him being blatantly ungrateful right in front of August, who had gone out of his way to welcome us into his home and provide us with every amenity imaginable. Guilt skittered around within me, crawling under my flesh, and I pushed it down like I had been doing a lot lately. Once I had him out in the hallway, I peeked back into our room. "See you this afternoon," I told August, who still stood there with a lopsided grin. It was nice to see the lightness in his face again. Following our trip to Emynor and his return home, he had spiraled. I had tried to comfort him to the best of my ability, but it was hard to know how. I'd led a hardened life myself, but it was nothing compared to what August had gone through... the betrayal by his family, the discovery of his true origin and real mother, all of the blame that had been placed on him for decisions he didn't recall being part of. Unlike me, he wore his heart on his sleeve, and it was painfully obvious when he was hurting. It was a relief when lightness started to find its way back into his face. I gave him one last look, soaking up the new warmth that radiated from him, and then headed to the door.

And just like that, we headed off into the day... and into domesticity.

NORMALCY

AUGUST

"Wait." I caught Max's hand just before she slipped out of the room again and pulled her to me. The way her body pressed up against mine immediately relaxed my muscles, any stress about the day to come melting away in an instant. She was small, but the effect was as if she had enveloped my entire body within hers; I just wanted to be near her, with her, consumed by her if I could. Even with her bullheadedness, I couldn't get enough of this woman. "Tell him you'll catch up to him."

Her lips parted in preparation for protest, as they often did, and I cut her off with a pleading smile. I could sense the exact moment it took effect. Max wasn't always outwardly expressive, but her cheeks went pink with the threat of a full-on blush, and she gave me an exasperated look before peeking out into the hallway. "Danny, go on! I'll be there in a minute."

"A minute?" I whispered with a laugh. "That's not giving me very much credit. Besides, he knows the way to school..." Even though Barrien was safer than anywhere else the pair had lived, Max insisted on walking her brother to his classes each day. He'd hinted that he wasn't enjoying all of the extra hovering, so holding her back was doing both of us a favor. I was enjoying the relationship I'd built with Danny; it was new to me to have that type of friendship with another male, and while I knew it was my job to be a figure of authority as well, we often shared secret eyerolls when being lectured by Max. I wasn't sure if we connected so easily because he was very grown up for a ten-year-old or because I had the maturity of a pre-teen boy, but whatever it was, our relationship worked. I only hoped that it was also a relief for Max that we got along and not just additional work to keep two rowdy children in check at all times.

"Well, are you sure you *have* more than a minute?" she teased, falling back into my arms easily. I remembered not long ago when I'd just wished she would look at me without hatred in her gaze; I never imagined I'd be lucky enough to end up here with her, laughing, teasing, joyful… she *wanted* to be near me and seemed as drawn to me as I was to her. "Don't you have all sorts of kingly duties to attend to?"

"They can wait a little… I'd rather attend to you," I told her, brushing a lock of raven hair from her face to tuck it behind her ear. The gesture exposed the golden curve of her neck, which made my mouth water.

"I'm one of your duties?" Her expression was a mix of curious and offended, another classic Max expression. She was quick to put up her defenses, even around me.

"Sometimes, when you're insatiable. But I'm nothing if not committed to satisfying you." She blushed again, and heat coursed through my veins. Ah, what a delight. I'd never tire of having that effect on her; it was only fair when she could snap her fingers and I'd bend to her will without protest. "What do you have planned for the day?" I took her by the hand and led her over to the main window in our shared room. I liked that it was *our* room, but I wished that Max would take more ownership of it. I'd tried many times over the previous months to expand Max's wardrobe, for her sake, and provide her with anything she wanted—trinkets or otherwise—to make the room seem more like ours and less like a bachelor pad, but she resisted. Either that, or she dutifully took the items and stored them away in the wardrobe I had brought in for her. At this point she was keeping a dragon's hoard of untouched items in there. Meanwhile, Danny wasted no time in accepting gifts to fill his room down the hall with. I liked that boy. Why not take what you can and let yourself enjoy life? I wished that Max had that tendency, too.

This window, though, was such a special part of our space...

"I thought I might take Wraith for a ride," Max mused aloud, following my lead. "She doesn't get out much anymore. She's getting kinda fat in the stables, though I'm sure she doesn't mind..." When she followed my gaze to the window, she added, "Looking for something?"

"Mmm." I pulled her up next to me and looked out of the glass with her, my fingers tracing lazy shapes on the fabric covering her hip. "Just sharing my favorite spot with you," I told her. I pointed out into the distance. "See, that's the spot where we got ready for the ball together and—"

"And the spot where I scoped out your room so I could kidnap you." I didn't need to look right at her to know that Max was watching me with a raised eyebrow and a curious expression on her face. I had no doubt that she was concerned by the way I romanticized my kidnapping. "Funny that you recall it differently than I do."

"*And*," I said, dismissing her need to dwell on the rather negative beginning of our relationship, and gave her hand a small squeeze, "that's where I saw you and Danny finally come back. I swear I looked out this window almost all day every day while you were gone, Nightshade." When we finally met each other's gaze again, Max's golden skin was pink again with a flustered blush. There was no way she'd expected this sentimental side of me when we had first met. I hadn't expected it—hell, I didn't even know that it existed within me, but Max had brought me face-to-face with many buried parts of my soul.

"I'm glad you're here," I said. And I was. So glad. Max looked up at me with such earnest curiosity, reminding me her past was as scarred and difficult as mine. I stroked her cheek with my thumb before kissing her. The oxygen left my lungs in a rush, and just like every other time I'd kissed Max the Menace, I thought it might not be such a bad way to die. She sucked on my lower lip and I growled in response. "You don't hate it when I'm sappy like this."

"Shut up," she told me, then pulled me to her again by the back of my neck. When she tangled her nimble fingers in my curls, I groaned against her lips again. I was pliable, loose, willing to do whatever. Only for her. When she pulled away, breathless, and ran a curious fingertip over the scarred mountain range of my ear, she said, "I don't hate anything about you."

"That's probably the sweetest thing you've ever said to me," I told her, grinning so hard that my cheeks were already aching. It sounded like I was teasing her, but it was true; Max was a woman of few words, and anytime she spoke of me, of us, about our life together, my cup overflowed. She didn't hate anything about me when there was so much that I could see within me worth hating... and knowing Max, that statement meant that she probably even liked some things about me, perhaps even... "You know, Max, I l—"

"What about that minute?" Max pulled me down by my earlobe and placed another kiss on my lips, this time small and chaste, an appetizer perhaps.

I cleared my throat. "Right." Once my wits were about me again, I placed a hand on her hip and swiveled her around so that she was facing out the window again, her back toward me. "Now, where were we, Nightshade?" I leaned over her a little to peek out the window, this time looking down toward the courtyard instead of into the distance. "It's a nice day," I mused just as a few members of the court walked by, discussing who knows what, probably something that they made to sound far more important than it actually was. The end of summer was approaching, and the last whispers of warmth streamed in through the open window. "Lots of people out. Our people."

Max turned to me and poked a finger into my chest, a playful smirk on her face. "What are you getting at?"

I nudged her a little further forward so that she was up against the windowsill, her ass pressed back into my lap. "I just think it's important for the people—our people—to see you, you know?"

"Uh huh."

"So just let that beautiful face be seen, okay?" I told her, my lips grazing the rim of her ears as I instructed her. "Say hello, give them a wave, let them know that Max the Menace is acclimating to royal life just fine."

She turned her face so that our mouths were hardly a breath apart. "And what will you be doing?"

"I'll be here," I told her, surprised at the way my voice had transitioned from joyous playfulness to low and husky. I made quick work of her pants, sliding them down her ample hips before she could protest, and when she turned back to look at me, I clicked my tongue at her. "You're supposed to be greeting your people," I said seriously, then gestured for her to turn her attention back to the window by drawing a circle in the air.

"But—"

"That's an order." When I looked down at her hips again, I had to wipe my mouth on the back of my hand to stop from drooling on her. Her flesh, so golden and warm, called out to me. And, oh gods, was that a thong? One of our attendants had filled her drawers with clothing I was certain she'd never wear, but now, seeing the thin lace fabric against her flesh made me so hard I had to grab her waist to brace myself. "Fuck, Max... what are you wearing?" I traced my finger along the outline of her panties and groaned, using my free hand to unbuckle my belt. "I really wanted to take my time, but you're making it difficult... Bend over," I told her, frustrated at my lack of control. "Bend over and look out the window."

Her breath hitched in her throat, but she complied. When I slid the fabric of her panties aside and swiped a finger down the warm, damp slit of her pussy, I realized that one-minute promise might've been accurate. "Max..." I plunged one finger into her, my cock straining against my unbuckled pants, and marveled at the way she squeezed it.

"August..." She whimpered slightly, and I wondered if she was keeping a straight face for the numerous castle staff that were puttering around on the grounds below. She was notorious for being serious and holding it together whereas I could be read like a book, but then again, I'd never tested her poker face under circumstances like this. I knew that those below us couldn't see me; between the curtains and the angle of the window, I was sheathed in shadow.

"I'm going to fuck you so hard, Nightshade, you're gonna feel me in your throat." I wiggled another finger inside of her, using my other hand to pull my pants down. My belt clinked against the floor, a warning that I was going to be inside her soon, and my dick twitched in excitement. I was powerless against her... existence? She didn't even have to try to excite me, to seduce me, the clenching of her cunt against my fingers was enough for me to imagine the same on my cock; I could've come from the sensation alone.

My Nightshade was breathless when she asked me, "You want your people to see me getting fucked by their king?"

My mouth went dry at the suggestion. "They won't. They won't know. You're going to keep saying good morning and waving at them, and they won't have the slightest idea," I told her as I withdrew my fingers from the most delicious place on earth and used her slickness to wet my cock. I lined it up between her thighs and gripped her hip again, notching myself between her plush lips. "Maybe one day they'll be lucky enough to watch, but for now I've got you all to myself. Feel me, baby? Throbbing against your pussy?"

A chill coursed through her body, I could tell by the way goose-bumps rose on the flesh beneath my hand on her hip. I stroked her skin lazily with my thumb. "Y-yeah…" she murmured.

"Go on, Max. Fuck yourself onto my cock. Take it."

Max took me slow, leaning herself back like a cat stretching after a nap in the sun, and I watched in awe as she took me inch by inch until I was sheathed deep inside of her. She sat herself back on me, her throne, and wiggled her hips a little to make sure I was as deep as she could take me.

"Oh…" I bit my lip hard. "How do you feel?" I leaned forward to slide my free hand around us, between her thighs.

Max's voice was timid. "Full…"

"See how good we fit together?"

Max sighed, a soft, feathery sound of delight.

"*Good morning, my lady!*" a voice called from below and Max tensed beneath me, a delicious feeling that caused her to grip my cock even tighter. "*How are you doing this fine day?*" The gardener. When I had planned to fuck her in secret while she greeted the common people and castle staff, I hadn't expected the gardener to be the first person on the list. He was fine at his job, sure, but he was also handsome. I'd heard maids swooning over him on more than one occasion, and he was not discreet in his flirtatious nature with Max. Hell, some time ago *I* had considered that he might be an enjoyable playmate. I groaned internally and focused on the fact that she was sitting on my dick, not his. That was where she belonged, no matter how attractive the royal gardener was. He was a little shorter than me and more slender, his arms sporting lean, carved muscles from days of manual labor… and he was *blond.* I tried to shake the memory of his glistening smile from my mind.

"Shh, it's okay," I told her, stroking her flesh with the hand on her hip. Reassuring her during sex caused adrenaline to course through my veins; there was something delightfully masculine about being the one to keep her safe while also pushing her limits. My other hand wiggled between her clenched thighs to find her clit and massaged it lazily. "Let me take care of you. Talk to him." I rubbed her softly, tenderly, then pulled out of her and thrusted slowly back in. I could've stayed there forever, buried inside her warmth, but part of me wanted to watch her squirm when I made her come over and over again.

"Doing… alright, thank you," Max managed, clearing her throat mid-answer so that the gardener could hear her.

Much to her dismay, I was sure, that wasn't the end of their conversation. *"And where is our king today? He's very busy, no doubt!"* That bastard was trying to see if she was alone.

I pulled out of her again before finding a pace I liked and fucking her steadily. I was bent over her, covering her small body with my massive one, as she attempted to maintain her composure. The curtains and darkness of our bedroom allowed me to continue to talk to her without the man noticing. "That's so good," I told her, fucking her hard enough that the sound of my balls slapping against her flesh echoed throughout our chambers. The way her flesh gripped mine, slick, dripping, filled the air with other sounds I wouldn't soon forget. "You take me so good. You're gonna come already, Max, I can feel it. Maybe I don't care if you can't hide it from him."

"Y-you want him to see me come?" Max was gripping the windowsill as if to anchor her to the earth.

"Only because I'm the one making it happen," I said harshly. "He'll never get the privilege."

"My lady?"

I was fucking her hard and fast now, my fingertips boring holes into her hip while I rubbed her in perfect synchrony with my thrusting. "Come now, Nightshade. Come all over my cock, let go, give me what I want."

In perfect Max style, she fought. I couldn't get anything from her without effort. She fought against it and leaned forward over the windowsill as if she could escape the onslaught of sensation, panting suddenly beyond her ability to hide it, and flustered, no doubt. "He's... around, sir," she squeaked out before I flicked my fingertip over her clit one last time and sent her tumbling over the edge. She whimpered at the same time she tried to finish her response to him: "Very busy these days!"

I couldn't help but laugh against her shoulder as she came, shuddering almost violently. I didn't notice when the gardener finally fucked off, but Max slumped forward hard against the windowsill, and I pulled the curtains across the window in front of them so that we were in the near darkness of our private room. I was still deep inside of her as we rode out her first orgasm and she whimpered in frustration, "You're an ass!"

I tsked at her, swatting her ass playfully. "You love me."

"Shut up," she told me again, then pulled herself upright a little more so that she could pull forward off of my dick. I gripped her hip hard, suddenly panicked that I might lose that plush warmth.

"Where are you—" but she pulled almost all of the way off of me only to slam back onto my cock again, nearly knocking the wind out of me. My injured leg ached as I braced myself against the impact. "That'll shut me up, ugh, fuck."

"It hasn't worked yet," she scolded me between frazzled panting.

"Keep trying," I encouraged her, pulling up my shirt for a full view of my cock stuffed inside of her. I pinned the fabric under my chin, then used my newly free hand to grip her ass.

"Like this?" she purred, glancing over her shoulder at me. Her cheeks were flushed, and the low light of the room reflected off of the silky darkness of her hair as it tumbled down her back. Again and again, she pulled off of me, then took me deeply again, as if she needed it as badly as I did.

"Oh, shit..." When she reached between her thighs and ran her nails down the flesh of my balls, then used her slender fingers to grip them firmly and pull me forward, I leaned over her and bit into her shoulder as punishment. "It's not fair... the way you unravel me so easily, Nightshade."

THE INVISIBLE CLIFFS, AGAIN

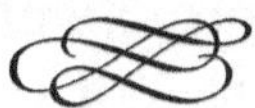

MAX

What's a mercenary to do when her little brother is off at school today and her boyfriend… er, lover… er, partner… is busy running a kingdom? That was a question I'd never in a million years imagined myself asking and yet, there I was, sufficiently fucked and with very little to do. I supposed other women in my position might spend the remainder of the day taking walks in the garden, or being tended to by chambermaids, or um, braiding… their… hair? Again, I'd never imagined having "little to do," given how the previous ten years of my life had required me to stay busy or die. You see, Barrien was shockingly limited on its number of monster infestations, and because I didn't have to worry about money for the first time in my life, I didn't go seeking out work in other towns. In fact, August had strongly advised against it, insisting that he'd be concerned for my safety the whole time I was gone… and Danny would throw a fit if he knew I was off slaying monsters when he was stuck at a desk learning arithmetic. I couldn't blame him. There was some part of our biology that longed for the chaos of the open road and the rush of fending for ourselves.

When I woke up a bit later after a brief nap, I did the next best thing… I packed up my usual gear and made my way to the Invisible Cliffs with Wraith. It had been a long time since we'd last been there. In fact, the last time had been with August, who had since condemned the use of the cliffs for mining the calcinite[1] (or the Neon Shackle). As a result, it seemed the elves of Emynor had taken his reign seriously and believed, at least to some extent, that he was attempting to remedy the horrific damage his parents had done. As far as I knew, August hadn't been back to the cliffs since we'd gone together. Perhaps his heart couldn't stand the reminder of what they had been used for.

Even with all of the healing we'd done together, there were some things that we simply hadn't spoken much about. His real mother was one of them. The last I'd heard about her was the night he'd confronted the former king and queen… and I found that I just didn't know how to broach the topic of his suffering. But I knew, deep down inside his carefree exterior, there was likely a man aching to face his past. Perhaps he wanted to know more about his mother, and understand if she was a good person or just as wicked as the woman who had adopted, butchered, and used him. I thought, perhaps, part of him wanted a chance to mourn her. Or was it better to let him push it deep down inside, as he seemed to do with most serious things?

Years of being alone had made me awkward at interacting with other people: a fact that being part of the kingdom of Barrien forced me to face on a regular basis. I just wasn't conditioned for social life, let alone royal social life. I was withdrawn, introverted, sure, but I had spent a lot of time on the road thinking. I'd come to terms with my demons, with the loss of my parents, with the hand I'd been dealt. I had made peace with the fact that I had killed many people in my career and as a result, there wasn't much in my past that kept me up at night. If anything, my current predicament as a newcomer in a society that was completely foreign to me gave me nightmares. August, in all of his genuine, good-hearted optimism and obliviousness, hadn't seemed to notice the ways I didn't fit in.

Wraith and I made our way to the cliffs, and I found that the farther away from the castle we got, the less worried I was about my appearance or the way I was holding myself. I settled into the saddle just in time for us to approach our destination, which was shockingly close; August, too, had thought we were miles away when I'd taken him there, when in reality we were just around the corner from the castle. The cliffs, now blocked off with an array of barriers and threatening signs, felt different than they had before. They were deserted, silent. No longer did the repetitive clink of mining tools echo through the valley of the cliffs. It was a good thing, but it made the place feel haunted… I suppose in a way, it was. There was no doubt that the ghosts of those who lay at the bottom of the rock face were trapped there forever.

Wraith huffed, snorted, then kicked a hoof into the ground. "You don't have to get too close," I assured her. Neither of us wanted a repeat of our last close call at the cliffs. "I'll go the rest of the way." When I hopped off of her back, she nudged me with her nose and huffed again. "I know, I know. It's a long shot, but what else do I have to do with my time these days? It's not like I'm going to go shopping or get my nails—"

A voice snapped me from my rant, probably much to Wraith's delight. "That's a long way down." I gazed along the rim of the cliff to find a figure ten feet away, staring carefully over the edge of the cliff much like August had when I'd first brought him there. The figure was short, lithe, built similar to myself, and mostly concealed in a long, black cloak. "Are you sure it's worth the trip?"

Wow, Juniper's contacts sure just… jumped right into conversation. When I didn't respond right away, the cloaked figure closed the gap between us and approached me with an outstretched hand. The sleeve of her cloak slid up during the gesture, exposing a slender arm covered in tattoos and a hand gloved in what looked like black silk; the clawlike points of her nails were obvious even through the fabric. "I'm Sidney."

"Max." I didn't shake her hand, but instead looked her up and down, my inner skeptic making itself known. "So, you're the witch."

Sidney laughed, a cheerful, honest sound that suggested she didn't fear me in the slightest. "And you're the mercenary. Just as welcoming as Juniper said you'd be." *Leave it to June to paint a far too accurate picture of me.* She withdrew her hand and laced it with the other in front of her lap before turning toward the rock ledge again. I had to admit that her nails looked cool, even through her gloves… kind of like a cat. Maybe I'd reconsider the whole manicure thing once I got back to the castle. "What… or who exactly are you looking for down there?"

I sighed, feeling defeated at the concept already. It was such a stretch that it felt silly if I thought about it for too long. "The body of an elf," I told her, unsure of just how much backstory she would need in order to help me. "I don't know anything but her name." Even that I'd had to pry out of August's dad. It hadn't been a pretty sight, but not in the dirty torture kind of way and more in the shockingly pathetic kind of way.

"You're telling me you don't even remember her name? That's disgusting." I wasn't outraged when I told him this through the bars of the Barrien castle prison, nor was I surprised. In fact, I was bored by how predictable King August II's nastiness was. I kicked my boots into the dirty ground of the castle prison before I remembered that I was trying to keep them clean. These were my *new* boots after all, the ones I had insisted on buying with my own hard-earned money from killing the Umbral[2], even though August had offered to get me a pair in every color for the rest of my life. These were my boots, and I would keep them clean. I kicked one last pebble toward the steel bars of the cell door and sighed in irritation at its inhabitants. The pebble ricocheted off the bars with a clink.

"It was a fling!" he argued, the flesh around his collar red with embarrassment. His wife stood silently behind him, arms folded across her chest, and I could only imagine what their time together in the prison had been like so far. I wondered if she was prodding him in the back to say, *Be careful what you tell her because you'll have to face me afterward. My wrath is far worse than any mercenary.*

"Sure, but then she came back with your child," I reminded him. "You didn't think to catch a name then?"

When he stammered an unintelligible response and glanced sideways at his unimpressed wife, I knew we weren't going to get any further with them in the same room. I swung the door to their cell open and pointed my blade at him. "Get out. You're coming with me."

The former queen was quick to argue, oddly protective of this man whom she could hardly stand otherwise. "What do you think you're—"

I silenced the former queen when I turned my blade to her, and she put her hands up in exhaustion. Why defend this man anyway? What good did it do her to protect him? Once I had escorted him out of earshot, I cornered him impatiently. "The name, let's go." I gestured for him to hurry up with outstretched fingers. It was late, and August would be wondering where I was if I didn't crawl into bed with him soon. Mmm, bed… that was a luxury I wouldn't soon take for granted. These idiots, meanwhile, probably had no concept of time this far underground… not to mention the former king was likely dying for a break from his wife.

"Callianthe."

"That was quick." I eyed him curiously and suppressed a sigh of disappointment; part of me had *wanted* to torture the name out of him. The name had come so easily, so smoothly off his tongue, as if he'd said it, or at least thought it, every day for decades. It hadn't been a fling. I swallowed hard at the thought and forced myself not to go down that rabbit hole; I didn't have the time, or a reason, to wonder what it had been like to see the woman he loved pushed off the Invisible Cliffs at the order of the other woman he maybe, sort of, tolerated. It was a sad story, to be sure, but he interrupted my musings with his own pitiful pleading. Whatever came of my attempt to provide August with some closure would not involve sharing this interaction with him. Knowing that his father had actually loved his mother and still marched her to her death would not soften the blow of his loss.

"You can't imagine how challenging this has been for me a-a-and… how much it has tested my marriage," he blubbered, his once stoic gaze now pleading, as if I were the sympathetic type… I wasn't.

I shook my head. "No, it's not that I can't imagine. I just don't care."

The former king wrung his hands together. "You won't tell Celine, will you? She'd never look at me again if she knew, and I—"

"This isn't about you, it's for *him*." I gestured up to the ceiling, knowing that August was somewhere higher up in the castle, far away from the filth that had called themselves his parents for so many years. I could've yelled at the former king for his narcissism; why should I care if being imprisoned had challenged his marriage? He hadn't given a second thought to ruining the lives of his son and his ex-lover.

"You really love him, don't you?"

I groaned, this time out loud, and rolled my eyes. "We're not going to bond over this, old man."

SIDNEY SCRUNCHED her nose in distaste. "That's it? You don't have… I don't know, something that belonged to her? A description? A lock of her hair?"

Ah, yes, let me just pull a lock of her hair from my pocket, I thought… *And here's a painting that the king happened to keep in his bedside drawer, as well as the exact coordinates of her body's location while I'm at it.* "Nope. Tough, I know," I muttered. I reached into my pocket and pulled out a small bag of crystals that I'd been hanging on to since I decided I wanted to find August's mom and lay her to rest. I tossed the bag toward the witch, and when she caught it, I assumed she was at least still somewhat on board. "Can you do it or not?"

"Oh, I can do it, babe," Sidney said with a chuckle. With that, she plopped down at the edge of the cliff and snapped her fingers. Almost immediately, a bag hovered over to her from gods-know-where and parked itself immediately next to where she was sitting. Cool. Really cool. I wanted one of those, too. Maybe I was cut out to be a witch and not a mercenary…

I looked at Wraith, who was also staring at the magic bag with a deep fascination on her dark face. It didn't have legs, and yet, it was walking. Bizarre. "You don't come when you're called, but a bag can do it," I whispered harshly in her direction. She snorted in defiance, and I rolled my eyes before turning back to Sidney. "Well, how am I going to find her? I can't bring up every skeleton I find."

Sidney was rummaging through her bag when she called over to me. "Well, you're gonna…" She paused, grunting a little as she moved items around within the vessel, the force she was exerting seeming inappropriate for how small the bag was. What could possibly be in there that sounded like she was rearranging boulders? "… climb that cute little mercenary butt of yours down the cliff. Is it still climbing if you're going down? Sounds like an 'up' kind of thing to me, but"— more shifting, moving, then she popped her head back up and looked at me—"you'll go down, and I'll help you find her. You're sure she's down there?"

"Yes, though I don't know how much of her is left. It's been thirty-something years, and the conditions at the bottom of the cliff can't be favorable..."

"And it's a loooong way down," Sidney commented, peering over the edge again curiously. She grimaced. "Lots of bumps."

"Yep." I tightened the straps of my pack and weapons, then attached a coil of rope to my hip. I'd need it to get the body back up. Afterward, I tied another rope around my upper legs and waist before anchoring it on a boulder at the top of the cliffs. I hadn't really planned much beyond that because I wasn't sure I'd even find her, let alone have a body to do something with after all was said and done.

"Seems unlikely that there are just... bodies..." Sidney mused, finally pulling a crystal sphere from the bag and holding it up to the light before polishing it with her robe. It glistened, even in the overcast light. "I mean, you'd know better than I would, but when was the last time a pit of death *wasn't* guarded by a creature from hell itself?"

"Not much I can do about that until I get down there." I shrugged. Then I looked to Sidney again when I noticed the long pause in our conversation. Her eyes were slightly narrowed and a finger bent on her chin. "What?"

"You love him, huh?"

I scoffed. "What is it with everyone and love?" I scrubbed my face with my fingertips before adjusting the straps of my pack and my weapons. Maybe I didn't need weapons to scale a cliff, but the likelihood of this pit being filled with living dead—or, as the witch had mentioned, a hell beast—seemed pretty high. "Just because he's all I think about and all I want is to make him happy and bring him peace and closure, doesn't mean—"

The witch was staring at me over the rim of her glasses, the half-moon shape of which seemed utterly useless to me. "Uh huh."

"How do you even know there's a *him*?" I blurted out suddenly, annoyed that I had told more than I'd wanted to tell this person I had only just met. "Never mind. Juniper. Just help me find this body, okay?"

Sidney waved me off. "We'll find her, mercenary. I just don't know what else you'll find down there while you're at it." She gave the glass sphere one more rub and then held it out to me, but when I grabbed it gracelessly and tossed it between both of my hands, she winced. "Be careful with that."

"Sorry…" I offered sheepishly, then tucked the orb into one of the leather pouches on my hip and gave it a soft pat. Leave it to me to toss around a witch's relic like it was an uninteresting rock. "Expensive?"

"You could say that. It's kind of like… an extension of my soul, so you know, don't drop it… or I'll haunt your ass forever." She winked at me.

I swallowed hard, then double-checked the strap holding the sphere's pouch to my body. Note to self: Do not drop the witch's soul sphere. "Got it."

I sort of knew what to expect to find at the bottom of the Invisible Cliffs because I'd been the one to tell August what was down there. Well, most of what was down there. It was his own adoptive mother that told him who else was resting at the base. I didn't know what almost thirty years of decay would leave of her—just bones, if anything—but if I could find any remnants of August's birth mother, I thought perhaps he'd like to lay them to rest.

Climbing down the cliffs was a feat. I tired quicker than I expected, and my grip wasn't nearly as strong as it once was. I wondered how so many workers had clung to the side of this cliff, swinging axes and other tools into the rough face to pick away green chunks of poison for the kingdom's bidding… and if they fell, they joined the piles of people below, doomed to be forgotten in the rubble. No one ever retrieved the bodies. The cliffs hadn't been off limits for long, so the lower I went, the more the scent of death increased.

It wasn't new to me, that smell, but it wasn't one I'd ever be comfortable with. The air was sickly-sweet and rotten, like bad meat mixed with odors that were unique only to dead human bodies. But something was off, wrong... yes, more wrong than the fact that I was approaching a pit of bodies. They should've been lower, less of them after this long. I should've been headed for sad piles of bones, crunching and dry beneath my boots, but instead I found a foothold much sooner than I expected, and what I stepped on gave in under my feet: bodies upon bodies upon bodies. Not the remnants of bodies... not a few scattered bodies on top of skeletons, but a mass gravesite of near-perfectly preserved bodies. When I exhaled, my breath briefly clouded my vision; it was cold down there. Cold enough to keep the bodies that had fallen from decomposing and instead, allowing them to pile upon each other. I took a steadying breath and dared to look directly under me only to be met by the bluish face of a young man, probably my age, which was distorted in the shape of a horrified scream. He was frozen in time with the rest of them.

On one hand, this meant that it would be possible for me to actually find August's mother's body. On the other hand, there were a lot of bodies down there... and many of them lay still with their eyes wide open in terror. I would have to face these ghastly onlookers in order to find what I was searching for... The kingdom of Barrien had carried out so many executions between Callianthe's death and the closure of the cliffs. Dead cliff workers would also be there, along with who knew what else. I didn't know enough about Barrien to understand all of the acts this area had been used for, but could imagine that murders were hidden there and one or more people who had jumped purposefully to their own deaths.

My head swam as I neared the bottom. The worst part, I decided right away, was that there was nowhere to land or stand except for the literal bodies of people. It felt wrong, disrespectful, and for some reason I convinced myself that balancing on their legs was kinder than stepping on chests or arms or heads, so that was what I did. It took me a moment to get my footing and pull out the soul sphere (I didn't know if it had a real name, but I'd dubbed it this in my mind). I looked up through the fog and could barely make out Sidney's shape at the edge of the cliff. "Witch! You up there?"

Her response came from the globe in my hand instead of above, and I directed my attention down to it as it spoke. "Where else would I be? You got abandonment issues or something?"

I grumbled to myself. Abandonment issues, yeah right. "I don't even know what I'm looking for!" I told the glass ball.

"Take a breath," the globe told me, Sidney's voice faraway and ethereal as it filtered through our conduit. "Calm yourself. This could take a while."

"That's what I'm afraid of!" I tried to take a steadying breath and failed, so I gripped the globe and rolled it between my fingers, savoring the smooth coolness of the sphere. I stopped only when I realized I was fondling Sidney's soul. "Sorry…"

"Show me what we're working with," Sidney chirped between chuckles.

I glanced around, the mist of the base of the pit shifting and revealing bodies left and right, all frozen in their last moments. Many were on their backs, but some were flipped over, as if they had landed still alive and attempted to crawl away. Others had fallen sideways, landing on limbs that crunched and snapped and settled in unnatural positions. "You sure you want to see this? It's… bleak."

"It's a pit of dead bodies," the sphere told me. "Of course it's bleak. Isn't that something you're used to?"

"I'm not a monster," I muttered, steadying myself as my weight cracked the shin of the body beneath me and I stumbled a little. I steadied the sphere and pointed it in one direction so that Sidney could get a clear view of my surroundings, assuming it was some sort of portal or looking glass for her to peer through. "You getting this?"

"Yeeeesh. All in the name of love, huh?" Sidney's voice was clearer now and no longer muffled, as if she'd finally tuned in to her special tool. "Give me a moment."

I waited as patiently as I could when knee-deep in death and followed her instructions as she told me to move the sphere left, right, and forward. "An elf, huh?" she asked after a few moments of silence. They were agonizing.

"Yeah, named Callianthe."

"Where are you, Callianthe?" Sidney asked no one in particular. "I'm not getting anything yet. Start walking, Max."

I leaned against the face of the cliff with half of my body and held the glass orb against my other side as I shuffled, trying my best to step on as few people as possible. "Not sure if I believe in an afterlife," I muttered to myself, "but if there is one, I'm guessing that stepping on dead bodies is sending me straight to the bad part."

Sidney chuckled. "Eh, I don't think it's that black-and-white." I could picture her shrugging.

Jagged chips of calcinite dug into my shoulder; they were too far down to have been safely mined by the cliffside workers, and despite their magical properties having no effect on me, their physical properties were cutting holes into my sleeve and the flesh underneath. I winced, the hot stickiness of blood trickling down the inside of my clothing and against my flesh. "Hope you don't have a weak stomach," I mumbled, my own insides turning when I inadvertently crushed the arm of another victim of the cliffs. There was a small path against the cliffside, the size of one of my boots, but walking on it alone was proving difficult. I was forced to decide between respecting the dead by not walking on them and preserving my own body, the strength of which was already waning following the climb. I still had to go back up, and with another body, when all was said and done.

"How'd she die?" Sidney asked, obviously trying to distract me. "I mean, I see how, with the whole thrown-off-a-cliff thing, but why?"

"Slept with the king," I told her, continuing my walk until told otherwise. As I leaned into the bodies and away from the cliffside, the cool air of the pit soothed my new cuts. "Got pregnant. Showed up with the baby. Queen found out, and well, here we are."

"Oh, Callianthe," Sidney lamented through the orb in my hand. Her tone was sad, sadder than I'd expected. It was a depressing tale to be sure, but neither of us actually knew the woman... and yet, I felt the same desperate heaviness when I thought about it for more than a moment. Did August feel it, too? Did he mourn his mother, her life cut short by greed, and all that she would have experienced with him had she lived? My heart ached at the thought of a young August growing up with a mother who truly loved him and not holed up in his bedroom until he'd discovered the only way to initiate human connection.

"Max, stop."

I did as I was told without thinking and snapped another bone when I set my foot down. My stomach lurched. "What is it? Are we close?" My heart thudded painfully in my chest.

"Closer, closer... yes, there. She's there." I shuffled slowly until Sidney's final statement, then looked down ahead of me. There lay a large man, older than me, and one who had obviously spent his life working in these cliffs; his body was muscled and scarred, and he was still tangled in the ropes that had failed him while working. One rope remained in his frozen hand, the palm of which bore a bluish-purple wound from where he had tried to pull himself up as a last attempt to save himself.

"I really don't have time for games, Sidney," I told the orb, squatting down to get a closer look at the man, "but I don't think that this gigantic man is August's birth mother."

I didn't have to see her face to know that she was rolling her eyes. "*Under*, Max."

"Shit."

"Set me down," Sidney instructed. "Or put me in your pocket. You're going to need both hands to move him."

I did as I was told and tucked Sidney's sphere safely into the pouch on my hip before crouching down into the mound of bodies again and attempting to roll the man over. Months of being a lazy royal really had made me weaker; even the calluses on my hands had gone soft. I yanked on his clothing and then shoved myself under his shoulder to get some leverage before flopping him gracelessly onto his front. A poof of dust escaped his clothes as I did so, but that wasn't all. I turned in time to see a small piece of paper, a drawing, flutter out of his shirt. When I picked it up, I found the familiar faces of two young girls that August and I had helped with their tooth faerie[3] infestation not long ago; we had been right in assuming their father had fallen to his death. I tucked the drawing back into the man's shirt, ignoring the way his stiff, cold body felt against my hands, and made a mental note to visit that family as soon as I could.

"Well?" came Sidney's muffled voice from my hip. I had been avoiding looking at what, or who, was beneath the townsperson's body.

When I found Callianthe, I cried. I didn't know what came over me, but I couldn't help it. I pulled her still, cold, lifeless body into my arms and her hair, frosty with the cold, crunched against my arms. It was curly, a warm brown that looked just like August's... and her gaze, a forever-open look of shock and betrayal, was softened only by the warm green of her eyes. They were a different color than August's, but their shape was the same. Now that I had found her, I would've known this woman anywhere.

Suddenly I wasn't so sure if bringing her back was the right thing. It was painful to see her, so young and so innocent, and I wondered if this would bring closure to August or just more heartache. When her frigid hair shifted slightly, I caught sight of the pointed tip of one of her ears, and a shuddering sigh escaped me. That was what August's ears would've looked like had he not been butchered by his adoptive mother. I wiped my face with the back of my sleeve, my snot and tears beginning to freeze to my face already.

I kneeled there for longer than I should have, in the silence of my own mourning, before Sidney gingerly piped up. "It's getting dark, Max. It's time to bring her up if that's what you want to do."

"Yeah, got it..." I muttered, not sure if Sidney had heard me, but not really caring, and began to fasten my rope around Callianthe. I wished her eyes would close, but they were frozen in place, so she watched me prepare her body for transport. I took as much time as I thought I had, wrapping the rope around her carefully and double-checking each knot before attaching it to the rope I'd used to lower myself down. I gave it a small tug to let Wraith know that I was ready for her to be pulled up. "Gently!" I called, putting my hands on the rock wall again in preparation for climbing it, giving my rope a swift tug to ensure it was still tied up at the top. I had barely gotten myself a couple of feet off of the bodies below when the cliffside rumbled. Yes, rumbled. I froze, and so did Wraith if the sudden halt in Callianthe's body was an indicator.

"Uhhh, Sidney?" I reached down with one hand to unsnap the pouch on my hip before quickly grabbing hold of the cliffside again.

"Yeah... remember my whole hell beast speech?"

I sighed. I sure did that a lot. "You're gonna have to speak up in there. What is it and where? How do I kill it?"

Sidney's voice was a little clearer now. "Well, definitely down below. I think you... woke it up? Not sure what it is, though."

A lot of help you are.

"Climb faster, Max."

I grunted; climbing up was a lot harder than going down, especially without a rope. I called up the cliffside when I noticed that Callianthe's body hadn't started moving again. "Wraith, pull!" When she started moving again, I tried to pick up the pace and follow, my brain scrolling through stories I'd been told to see if I could even imagine what was at the bottom of the pit buried under all of those bodies. And why had my movement woken it up? The cliffs rumbled again, and up above me, Callianthe's body swayed as it was pulled steadily up by my horse. If they could just get her onto the surface, I could focus on climbing and not on being afraid that one of her arms would be lobbed off if Wraith pulled her against the cliff too hard. The last thing I needed was to bring her body back damaged.

I didn't need to look down to realize that the frozen bodies below were shifting, almost as if they were bubbles in a pot of boiling water, and something beneath them was preparing to emerge.

"Faster, Max," Sidney ordered, panic now apparent in her voice. It's always a bad sign when people who are usually carefree suddenly sound worried.

"This is," I grumbled as I continued to hoist myself up the cliffside, "as fast as I can go, witch!" Callianthe's body was nearing the top, and I was about halfway up myself when the wet smack of something thick and wriggling hit my back and knocked one of my hands loose. I screamed. "It has tentacles?" I yelled, annoyed that Sidney's witchy powers couldn't have given me some sort of heads-up about what I was dealing with. I regained my hold on the wall just in time for the tentacle to slide down my back and return to the body it belonged to, obviously temporarily. I looked down beneath me to see that the shifting bodies had made way for a mouth, a gaping maw with a giant, glistening beak inside. The creature at the bottom of the cliffs was some sort of giant squid. If it had been any smaller, I might not have been so worried, but the beast was massive. As its mouth opened wider and wider, bodies threatened to fall in, but it pushed them away with more of its tentacles, which worked in perfect harmony to keep its beak clear. The monster hunter in me wanted to get a closer look at it, but I also wanted to live, so I kept climbing as fast as I could.

"Are you close?" Sidney yelled from the top of the cliffside, where she peered over curiously as Callianthe's body disappeared over it.

"Uh... trying!" I struggled to find another handhold as I neared the top third of the cliffside, which had been picked clean by so many miners trying to stay away from the bottom of the pit. I had just shoved my battered fingers into a crevice in the wall when the wet slap got me again, this time accompanied by searing pain—the tentacles had retractable hooks in them. I screamed, and to my horror, my grip on the wall slipped, and I was pulled back down into the pit toward the creature's mouth. I scrambled for my weapons, trying to ignore the fact that this beast was tearing the flesh off of my back, and grabbed a blade just as the rope that had been holding Callianthe came flying over the cliffside toward me. I grabbed it, then swung around to dig my dagger into the tentacle, which caused the creature to shriek and temporarily release me but not without removing some of my flesh in the process.

"Max, hold on!" Sidney shrieked. "Wraith, pull!"

And she did. My big, strong, stubborn steed pulled my flailing ass up the wall as steadily as she could without bashing my head.

"What does it want?" I groaned in pain, struggling to hold on to the rope and my weapon. The pouch with Sidney's sphere in it swung on my hip, and I realized that it was still unbuttoned, causing the ball to teeter on the edge of falling out. I put my blade between my teeth and snapped the pouch shut. I would not be responsible for dropping a piece of someone's soul.

Sidney's face, peering over the edge of the cliff in helplessness, looked exasperated when she replied, "What does every beast want? She's hungry!"

"There are thousands of bodies down here, Sidney!"

"Yeah, but they're all cold and dead. Hang on... you're almost here."

The earth shook again, and as I watched, the beast sent up another tentacle. This one was longer, thinner, with a bulbous tip that looked a lot like an oyster or clamshell. As it slithered its way up the cliffside toward me, my stomach turned and my flesh crawled; I didn't like the look of this appendage. "What the *fuck* is that?"

Sidney peered over the edge of the cliff again. "Babies."

I didn't know exactly what she meant, but I didn't want to wait around and find out. "Ah, hell, Wraith, faster!" The horse did as she was told, but the tentacle, shorter than the cliffside but long enough to reach me, managed to wrap around my leg and slither up my body. I juggled my dagger and the rope again, struggling to sever the tentacle, but not before its clamshell head got right up onto my chest and opened. It… belched, letting out a puff of noxious fumes, and then the screech of hundreds of tiny little squid monsters filled the air as they poured out of the tentacle's tip onto my chest and head. I flung the remainder of the tentacle back into the pit, where it went toward the creature's still-open mouth, just in time for Wraith to pull me onto the ground above the cliff. Much to my dismay, Sidney didn't rush over to help me rid myself of my hundreds of new companions and instead was busying herself with making a fire.

"A fire? Right now? I'm not worried about getting warm!" I complained.

Callianthe's body lay in a grove far from the edge of the cliff.

I scrambled to my feet and began flicking the small squids off of me, back toward their mother; they leaped and screeched loudly as they fell down the cliffside. They were everywhere… under my clothes, in my hand. I even found one behind my ear.

"It's the only way to kill those little buggers," Sidney explained once the fire was going. She then approached me and dragged me over toward it as I was still plucking the beasts off and sat me by the fireside to help me pick each one off and flick it into the flames. They exploded like popcorn and smelled like death.

When it felt like my skin had finally stopped buzzing with the sensation of so many tiny suckers, I ventured a question. "What is that thing?"

"Karuga,"[4] Sidney said simply as she plucked a few more tiny squids from my hair. "The babies are pretty harmless, but they grow quickly and then turn into"—she jerked her chin toward the cliffside—"that. And *that* will eat anything living in sight: humans, dogs, livestock, trees. They're also pretty impossible to kill once they get to that size."

We sat in silence as Sidney dutifully groomed me like we were a pair of cohabitating monkeys, tossing the squids one by one into the flames. The resulting smell made me both hungry and nauseated. When the process took longer than I expected—and probably longer than I had paid her for—I couldn't help my curiosity. "Can I ask about your… magic seeing stone?"

The witch chuckled a little, a noise I had grown to associate with her. "Sure, what about it?"

"You said it's an extension of your soul," I commented, picking at the dirt under my nails to busy myself while the witch did all of the work; it appeared that most of the squids had found shelter in my hair or on the back of my clothing. I resisted the urge to scratch whenever the wriggle of tiny tentacles caressed my bare skin. I'd faced far worse monsters, but something about these being so tiny and easy to go unnoticed made me uncomfortable. At least I could see the tooth faeries and Umbral.

"Right."

"How does that work? Do you…" I struggled to make a guess; I knew very little about magic beyond potions. And those, I relied on Beatrice for. I could use them as tools rather efficiently, but couldn't even begin to imagine what steps were involved in actually creating the concoctions she crafted. "Do you cast some sort of spell that allows you to exist within the stone?"

Sidney wasn't really laughing anymore. It felt odd that *this*, of all things, would change the tone of our conversation and not the dead body lying a few yards away. But then again, the lady wrapped in cloth had very little to do directly with me, let alone the witch, so it only made sense that it wouldn't feel all that personal. It was clear that I'd touched on something that was sensitive to the witch, however.

"No, not exactly," Sidney said, her voice low and thoughtful. She flicked another demon squid into the fire, and after it popped, she paused her preening. I imagined her with her long-nailed hand resting thoughtfully on her pointed chin behind me. "Truthfully, and I haven't told many people this, I don't know how much longer my body will last on this plane."

"Does anyone?" I quipped back, not meaning to argue, but genuinely curious.

"No, but..." Another pause. More rummaging through my hair, then another crispy pop. "I'm not well, I guess, and not too long ago I was pretty certain that I was nearing the end of my time." Sidney sucked her teeth as if unsure how to continue such a delicate topic. Most people were uncomfortable with the mention of death, of illness, of having an expiration date. I was probably more comfortable than most, but then again, I wasn't having to discuss my own mortality with a stranger. "I still have a lot of work I need to do, Max. I'm not ready to go. So I figured out how to split my soul into another vessel— the sphere—just in case. I don't want to be limited by the expiration of my physical body. I don't know when I'll have to rely on it beyond being able to see things in places my body can't go, but I am glad to have it as an option."

I mulled over her admission for a while, considering how serious of a decision it must have been to split one's soul into an inanimate object and then let a stranger carry it down a cliffside. "Why me?"

"Huh?"

"You let me carry that thing down into the pit, and you hardly seemed worried. You said you don't normally share this story with people, so… why me? Why trust me with this information… and the sphere?"

"Oh, mercenary," Sidney said with an exasperated sigh, but I could tell she was smiling behind me. "You risked your life to go down there because laying Callianthe's body to rest is the right thing to do. I'd say you're pretty trustworthy. I told you that the sphere was special, and you kept it safe. What more could I ask for in a confidant?"

As night crept in, I realized the task I had before me.

I had found August's mother.

Now I needed to bring her to him.

---

1. Calcinite (also known as the Neon Shackle): a neon green gem mined from the Invisible Cliffs. It is harmless to most beings, but depletes the magical abilities of elves and for that reason was weaponized by the kingdom of Barrien during their war with Emynor. The gem is no longer mined, sold, or utilized.
2. Umbral: a giant wolf with two sets of eyes, huge claws and teeth, and toxic saliva. Their saliva is deadly to humans and many other races; elves can recover from an Umbral bite, but the pain of the wound itself is agonizing. Only spotted in the Grimmaker Woods, possibly extinct.
3. Tooth Faerie: cat-sized spider-like creatures which feast on teeth and are typically drawn into a home by those left under children's pillows. Once they identify a target, however, they won't rest until they have extracted all of their teeth. They make a tinkling sound when they move as a result of all of the teeth inside of them clinking together.
4. Karuga: a giant, pit-dwelling monster with a mouth that resembles a butthole. It has an affinity for anything living and produces babies through the ends of its tentacles, which contain buds that grow them. The karuga's tentacles also have hooked claws within each sucker.

I DON'T KNOW, CLOSURE?

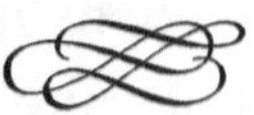

AUGUST

It was late when I realized that I hadn't seen Max in quite some time. It wasn't unusual for her to go off and wander on her own. I'd come to terms with the fact that I'd fallen for a free spirit who, despite having all of her needs met within the kingdom, would always feel the pull of adventure and the outside world. But hell, it really was late. Where was she? Danny was back, had eaten dinner, and was holed up in his room doing gods know what. When I asked him if he'd seen his sister, he just shrugged. "She comes and goes. That's kind of her thing. Don't take it personally."

I was standing against the doorframe of his bedroom, but shifted on my feet at his commentary. It made me nervous, and I wasn't sure why. "What do you mean, take it personally?"

"I dunno," Danny mumbled as he lay on the floor of his bedroom using a small wooden knight figurine to beat the hell out of a matching wooden dragon. When the dragon had been sufficiently pulverized into the floor, its form lying on its side, he looked up at me. "She's not, like, running away from you. She just does her own thing."

"Huh, yeah…"

I hadn't even considered it could be me.

I turned to leave, but my curiosity and now concern got the better of me. "Has she… mentioned running away?"

Danny was setting the dragon upright again. "Huh?" he asked, making eye contact with me briefly before waving me off. "Nah."

"Are you sure?"

When he turned his attention to me again, he looked annoyed. "Don't you think I'd know? It's not like she's gonna leave *me.*"

"Yeah, you're right."

Then I was back in our shared bedroom, having been ushered out of his by his glaring. I flopped onto our bed and rolled over so that I was face down, where I could smell her perfume from that morning and the faint scent of our shared sweat. Any longer than that, and I would've ended up not only concerned for her wellbeing, but irrationally horny from thinking about her, so I got off the bed and went to my spot by our window. Summer was sleepily crawling to an end, and the air was still warm, the sun having gone down not long before.

There she was, faintly lit by the glow of the moon, standing in the distance as I had seen her several times before. Many of those times were in a dream, it seemed. I wondered how long she had been waiting there to get my attention because when she saw me, she waved her arms frantically and gestured for me to join her. It seemed odd, unlike Max, but I was so relieved to see her that I pulled on my boots and sprinted outside toward the stables. I was nowhere near the confident rider that Max was, but my time with her on the road had given me more familiarity with horses than decades in the kingdom, and I was able to mount a horse and ride out to meet her with a surprising (for me) level of ease. I'd even taken the time to familiarize myself with my own horse, whom I'd previously only rode during royal "hunts"; he was a bay Hanoverian named Heckle, and his average size made him look petite next to Wraith. We didn't have the same bond Max had with her horse yet, but I hoped I'd find that in an animal companion one day.

Meeting in the woods in the middle of the night was strange enough, but I certainly hadn't expected to find Max the way I did. I dismounted as soon as she came into view and was shocked to see both her and Wraith looking… exasperated, not to mention dirty.

"Where have you—" Before I could finish my thought, I noticed the shape flung over Wraith's back and covered with a tarp; it was obviously a body. "Who is—" When I looked at Max again, it became clear that she wasn't just dirty, she was *injured*. "Ah, hell, Max, what happened? Who did this?" I closed the gap without waiting for a response and pulled her into my arms, only loosening my grip a little when she winced at the contact. "Tell me what happened, Nightshade."

To my complete shock, she smiled up at me. Smiled. And my body relaxed, as if I hadn't spent the evening worrying about her or seen a dead body on the back of her horse or found her covered in scrapes and bruises and—shit, what had happened to her back? "Max?" I nearly shook her when she didn't respond.

"I'm okay, I'm fine," she told me finally, the faint smile lingering on her lips. I wanted to kiss her. When did I not?

"Are you going to tell me what happened?"

"It's kind of a long story," she said softly, then placed her hands on my chest. I liked them there, so I placed mine over hers as if to ask her to stay. Her smile faded, and my worry returned almost immediately. It felt unfair that she could pull me through the full range of emotions with no effort.

"I have time," I told her.

"I found your mom."

I laughed. I laughed because what the hell else do you do when someone tells you they've found your mother, who you both know has been dead for most of your life? It had to be a joke, but Max wasn't the joking type, and this wasn't a joking matter. My mouth must've been hanging open because I found it dry when I attempted to speak. "What are you talking about?"

"Sorry, I, um… I wasn't sure how to tell you, so I just… said it, and now I'm thinking that wasn't the best way to go about this." She shot a nervous glance over to Wraith, who huffed in what I assumed was agreement.

"Did you hit your head?" I managed finally, then put a hand on her chin and forced her face down so that I could see the top of her head. It was hard to see in the night air, but it didn't look like she'd injured herself.

"No, no," she argued, swatting my hand away so that she could face me again. "Please…" Her dark eyes were pleading.

I swallowed hard, struggling to find words to address the fact that she'd found my mother's body. "Why? How?"

"I climbed down the Invisible Cliffs—"

"You did *what*?"

Max put a grimy finger over my lips to silence me. The scent of dirt and blood was thick in the air between us. Then she rambled, which was wildly unlike her, so I knew she was telling the truth… a hard and heavy truth, a truth that could shatter me. "I climbed down the cliffs, and I found her body… and I brought it back. I thought you might want… I don't know, closure? I didn't know what I'd find of her, but her body was okay, it's really cold down there and I thought you could maybe…"

When I brought myself to look at the body slung over Wraith's back again, my heart was pounding so hard that I couldn't hear anything else. I must've released Max at some point because the next thing I knew, I was reaching out to the cloth covering the body.

"Wait!" she whispered harshly, reaching out to place her own hand on top of mine and halt its movement.

"I want to see her." I set my jaw firmly, unable to look away from the covered form.

"You will, just let's get her off the horse and…" I didn't look at Max while she spoke, but she proceeded to gingerly lower my hand from the cloth. "You should see her lying peacefully, not over the back of the horse like she's a bounty. I just didn't have another way to take her body with me. I'm sorry."

I couldn't face her. "Why did you do this?"

"I didn't want her to spend eternity there, August. She deserved better… and so do you." When I didn't respond, she took the hand she'd lowered into her own and stroked it tenderly, and without forcing me to look away from my mother's still-covered body, asked me, "Do you want to follow me? I think I've found a nice spot to bury her. You can take your time. I can give you space with her… I don't know. Or I can… bury her, if you'd rather just go back to the castle. I'm sorry. I should've asked before I went looking and I—"

"Lead the way."

She dropped my hand and nodded; that much I could see from the corner of my eye. We loaded up onto our respective horses, and I followed her, in silence, for what must have been a very short distance but felt like a million years. During the entire ride I struggled to organize my thoughts. I couldn't decide how I felt. Was she foolish for doing such a thing? Invasive, pushy, to expect me to welcome this confrontation with open arms? And why would she put herself in harm's way like that? For what, a dead body that I had little to no connection to? I cleared my throat when I caught myself spiraling and realized that I didn't recognize the wooded area we had entered. But then again, "the big idiot" didn't know much beyond the castle walls, even with his recent grand adventure.

"Where are we?"

"Just a few miles from the castle. I can show you how to come back here, if you want. It's far enough away that no one will find it and close enough that you could ride or walk if you wanted to…"

"Yeah…"

She slid off her horse in front of me and looked back, past the white cloaked figure on the back of her horse. "You're upset with me."

I sighed and ran a hand through my hair in exasperation. "Max, I'm… I'm really not sure."

The way Max reached up and wiped the sweat from her forehead with the back of her arm caused guilt to prickle within my chest. She was exhausted, dirty, covered in scrapes and cuts and gods knew what else, because she had done this work for me. I couldn't even approach the Invisible Cliffs—not that I'd considered it—and yet she had braved them to find a single body in what was certainly an ocean of death below. Still, I felt detached, defensive, unsure of myself. She understood. She didn't protest. Instead, she nodded, and led Wraith to a clearing where she had already dug a grave for my mother's body. The shovel remained propped up against a nearby tree. After all of the effort it would've taken to descend into the pit at the bottom of the cliffs, find a body, haul it back up, and then dig a grave, I had no idea how Max was still standing.

I hopped off of my horse, dropping his reins carelessly, and once again, approached the body on the back of the Percheron. If Heckle took off, I'd walk back. I didn't care. Together, we pulled my mother off of the horse and laid her down, still covered, next to the grave. Max was tender, soft, and loving in the way that she undid the fabric covering to expose the body inside; she tucked the white cloth in a way that framed my mother's head and face, leaving her like a sleeping angel in the darkness and dirt. It reminded me of the way she had cleaned and bandaged my wounds at the Beast's Breath Tavern while I fought silently for my life after the Umbral attack. The memory was hazy—after all, I had seen it through bleary and half-conscious eyes—but it would forever be ingrained in my mind. For someone who often appeared rough around the edges, she had a hidden tenderness that most would never see.

My birth mother's face was soft and peaceful, as if she were only resting temporarily… and she was young. Hell, she must've been younger than me when she died. If I had encountered this woman elsewhere, we might've been friends. I wondered what she would've done with her life had it not been cut so tragically short. Perhaps she would've been extraordinary, but I decided then that her life, ordinary or otherwise, would have been very special. She had deserved to live more of it. "I'm sorry…" Max said again, her voice still muffled beneath the thudding of my heart.

My mouth was dry when I told her, "You should go."

"I don't want to leave you."

"I need you to." Again, there was that tenderness that I was certain only I had experienced from Max the Menace… and it only added to the new ache in my chest. Time and time again, she'd stripped me bare and left me exposed, to face whatever darkness had been lurking within me. This time I just couldn't have her see me like that because I didn't know what *that* would really look like. This was different than confronting the parents I'd learned had betrayed me. I hadn't thought of my birth mother much… even after learning how she'd been taken from me. Until the moment I saw her face, in fact, my elven mother had always been a closed door in my mind. Why explore it when there was nothing that could come from it? Better to board it up, leave it shut, and never wonder what could have been than to mourn that loss. But that was no longer an option.

I didn't look up as she did as she was told, nor did I turn at the sound of Wraith's hooves against the soft dirt of the forest. Soon I was in silence again, and I stared down at my mother, my mom, and realized just how much that closed door had been festering over the past year. It was a wound, not a safe, and I had left it to rot instead of tending to it, just like I had done with many things before Max. I let myself crumple to my knees next to the body and pulled the elven woman's hand into mine, realizing I knew nothing about her, not even her name. I pressed my forehead to the back of her hand, letting the limp coolness of her flesh soothe the heat in mine. Had Celine Theodoric of Barrien ever loved me like this woman would have? Had she ever held me close or soothed my tears as a baby? Did she have a nickname for little me, or was I always August Theodoric III? Had she ever felt pride toward me… or concern? I didn't know. I couldn't recall a time that either of the parents who raised me had expressed those things. And while I didn't know if the woman before me would have been that type of mother, I mourned the loss of what might've been. I mourned the loss of a life that could have been many things, one of which was a loving mother, and held her hand as I cried. It felt only right that I'd cry for her then like I'm sure I did as a baby when I first realized she was gone.

GOOD DEEDS

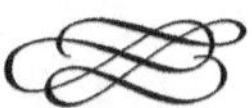

MAX

Why I ever try to do good deeds is beyond me. This one was a big gamble. Could I not have purchased some racy lingerie at the market or finally gotten August that micro dragon he'd always wanted? No, of course not. Instead, I had to go and dig up his dead mother's body and bring it to him out of nowhere. It'll be great. It'll bring closure. We'll bond. He'll know how much I lo… long for his healing and peace. Who *does* that?

Nope, not so. And then of course I'd tried to explain myself to him only to stammer and say "I don't know" repeatedly. That had not panned out the way I'd expected. You do something that big for someone, you think you'd be able to accompany it with some sort of eloquent dedication.

"Not sure how I could've gone about that differently," I muttered to myself as Wraith and I slowly headed for the castle. I wasn't in a rush. I had no clue what I'd find the next time August and I were together, and part of me just wanted to erase this whole day from history. Why hadn't Sidney told me it was a foolish idea? I didn't know enough about normal human interactions; I needed a voice of reason to chime in on these things!

Wraith tossed her head back in protest.

"I know, it was a long day," I told her with a sigh. I leaned down to pat the side of her neck in appreciation. "You worked hard."

She snorted defiantly.

"Listen, you didn't have to climb down the freaking cliffside, okay? And did you see that squid thing? It was like a giant asshole with tentacles. Just consider yourself on the lucky end of that adventure." A shiver ran down my spine at the memory of the creature's tentacles, and in response, I winced when the movement made my back ache.

She huffed again.

"At least I didn't bring you *your* dead mom's body."

We carried on that way for longer than we would've had we not both been hungry, tired, and slightly delirious. Our conversation, or lack thereof, reminded me of our time on the road together. Pre-August. Pre-kingdom. Pre… complex living arrangements and societal expectations and romantic feelings.

"No, that's not a threat," I told Wraith. "Would you *like* it to be a threat?"

"I'm just saying, it doesn't seem like the type of gift I thought it would be. Maybe he thinks I'm trying to break up with him."

"What if he's out there completely falling apart, Wraith? I brought his dead mother's body to him and just *left* him there. I should've stayed. What if he *needs* me?" Then, I quickly realized how ridiculous I was being. He didn't need me. He wasn't a child. I wasn't his protector. Why was I acting like this? "He's probably just annoyed that he has to fill a grave… and wondering how to tell me how stupid of a decision that was."

Eventually we came upon the castle again, at the same spot that we had met August not much earlier. I didn't feel like going back to the castle, so we just sat there. Sure, we were hungry, but food could wait.

In fact, it was more tempting to starve than to risk facing whatever might be inside that building. I flopped forward on top of Wraith and rested my cheek against her neck, letting the deep whooshing of her breath calm me.

I woke some time later to Wraith moving without my instruction, and though my body was immediately on alert, I was so exhausted that I could barely lift my head enough to see August and his horse leading us back to the castle. Either I was out of shape from months of not needing to fight for my life on a regular basis or the day's events really had pushed me to my limits. My eyes were so heavy that I drifted off again before we arrived at the stables. If we'd been headed somewhere strange, Wraith would've refused to move... At least, that was what I told myself. She had learned to follow August wherever, though.

"Grain, carrots for Wraith," August said to the stable hand before handing her reins off to him. I had hardly lifted my head again before I realized that he was pulling me off of my horse's back to... carry me?

"I'm sorry," I murmured.

"Don't be. Sleep."

I rested my head against his chest, my favorite place to be, and let my tired body be carried through the castle to our bedroom. August smelled like sweat, wet earth, and a somewhat recent shower all in one. We were ascending a flight of stairs when I opened my eyes again and stared up at him. I couldn't get a read on the situation or how things were between us. I had wanted nothing more than to heal his heart, which I'd learned was pure and beautiful even though it was as full of mistakes as anyone else's. My gaze traced along his jawline, the sharpness of which I'd always admired; it was clenched tight. He must've felt my gaze on him because he asked, "What was her name?"

"Your..." I cleared my throat, expelling the sleep from my voice in a sharp gust. "Your mother's?"

He nodded.

"Callianthe," I told him, repeating it with the same cadence that his father had told it to me. It was a name I'd never heard before, but I liked it very much.

He smiled a little to himself. "Beautiful."

"Yes," I murmured, resting my head on his chest again as we approached our room. His steps were hilted, like they had been ever since the Umbral attack, but he didn't complain about the discomfort that must've accompanied going up the staircase with an additional body to carry. We passed Danny's room, and I noted that the light was off, so he was either asleep or hiding under the covers with a book and a candle, risking a fire for the sake of late-night entertainment. "She was beautiful, August, like you. I wish so much that you two could've had more time together."

He shifted me in his arms just enough to open the door to our chambers. Before responding to me, he nudged a bell near the door to summon one of our attendants.

The responding attendant was alert and attentive, his voice coming clearly through the small cone at the entrance of our room: "Yes, Your Grace? Is everything alright?"

August cleared his throat. "Apologies, I know it's late."

"It's no matter, King August. Whatever you need."

"I need a basin of warm water, some bandages, Savers Salve[1], please." August had ensured the latter was kept stocked at the castle.

"Is everything alright? Shall I call for a doctor?"

August paused and looked down at me. I shook my head in a hurry. "That won't be necessary," he said as he turned back to the speaker.

"Right away, Your Grace."

August set me down, then removed his coat and boots and stood before me, but said nothing. His clothing was dirty, not nearly as disgusting as mine, but his boots immediately left a patch of dirt on the floor of our room, and the knees of his trousers were damp and brown with earth. I imagined him burying his mother and had to shake the thought from my mind before despair overtook me. I'd left him there. But then again, he'd asked. Guilt bubbled inside of me despite my attempts to suppress it.

"What is it?" I asked, suddenly hyper-aware of the fact that we were in our usual place, but everything was anything but. I had forever altered part of our history and potentially our future... there wasn't really any going back from what I'd done, for better or worse. I wasn't sure if I was prepared to live with that.

August was so matter-of-fact in his response that I was certain I had ruined everything we had with each other. And to think that only hours before we'd been making love by the window... Why had I thrown that away? "You should take those clothes off," he said gruffly. "They're ruined." Normally it was a feat to get August to shut up, so the fact that he was shutting me down with his conciseness hurt.

I looked down at myself in confusion. I'd worn worse. Slept in worse. My clothes were the absolute least of my concerns. I'd sleep in bloodied, dirty clothing for the rest of my life if we could get through that night without everything we'd built being demolished. "I... they're fine, we should just get to bed." *Please, please, let's just go to bed and pretend none of this happened.*

August shook his head, his expression hard and unreadable. "No. Let me take care of your wounds."

"Will you talk to me then? If I let you clean me up? Will you tell me what you're thinking?"

"I don't know, Max." Ruined. Ruined. Ruined.

I was wincing in pain as I peeled what was left of my shirt off when there was a knock at the door. I left the torn and bloodied scraps of fabric in a pitiful pile on the floor, then crossed my arms across my chest; I hadn't thought to cover myself in front of August in almost a year, and yet now I felt as vulnerable and exposed as ever. Despite me being deep in the bedroom, August covered the gap in the slightly open door with his big body while he retrieved the items from an attendant. Then, he locked the door behind him and set up a makeshift nurse's station on one of our nightstands, still speaking so little he hardly seemed like himself. I watched him in curiosity as he replicated what I had done at the tavern while tending to him.

"Turn around."

When he brought a damp cloth to the gashes on my back and dabbed at them cautiously, as if he were caring for a wounded wild animal, I hissed in pain. "Why are you doing this?"

"It seems only fair," he said seriously. The sound of water being wrung out of the spent washcloth followed.

"To punish me, because I hurt you?" I winced again as he wiped more dried blood from my skin and picked what was likely a claw from one of the wounds on my back. It made a plinking sound when he discarded it into the basin. Gross.

August was quiet for a moment as he wrung the cloth out again and worked lower on my back. Once he had cleaned me off, I heard the jar of salve open, and he carefully but methodically worked his way from the top to bottom of my back, smearing the thick paste across every bit of battered flesh as he went. The discomfort was enough to distract me for a while, but eventually I realized that he hadn't answered my question. The entire interaction felt so unlike him, so unlike us, or what we had grown to be over the past year.

"Well?" I choked out, arms still crossed over my chest. I gripped my upper arms to still myself despite the chill that was coursing through my body. "If that's what it is, just tell me. I can take it. If I made a mistake—"

"To try to heal your wounds, because that's what you're always doing for me, Max."

The rest of our interaction went by in silence.

August pulled the remainder of my shredded clothing from my body, leaving me bare before him, and washed me from head to toe, medicating and bandaging every wound he spotted on me, no matter how small. I watched him through curious, but worried eyes, wondering if there was something I was missing. He'd always been honest with me, so I told myself to trust what he had said. That I was helping to heal him, that we were healing each other. That I hadn't hurt him more by bringing him face-to-face with his past.

When I'd been cared for to his satisfaction, he pulled soft pajamas of silk from one of the drawers he'd given me, and helped me into them in silence. I knew the drawer was filled to the brim with pieces just like it that I'd been too nervous to wear for fear of being too comfortable with royal life. Hell, I had only branched out to the underwear section of my dresser that morning alone. The sight of August before me, pulling the pants up my legs like it was his duty to dress me, struck something deep inside of me. He was acting... not defeated, but submissive in a way I hadn't expected. It surprised me.

I let him pull me into bed with him, and we lay side by side on the fine silk sheets, both staring up at the ceiling unlike any other night we'd ever spent together. My body ached and my wounds felt sticky and irritating. "I feel like I broke us," I confessed finally, certain that speaking my fears couldn't do any more damage than I'd already done. "I didn't mean to break us, August."

"You didn't."

"What can I do?"

August was quiet as he searched for a response. "Tell me what did that to your back."

My head popped up before I could control my reaction, and I looked at him incredulously in the near dark of our bedroom. A few remaining candles were all that lit the space around our bed. "That's what you want to talk about?"

August didn't turn to me, but I could make out the dampness of lingering tears in his gaze as he kept his eyes trained on the ceiling.

"Yeah," he said with a shuddering breath. "That's what I want to talk about."

Before lying back down, I pulled August to me so that his head was on my chest and immediately felt him relax into me. I took a steadying breath and ran my hand through his hair like I often did, tracing my fingertips over the ridge of his scarred ear, where long, regal points should've been. "It's a really ugly thing," I told him finally, mustering the energy to talk about something as trivial as a monster given the circumstances. "And a prolific procreator, apparently, which is shocking, given its appearance."

The bed shook with his silent laughter, and my heart rate slowed a little in response.

---

1. Savers Salve: general first aid, used for cuts, scrapes, and other minor injuries. Can disinfect serious wounds like an Umbral bite, but cannot heal them.

THE BACK ROOM

MAX

We tried to get back to life as usual after that, part of which meant shopping. I get it—what else is there to do with your free time when you have tons of money at your disposal? Because our relationship started with shopping in the Dalcester Street Market, we occasionally headed back, and during those trips, we often went to see Beatrice. Now, I didn't know this before meeting August, but in the back of Beatrice's apothecary, there is a small, dark room. You'd think that's where she keeps all of the really dangerous stuff, but nope, she keeps those items front and center, right where any old fool or mercenary can buy them. What she keeps in the back room has nothing to do with potions or elixirs or perfumes, even. At least, that's what I'd heard; I had never had a reason to go back there myself until I brought August with me.

"Sex toys? Wow, I hadn't pegged you as the type, Max," August purred at me as we were led past the aisles of glimmering potion bottles and through a thick velvet curtain that separated the store from this secret back room. The contrast between the two spaces was jarring; it truly felt like another world past that curtain. The gaze of the other patrons had me sweating and mortified as the curtain closed behind us, but August, of course, was perfectly at home. "Get it, 'pegged'?" I must have been bright red because August grabbed my hand and squeezed it a little. "Though I guess you wouldn't be the one getting pegged if—sorry, I know you're just trying to appeal to my interests"—his interests primarily being banging—"but really... I don't need fancy toys." Even though I was horrified internally, I was mainly glad to see August back to his old, flirty self. I hadn't broken us. At least not all the way.

I struggled to find the words to reply. Why exactly had I brought him here? Beatrice and Morgan had suggested it as a natural next step —exploration, they said—but it felt strange to be at this point in a relationship with someone. Too domestic for Max the Menace. I could try, though, right? Max the Menace could be adventurous in different ways if she wanted to. "I want to make sure you're... you know, into it."

August didn't seem to be thinking as far into it as I was. "I'm into you," he insisted, pulling me into his arms once we were behind the curtain. Beatrice had left us almost immediately, which led me to wonder what typically happened in this back room aside from shopping. I didn't have to think for too long when August pressed his big body up against me, pinning me to a row of dark shelves. His gaze was heavily lidded when he pulled away, his molten irises boring into me like they tended to do, and all I could think was that I wanted to please this man, to be the person he needed. I savored the sly curve of his lips, the rigid sharpness of his jawline, and the twinkle in his soft, honeyed gaze.

Unwilling to admit my self-consciousness after our recent close call, I tried to shove it deep down inside of me with the rest of my big feelings. "Yeah? Let's look around, then."

Did you know there are tons of different types of sex toys? I used to think it was pretty straightforward—stuff to stick in your parts or stuff to stick your parts in—but apparently it's way more complex than that. I felt a little prudish not having known; it wasn't like I didn't have sex or masturbate, I just… had very tame experiences, apparently. The back room was small, sure, but each shelf was brimming with items of all shapes, sizes, colors, and materials. I knew enough to infer that several rows were the "stick in your parts" kind of items, but the shapes caught me off guard. There was no way half of these were modeled after human penises… and hell, why were they so big? Surely some of them were just asking to shamelessly rearrange your internal organs. Did that actually feel *good*? August must've caught me looking because he chuckled a little to himself. "Looking for something bigger?"

"N-no, not at all," I stammered.

"It's okay. I know mine is average." He shrugged, seemingly really, truly okay with the fact.

"It's just right," I told him honestly and suppressed a shudder of enjoyment as I recalled the last time I had encountered "it." August's body was built for mine.

He gave me a soft smile and went back to browsing, occasionally making comments about particularly absurd or interesting items. We were lazily looking over the many shelves in the back room when August's commentary lost my attention and another sound felt like it was prying into my brain. Didn't anyone else hear that? That… skittering, squelching… My ears felt like they were twitching as they followed the sound.

"What is that?"

"Huh? That's, uh…" August picked something up off of one of the shelves and turned it over in his palm until he found the tag. "*Bloob*. Blueberry-flavored lube, apparently—funny, I get it. Blueberry. Lube.

Bloob. It says it's made from locally sourced berries." He shrugged, then tossed it in the small shopping bag in his other hand. It clinked against some other items in the bag that I hadn't noticed August pull off the shelves. "Worth a try, I guess. I love blueberries."

"Yeah, yeah…" I murmured, still distracted by the fact that the noise was so uncomfortably familiar, but I couldn't place it. "I'll be right back." I didn't stick around to make sure that August was okay with me leaving, but instead followed the noise as it got louder and louder. My brain was buzzing. Before I knew it, I was outside of the shop, following the offending sound down a cobblestone alleyway. I knew I'd heard that sound before, at least once… maybe recently? It was so familiar. In fact, it reminded me of the tooth faeries we'd dealt with not too long before, but it wasn't accompanied by the tinkling of loose teeth, nor was it the right time of day for such creatures. No, no tinkling… no scuttling… squelching, squishing, tiny suctioning noises… like a bunch of little—

"Tentacles!" I hissed, following the noise down an alley between two storefronts. Oh, shit. "You tiny, tentacle-having, asshole-born demons!" It was me. Somehow, I'd brought some of the tiny little karuga babies back to the surface with me and into the city. I didn't have enough time to figure out how they'd hitched a ride back with me—it could've been in my hair or in one of my weapons bags or even on Wraith—but they were here. I turned the corner into the alley just in time to see several of them scurry up the side of a building and squeeze their way into a crack in the wall. They were bigger than they had been a few days ago at the cliffs… and if what Sidney had said was true, it wouldn't be long before they were the size of their mother and big enough to consume the town whole. If one of them was that massive and foreboding, I could only imagine the capability and insatiable hunger of multiple. Their mama had craved human flesh… Barrien was full of that. My stomach turned at the thought of the entire city being eaten just because I hadn't shaken off my clothes thoroughly enough. Families. Children. Pets and livestock and… Danny and August. I had to do something.

I was so determined to "do something," in fact, that I had completely forgotten I wasn't alone on this outing *and* that I hadn't come prepared with any tools or weapons. It had taken me months to get used to leaving my weapons behind at the castle during outings, but August insisted that it was better for appearances if I was unarmed in the city. It didn't look right for the king to be with a hardened mercenary who was ready to pull a blade or poison on someone at a moment's notice… He didn't want people to think I was still a hired hand or that I was fully armed and dangerous. I had to demonstrate a level of comfort and trust in the people of Barrien that I simply didn't have; it wasn't them, I just couldn't see how one could trust an entire city of people as a whole. I sprinted back toward the apothecary and poked my head in, shouting past customers that Beatrice was serving to ask, "Do you have anything that works on karuga?"

Beatrice didn't look up, just smiled a little to herself as she wrapped up a potion bottle she'd been showing a customer. Her partner grumbled somewhere behind her, jumping as she yelled in response, "No clue what that is, sugar!"

Shit. "Thanks, Beatrice!"

As I popped back out, likely out of the sight of the "back room," I heard Beatrice shout, "You bet!" August must have still been distracted by the vast array of toys; he had hardly noticed me slip out in the first place.

I grumbled to myself as I headed back toward the alley, still unsure of what I was going to do once I got there. The uneven and occasionally crumbling cobblestone of the road shifted and grinded under my boots; it felt more familiar, more normal to me than the sturdy pavement within the castle grounds. Even though I was mentally berating myself for bringing the little demons into the town (and possibly into the castle) without realizing it, I felt in my element again, much like I had at the cliffs. It was invigorating, purposeful, to be on the prowl again. Now, to figure out what the hell I was actually going to do about the monster babies…

The only thing I remembered working on the babies was fire, but I couldn't very well just set the building on fire and hope for the best. I needed something more precise, something concentrated. I needed to act quickly… the babies wouldn't grow to be the size of their mother in a matter of minutes, but I didn't know what it was they ate in the meantime to help them grow… bugs? Cats? Kids?

When I headed back out into the market square, I spotted a booth that immediately gave me an idea that August would probably scold me for. I would've approached it slower—or run the other way—if the situation wasn't literally life and death.

"Ah, yes, young lady! Come to see the world-famous micro dragons?" The shopkeeper looked a lot like the last time I had seen him, but he'd opted for heavier-duty glasses with a metal visor that flipped down over them, and his oven mitts, still dutifully stuck to his hands, looked to be reinforced with something a little thicker than the regular oven-handling fabric he'd had before. Surely the little dragons weren't *that* ferocious, but it was promising that he still sported so much gear and so many burns on his clothing and tent. I was already scanning the rows of pitiful tiny lizards while he continued his spiel. They looked just as sad and miserable chained up as they had last time.

"They come in a wide array of colors, guaranteed to match your daily fashions with ease! You'll be the talk of your friend—"

I didn't bother telling him that I didn't have a friend group and was actually trying to save the entire town (from my own mistake). "That one!" I snapped, pointing out the only dragon that wasn't struggling to hold its head up. It was a dark green, almost black. Typical dragon color, I guess. Maybe he'd been discounted.

"Just one? They're two for—"

"Just one!" I interrupted again, fishing in my pocket for a handful of crystals and pressing them into the shopkeeper's mitted palm. The sum was likely more than the asking price for the dragon, but I didn't care. In fact, if I hadn't been unarmed, I would've threatened him to get him moving quicker. Couldn't he sense that I was dealing with something urgent and important? It would affect him and his silly little pets, too! If the karuga babies got any bigger, they'd likely eat the micro dragons as a snack. "Now, please!"

"Oh my, you're in quite the hurry." He chuckled, his big belly jiggling as he struggled to shove the crystals into his pocket with his mitts still on. "Patience, patience. I'm glad to see you're so excited by our top-of-the-line product!" Despite the struggle and the fact that his attire had him sweating profusely, he never once dropped his marketing persona.

I held out my hand impatiently, and when the scaly creature was turned over to me, I took off back to the alleyway once more. The creature wriggled in my hand, no doubt feeling lighter now that it wasn't relegated to a small perch and probably confused by the speed at which it was being transported, so I held it tight. *Don't crush this little thing, Max.*

"Tell all your friends!" the shopkeeper shouted after me.

The little dragon was warm in my hand as I reexamined the crack in the wall, peering in to find what appeared to be a nest of the escaped karuga babies. Thankfully, there appeared to only be a few. I grumbled a little to myself as I realized that I'd have to scour the rest of the town and the castle somehow to make sure there weren't more. They couldn't reproduce at this age, and the likelihood of me not noticing an entire swarm hitching a ride in my clothes or on Wraith was slim, but not zero. I peered into the hole again, the lizard still tight in my fist, and attempted to lure the karuga babies out. "Pspsps... come on little... fuckers..."

They screamed, an ear-piercing noise that made my skin crawl, and retreated farther into their dark cave in the wall.

I groaned. "Fine." When I put the dragon up to the crack in the wall, I realized I probably should've asked the shopkeeper about controlling its fire-breathing abilities. "Uh... help me out here?" I asked, looking down at the creature in my hand. "Could you maybe, I don't know, cough up some flames?"

The dragon cocked its head to the side in confusion.

"This is literally the worst beast-slaying performance I've ever had," I confessed to the tiny forest-green dragon. "I'm usually a lot better at this. Is there a special phrase or something? It looked like you weren't skimping on the fire with the shopkeeper..."

Nothing.

I twitched my fingers around the small dragon in my grasp again and noticed that it reflexively shuddered away when my fingertips rubbed its side. "Are you... ticklish?" I tried again, and the lizard shook its entire body as if it could shake me off. It wiggled again and, to my surprise, coughed out a tiny gust of flames from its snout. "That's... not how I expected this to work." Inside of the crack in the wall, the tiny squid-like creatures curled up against each other without a care in the world. I shrugged, realizing that I had at least figured out how to use the dragon's fire, even if it was weird, and held the little lizard up to the wall once more. Then, I gave it what I could really only describe as a more enthusiastic tickle, which caused it to protest, then cough and sneeze until a small fireball exploded from its face and went straight into the crevice.

The resounding screeches from the baby karuga was reassuring, but when they didn't immediately explode, I realized that the fire had only cornered them in their nest. "Again!" I told the dragon, repeating my actions so that it would release flames once more. I owed this little beast. Again, a stream of flames flew into the crack in the wall, blackening the surrounding brick. I felt guilty for putting this little reptile on the spot when I had pitied him and the others at the shop, but I continued my assault until I heard the assuring pop of the baby squids, then relaxed my tickling and loosened my grip on the micro dragon. I slumped back against the brick wall, shockingly out of breath despite having been standing in one place, and wiped my forehead with my free hand before sliding down to the ground. I set the dragon loose on my lap. "Sorry, little guy. I promise to never do that again."

The lizard wiggled out of my grasp, and I let him go without a fight. Then, it crawled across my lap and sneezed once more, in defiance, sending a spark toward my chest. "Hey!" I protested, desperately patting my blouse to put out the small fire it started. "I guess I deserve that..." When the tiny creature didn't fly off (not that he had the strength) or scurry away down the alleyway and instead settled onto my leg, I was surprised, but oddly pleased. Aside from Wraith, it often felt like I didn't have much in the way of friends. Perhaps this was the start of some sort of friendship... Maybe August had been right about the micro dragons. Oh, shit. August. I groaned, then scooped the dragon into my hand and hoisted myself to my feet. "You're welcome to tag along," I told the dragon before sitting it on my shoulder. "But if you want to take off, that's okay, too. Thanks for your hel—"

It was then that I realized that the alleyway was... hot. Hotter than it should've been from a single blast of fire sent into the squid nest; it should've set the creatures alight and then burned out since the nest was encased by brick. I hadn't seen any actual nesting material in there with them, probably because they were used to the cold and empty nature of the base of the cliffs. Yet, in fact, the heat was increasing. I stood in time to catch a flash of red and orange from within the wall; it was still burning. The smell of smoke filled my nostrils before I could even think to react. "Shit, shit, shit!" I had no idea what was on the other side of that wall, but it was clearly much more flammable than brick, and the crack must have gone right through to the other side rather than just creating a cavern like I had originally imagined.

I didn't have much time to muse over what I'd done because the street soon filled with the sound of panicked yelling. My head had hardly stopped swimming from the irritating noise of the karuga babies and the blood rushing in my ears, just to be replaced by yet another assault on my brain. The micro dragon dug its small talons into my shoulder as I ran, hanging on tight, especially when I halted abruptly to see the open space between shops filled with shoppers and shopkeepers alike.

"Everyone out!" one man yelled, holding the door open to the shop as patrons hurried out.

"Someone, help, get water! Please!"

"My shop, oh gods, my shop!"

I sprinted around the corner and came face-to-face with a nearby storefront, the entrance of which was already smoking. I recognized this shop as a small bakery that I would occasionally swing into when I had the crystals to spare. It was cramped and run down, much like many of the shops in Barrien (aside from Beatrice's, apparently, now that I knew it had a cavernous and mysterious back room with additional stock), but it was popular, and for good reason; the owner was a little old lady who must have been over one hundred years old. She had connections to rare and expensive ingredients from all over the world. Though she created pastries and breads with ingredients such as unicorn milk and blue lavender, my favorite treat from Yeast to West Baked Goods was their apple tart, a cheap and tasty little dessert made with a fruit that didn't grow on this side of the continent. Oh, gods. Not only had I damaged a local shop, but it was one of my favorites, no less.

I scrambled, looking everywhere for a source of water, and disregarded the fact that the dragon on my shoulder labeled me as the obvious culprit. Townspeople bustled around me, not noticing that I, too, was trying to help as I sped for the small well in the center of the town square. The path toward the well was difficult to travel, especially at my size, with people repeatedly bumping into me in their panic. I was finally able to duck past a few people and head for one of the buckets on the well's edge, then grabbed a worrying townsperson and shoved the filled bucket into their hands. "Take this to the shop and then come back!" I instructed them. People around us seemed to get the message because they, too, reached for buckets, which we filled one at a time in the well before handing them to others who went to the shop. My hands were clammy as I worked, the claws of the dragon digging into my shoulder a constant reminder that I had literally set fire to a local shop with seemingly no regard for the outcome; I had been less nervous than this when I'd gone toe-to-toe with the Umbral.

When the people stopped returning with empty buckets and the air was no longer fuming with active smoke, I seriously considered slinking away to the castle and hiding my shame there. Maybe no one needed to know *who* had started the fire. Perhaps it was enough that it had been put out so quickly... but I knew it would be wrong to do anything but face the truth and that my guilt would eat me alive otherwise, so I took a deep breath and joined the group gathered around the shop front in a half circle. The air was quiet aside from tense mutterings and whispers that caused the hair on the back of my neck to stand on end.

"How did this happen?" *I tried to kill invasive monsters that I actually brought into town myself.*

"What started the fire? Did anyone see…?" *Me. Me, it was me!*

"Oh, poor Gladolia, this shop was her whole life. It's been in her family for centuries!" *Oh, hell, centuries?!* Could it have been any worse? Did her pet kitten also die in the fire?

Again, I weaseled my way through the crowd toward the front and leaned over to the person next to me to whisper, "Is everyone safe? No one got hurt, right?"

The woman next to me, a short and squat lady who was probably a little bit older than me, began to respond before she turned to look at me. "I think so, just—hey, what're you doing with that dragon?" Her voice rose immediately. "I saw you come out of the alleyway... did you do this?"

"No, I—" I stepped backward, immediately running into another townsperson, which caused me to stumble and hit the ground. I instinctively caught myself on my hands and was left looking up at the townspeople, who quickly moved to surround me. The little dragon remained perched on my shoulder, no doubt looking up at the crowd forming around us. "I didn't mean to, I was just—"

The group began to chatter again.

"Leave it to a mercenary to destroy the town! Just because they don't belong to any place, they think they can treat cities however they want!"

The townspeople began to close in on me, and I found that there was nowhere for me to get my footing, not even enough to stand up. The dragon arched its back in defense and hissed. My heart pounded in my ears, and my vision blurred. I wished instead that I was being cornered by anything but humans... *Take me back to the pit of the Invisible Cliffs, please*, I begged the universe internally. *Take me back to corpses and man-eating assholes.*

"She's going to burn down the whole town!"

I opened my mouth to defend myself, even though I knew it was pointless. I was an outsider, no matter what was happening between me and August. I'd always be an outsider in Barrien, in Dalcester, in the world of normal people and their normal lives. Sweat rolled down my back. "No, that's not what happened, I was trying to—"

The shopkeeper appeared in the crowd, her face stained with soot and the dried trails of what I'm sure had been tears shed over the loss of her shop. She raised a shaky, wrinkled finger in my direction. "Hey! What makes you think you can come in here and set fires to people's shops? Don't you know this place was my whole life? I've been making treats for the people of Dalcester since I was a little girl!"

I *tried* to explain. "There was— I was trying to—"

Another townsperson spoke up. "Get out of here! You can't threaten our livelihood!"

It was useless, but it was my turn to speak again. "I'm sorry, let me explain—"

"Try explaining how we're going to feed our families now!" said a younger man I'd seen working at the counter of the bakery a few times. "My daughter's birthday is coming up!"

I shuffled backward on my hands and feet, dragging my butt against the rough cobblestone of the street, until I couldn't shuffle any farther. I was fully surrounded. Everywhere I moved, I bumped into the shoes of townspeople around me, and several of them carelessly stepped on my fingers. I winced, immediately pulling my hands in closer to me. I was just about to consider lying on the ground in defeat when someone grabbed me by the shoulder and pulled me onto my feet.

"Give her a chance to answer!" a familiar voice scolded the crowd. "I know this woman. She wouldn't have intentionally damaged a shop." Her hand remained firm on my shoulder, and when I turned to look at her, I realized that the person helping me was Ermaline, whose family I'd helped rid of their tooth faerie infestation. Her daughters were nowhere to be seen, thankfully; we'd left things on such a good note that I would've hated for them to see me like this.

"What makes you so sure?" one man challenged her, pointing a thick, grubby finger in my face.

"She's helped my family!" Ermaline bit out through clenched teeth, clearly maddened at the blatant mistreatment the villagers were directing toward me. "And for *free*, no less." Her grip on my shoulder tightened and she pulled me closer to her, swiveling us around so that we could look at the entire group now surrounding us. "I know for a fact that she's done the same for many of you ungrateful lot as well!" As we moved, I made eye contact with several people that I had, in fact, helped over my years traveling through Dalcester and the surrounding cities. I'd found people for them. Killed monsters. Done odd jobs for some pocket change or less. Their blatant disregard for my proven trustworthiness caused both sadness and irritation to bubble within me.

One voice boomed above all of the others, causing any arguments to cease immediately. "That's *enough*." A chill coursed through my body. Another familiar voice, and this one, I was more concerned about than Ermaline's.

The crowd went silent, the last few wisps of smoke trickling from the shop behind me; I was certain I looked like an omen to the people of the town at that moment. Fire. Dragon. Mercenary. Distressed townspeople. The group cleared in time for August to enter the center of the crowd and come to my side. While Ermaline's presence was the comforting, motherly, feminine energy of someone that potentially understood my struggle and stood with me in solidarity, August stood with undeniable male power and privilege. The tooth faerie mom and I stunk, no doubt; her from her daily life and me from hauling ass through the entire town to first set a fire and then put it out again. August, meanwhile, was still immaculately dressed and smelled like the clean royal that I fell asleep with each night. Much like seeing him on the throne, the position itself did nothing for me, but what he did with that power set a fire (okay, bad choice of words right now) within me.

"I'm sure there's a good reason for what transpired here today," August said clearly, his voice loud enough for the entire group to hear. He was as diplomatic as ever, and the interaction, the way that he commanded the crowd, reminded me of our vastly different upbringings. "While it's truly a shame that your shops were damaged, no lives were lost, and that's what is most important—the *people* here at the market and in the surrounding cities. The rest can be replaced and the kingdom of Barrien will ensure that the damaged buildings are repaired immediately." It was true that the kingdom could afford to help its people; the kingdom had always been able to afford it, but now that August was in charge, he was more willing to allocate funding to those who needed it instead of sitting on his hoard like his parents had. I knew that it had been on his list to connect with and assist the townsfolk more, along with restoring the city's relationship with Emynor, which had been August's primary work since our return home.

The townspeople muttered amongst themselves.

Meanwhile, August gestured to a group of soldiers that had been holding the people at bay. They wore full armor adorned with the buzzard symbol of Barrien, an apt icon for a city made of scavengers. Perhaps one day when Barrien was fully revived in the way that August intended, they could give another thought to their town mascot. "Help the people clean up the damage to this shop." He turned to the people again. "I won't hear another word against her now," he warned. "Please, help your neighbors and await assistance from the kingdom. I will arrange for help upon my return to the castle."

Somehow, despite all of the good that August was doing and continued to do, I felt shame. Fear. Emptiness. I didn't belong there. I was torn. When he took me by the elbow to steer me from the crowd, I put my hand over his to stop him. "Wait, I need to speak with—"

"Max, it has to wait. We need to leave and give these people time to cool off," August said under his breath, a warning in his tone and his grip on me firm.

I pulled against him again, feeling almost like I had nothing to lose, and turned to Ermaline for a brief moment. "Thank you. I'll come see you when it's safe, I have something for you." I had told myself in the Invisible Cliffs that I would tell her about her missing husband and put her worries to rest once and for all. Would there ever be a time that I wasn't the bringer of bad news?

She gave me a knowing look, though she was also rightfully concerned, and nodded before letting me go.

August was silent as he helped me onto Heckle, whom we had ridden into town that day because Wraith could be intimidating, and led us back to the castle. I sat behind him on the horse, my arms wrapped around his waist as usual, and rested my cheek on his back. The dragon, meanwhile, rested its head on my shoulder and clung to me as we rode. Just when I'd thought we were back to normal, I had made a mess yet again. "How angry are you?" I asked, a bit put off by my own question; since when did I report to King August like that? He wasn't my keeper. For someone who had spent so much time in direct opposition to any form of government or ruler, to be so close to the head of those structures felt bizarre to me, especially since all I wanted to do was be close to him, to please him. It had my internal dialogue completely at war with itself.

"Nightshade," August said with a sigh, his tone as warm as ever. "Mostly I just want to know why you're allowed to have a micro dragon and I'm not."

I huffed out an exhausted laugh and sighed. Yes, *that* was why I lo —felt allegiance to this man. He was really and truly good, a good person through and through, despite his past and the conditions under which we'd first met. Looking back, I would have never imagined that I would fall for my captive, but August made it difficult to resist his charms. "You can have it."

August's back vibrated with his own laughter, and I closed my eyes, soaking in the familiar, comforting sensation. "Then there's nothing to be angry about, I suppose."

"You don't want to know what really happened?"

"Of course I do," August said with a nod as the castle came into view. "I look forward to hearing all about it over a drink."

"A drink?" My head popped up as we neared the stables. As August helped me off the horse, a feat I still found amusing given his previous gracelessness with riding, I noticed that the saddlebags were significantly fuller than when we went out. We didn't usually go shopping together, and instead, August would have the castle staff run errands or acquire items for him, much like I assumed he had done prior to us meeting. Now that we'd gone out into town ourselves, however, it was clear that he had a knack for shopping on his own.

"Yes." He kissed the back of my hand as he lowered me onto the ground. "You know, I haven't seen you drink since you won that bet for killing the Umbral... and I'm *sure* that grog wasn't anything special. I figured sampling some of the flavors of Barrien with me might help you relax a little. I promise it'll be good, no Hippity Hops[1] or anything."

"And I need to relax because...?" Gods, would I ever stop questioning his generosity? Probably not.

"The fact that you're even questioning it is reason enough alone, Nightshade." He reached down and placed his hands on my shoulders for a firm squeeze as if to indicate he could feel the tension in them. He smirked a little. A stableboy took the horse from him, and another stepped in to begin unpacking his saddlebags; unsurprisingly, he withdrew several bags of items, all of which remained a mystery to me. "Up to our room, please," August instructed the attendant.

"Yes, Your Grace."

"Well," August began again, holding out his arm for me to take it. I pushed it down and took his hand instead, lacing my fingers in his and relaxing a little when he squeezed my hand in response. "Tell me all about it." He gave me a curious look before leading us out of the stables and toward the castle; we'd have a short walk ahead of us to talk before we had to face those bustling around in the castle.

I sighed a little, averting my gaze as we walked. "Remember the karuga?"

"Yes, the hideous but effective procreator. Can't relate to the first part, not sure about the second just yet." I didn't have to look at him to know he was smirking at his own jokes; leave it to August to try to lighten the mood no matter what. He stroked the side of my hand with his thumb.

I nodded. "Right, well, when Sidney was helping get all of the babies off of me, we must have missed some… I'm not sure how. It was a long night, but they got into the city somehow."

August grimaced, clearly disgusted by the thought. My description a few nights before must have done the creatures justice.

"Exactly. When we were shopping, I heard them…" I stopped, staring off as I remembered the noise, then shuddered. "Skittering and squelching."

August tugged me forward again, trying to spur on my storytelling as we continued toward the castle. "And you had to get rid of them because—"

"Because that's what I do best! Fight monsters. Right."

"Well, you're good at a lot of things, but—" He tried to keep going, but failed. Not much could stop my frantic mind.

"If I didn't kill them, then they'd grow huge just like the one in the Invisible Cliffs, only they'd have more to eat than that one"—I was rambling as if I couldn't get the words out fast enough—"and they'd eat the entire city if they could, everyone, all of the people, all of the livestock and the trees, even the rats in the walls, and the only way to get rid of them quickly was with fire, so I got the dragon and almost burned down the entire city myself. Not only that"—I was out of breath—"but now we have a micro dragon to deal with, and all of the townspeople think I'm just going around setting fires. I even ruined my favorite bakery!" All the while, the tiny dragon watched our conversation from its spot on my shoulder, where its head swiveled back and forth between us, depending on who was speaking.

"Max, it's okay!" August stopped us both and turned me so that he could hold my shoulders in his massive hands and force me to face him. He squeezed me again, but I was spiraling too far.

"The shopkeeper is a tiny old lady!" I argued, wiping my face with the back of my hands. I had wanted to cry since I realized what I had done. "She's been selling rolls there since the dawn of time, August! She's probably the person who *invented* rolls in the first place!"

August pulled me close to him for a hug and held me tight. "She's fine. No one was injured. Everyone is fine. It's going to be okay."

"It's not! I… it's my fault those things even got into the city to begin with, all because I had to make some grand gesture of… of… I don't know!" I buried my face in his chest in desperation, trying to calm myself but not knowing how. Everything lately had felt like *too much*.

"But you got rid of them before anything too terrible could happen," August reassured me. When he pulled back to look at me, he scratched the head of the little dragon, who had since taken shelter behind my hair. "Maybe this little guy can help search for any remaining freeloaders and blast them away."

I kept arguing. "I destroyed an entire storefront, someone's livelihood!"

August was exasperated as I shot down all of his attempts to help. "It's already taken care of, Max. The kingdom has already paid for it, and they'll have help rebuilding, okay? Please, please, go easy on yourself. You didn't do anything wrong!"

"All I've done since I got here is make things more difficult for everyone," I forced out finally. Now that the words were out in the open it felt like I could breathe a little more easily; now he knew that I knew just how not-made-for-royal-life I was.

But, in true August fashion, he dismissed it. He didn't let me fall into that hole… "People make mistakes, Max. Accidents happen. You've told me that on more counts than one. If it's true when you're reassuring me, why wouldn't it be true when it applies to you?" When I didn't respond immediately, he smiled. "That's what I thought. No witty comeback." He stroked my hair and kissed the top of my head before taking my hand again. "Let's unwind and relax. It's been a uniquely challenging few days, and I know we could both use a break before we face any other… adventures together."

---

1. Hippity Hops: beer made with frog legs. Causes loud belching that sounds like a frog croaking.

YOUR ASS OR MINE?

AUGUST

*B*ack in the safety of our bedroom, I couldn't wait to get into the small paper bag we'd left Beatrice's with. Because Max had taken off to do tasks far more important than exploring sex toys, I'd taken the liberty of purchasing a few bits and bobs based on Beatrice's recommendations. Max, ever deliciously aloof, would have likely never participated in that part of the outing anyway. Now that the day had finally wound down, I hoped that we could share in a new type of excitement together: one that was safer, more predictable, and didn't include the entire kingdom. "Check this out," I announced, shoving my hand into the bag once the door to our bedroom was locked. When I pulled out a small object of glittering blue glass, she stepped closer. I could tell she was holding her breath.

"What is that?" Max asked in a voice so quiet, so breathy, it would've been easy to miss. My cock twitched. She was intimidated, but curious. I liked that. Of all of the people I had slept with and all of the toys I'd had the pleasure of exploring, nothing would ever beat the anticipation of *this* interaction.

I held out the toy. "It's a butt plug."

Max looked from the toy, to my face, then back again. Her cheeks were ruddy with a scandalized blush. I couldn't take my gaze off of her. "Whose… butt?"

I pushed the toy into her palm, the colored glass heated by my flesh, and told her, "Yours." When she didn't respond immediately, I felt the need to explain. After all, what experience does a hardened mercenary have with the likes of sex toys? It wasn't like she had a special saddlebag for her dildo collection. If she did, I would've liked to explore the depths of it with her. "This part," I told her, tracing the teardrop-shaped end, where the finely shaped glass swirled inside with glitter that looked like a galaxy, "goes inside you."

Again, her voice came out in barely a whisper. Was she panting? "Why?"

I shrugged a little. "It'll make you feel… full. Stretched."

"I already feel that way with you."

I wanted to kiss her. I wasn't insecure about it, but we both knew that I was plainly average when it came to size. Still, she was small and tight and… I suppressed a groan, remembering the deliciousness of her warmth and loving the fact that she was probably telling the truth. "This is different. And when you're riding me like a goddamn stallion into the sunset, it'll rub against my cock from the inside. Some people like it… and I'm determined to learn everything you like." I was mesmerized by the way her thin fingers traced over the shape in her hand. When she looked up at me, the curiousness from seconds prior vanished, and she pressed it back into my palm before crossing her arms across her chest.

"Ah, there's the mercenary I know. What is it? Not your style? We can always find other things to try." I couldn't help but laugh. Admittedly, I much preferred Max who was mad that I was teasing her about sex rather than the one who was questioning her entire existence within my kingdom. I hoped we had moved past the latter, for both of our sakes. "I mean, you saw the… vast array of options at Beatrice's."

"If it's so *your* style, why don't *you* use it?" Her beautiful face screwed up into a scowl, and I wanted to kiss her so hard it would make her lips raw.

So I told her. "I really want to fucking kiss you, Nightshade." Before I could answer her question, a knock sounded at the door, and I held up a finger. "Hold that thought, I'm going to answer your question in just a second." When we were face-to-face again, I had a bottle of magically chilled sparkling wine in one hand and two wine glasses balanced between the fingers of the other. "Thirsty?"

"Is that... sparkling wine?" Max looked overwhelmed at the onslaught of novel experiences I was bringing to her.

"Kind of. It's Wysterum, from the Wysterum region of the continent. It's delicious, I promise," I told her as I set the glasses down on our dresser and poured us both drinks. When I turned to her, both glasses in hand, and she didn't take hers immediately, I took a long sip of mine, savoring the cool effervescence. I was glad when Max didn't reject my advance and instead melted into a soft kiss from me before relenting and taking her own glass.

"Good girl. Now... would that make you happy, if I used it on myself?" Not much was off limits for me when it came to the bedroom... aside from sharing. Before Max, I was all about it; I liked sharing and liked being shared. But it was no longer an option... I'd since realized that I was made only for Max and she for me. In fact, the idea of someone else—anyone else—putting their hands on Max ignited a new sort of rage within me. I slid the toy out of Max's hands and tucked it into my pocket so that it was out of sight, certain now that such direct confrontation had not been the best approach in our bedroom affairs, and pulled Max close to me with my free hand. The weight of the glass against my thigh still had me reeling with possibilities.

"I..." Max's mouth was parted with words unfound, her brows still knitted in the middle as if this was a conversation she'd never expected. The way her shoulders were tense and her fingers in mine felt clammy and cold had me suddenly worried.

"Before you answer, drink," I suggested. When I saw her attempt to speak again, I cut her off so I could explain myself. I could see how, from the outside, it seemed odd that I would be pushing alcohol on her in conjunction with a new recreational activity. "If you want. I'm not trying to get you drunk, I'm just trying to get you to… loosen up a bit. For your own sake. You can still say no… you know that… at any point."

She complied and sighed a little after she swallowed. It *was* good, after all, not that bottom-of-the-barrel pub ale. Better than anything Florian could buy her.

"What's scaring you? We don't have to do any of this, Max," I told her honestly, willing my prick to obey the shift in tone. We could sit in bed and talk, for all I cared; my dick might never learn to get over its obsession with Max, but I could keep it at bay when needed. I placed her free hand on my chest and stroked it with my thumb. "It was just an idea, nothing more. Not a requirement."

"But you've done this before," Max commented, seemingly testing out each word before she let it slip from her lips. "You've experimented with plenty of other people… and now you want to do that with me because… because it's part of what you're into."

"I'm into *you*," I told her again, echoing my sentiment from Beatrice's shop. "That's it. I'm into doing anything and everything with you. It's you, not the toys, not the experimentation, Max."

"But you've done all of this before," she repeated. My heart crumbled. What did she want from me? Couldn't she see that our relationship, as unorthodox and undefined as it was, had pushed me to new places in the best ways? That I was a different, better person because of her? I hadn't told her that in those exact words—I hadn't told her a lot of things I probably should have, of course… but I thought she knew.

I closed my eyes, willing my stupid, horny brain to articulate what I truly wanted to say. When I opened them, Max was staring up at me expectantly. "Not all, no."

Max's hands slid from mine, down my chest and abdomen, to my slacks, where she fingered the outline of the plug in my pocket. A chill trickled through my body, like ice was beneath my skin. *Oh, fuck, is she actually considering it?* "And using one of these on yourself… would be new to you?"

I swallowed hard, then nodded. "Yes… and I know enough about myself to know that I'll likely be reduced to a blubbering mess if I'm inside of you while wearing it. Is that what you want?" I found that part of me wanted her to say no—the part of me that still struggled with feeling vulnerable and on display—while the rest of me was begging her to say yes. *Please, please, please… tell me how much it pleases you to see me let loose, to have me at your mercy.* I prayed silently that the pleading in my gaze was as obvious to her as it was loud to me.

I was a column of solid steel by the time she unleashed me from my slacks, both of us frantic in the way we undressed one another. Our glasses had been left hastily on the bedside table, neither of us caring if they shattered on the floor during our lovemaking. I had Max naked in seconds, leaving a trail of blazing kisses across her golden flesh as I tore each garment from her body and tossed it over my shoulder. They may have been some of the underwear that I'd purchased her, but I'd discarded them so quickly I hadn't noticed. I didn't care. She could be wearing a paper sack or a couple of leaves and still be the most delicious sight I'd ever laid my eyes on. When I stepped back, I must've been straining against my boxers because she gasped at the sight of me. "August!"

I groaned. "Don't… say my name."

"Wha—"

"I don't think I've ever been this hard in my life," I confessed, pulling off my socks and tossing them aside. I didn't give a shit about my socks, but I needed to distract myself somehow. I wanted to try everything, do everything, go everywhere with Max. With my Nightshade. If she wanted it, I wanted it, too. Anything for her. "If you say my name again or… hell, if you look at me the right way, Max, I might come."

The way she looked at me then, her head held high in triumph and her perfect body on display, was exactly what I was talking about. Either the wine had loosened her up or she was finally beginning to realize the power she had over me. "Shut up," I told her.

Max shrugged. "I didn't say anything."

We hit the bed in a tangle of limbs, already breathless, already desperate, and I crushed my mouth to hers in overwrought desperation. She sucked on my lower lip, pulling it between her teeth as she straddled me, and I groaned again at the contact of her body against mine… the perfect, warm, delicious pressure. I was vibrating, buzzing with the excitement of just having the privilege to be near her.

"You're shaking," she murmured against my lips, soothing me with soft hands on my neck and shoulders. Divine.

"Every time with you is as exciting as the first time, Nightshade."

"I hope it always is—ah, August!" She gasped as I took one of her breasts into my hand, kneading it as I kissed a path down her throat and licked at a single dusky nipple. Beautiful. I couldn't wait. She was easy to lift and maneuver so that she straddled my face, her torso against mine. She wiggled against my grasp, protesting weakly. "You don't—"

I growled at her. "Let me eat." And because she couldn't let me have my fun in peace, she dove for my boxers, shoving them down my legs in an instant so that my cock sprang free. I knew without a doubt that it was throbbing, thick and hard, and precome dribbled from the head like a leaky faucet. It wasn't right, what she did to me, but who was I to argue? I wanted her to revel in the undeniable proof that she had me wrapped around her finger. "Careful, Nightshade," I warned before pulling her onto my face.

Max whimpered as I lapped at her. It took her a moment to gather her wits before responding, but I was in no hurry to leave my spot or be distracted from the task at hand. She smelled and felt and tasted divine, no longer the sweat-slicked, fatigued traveler I'd been captured by, but still Max. Mine.

"Don't worry, baby—" I stifled a groan again at this, her first time calling me any sort of pet name aside from "big idiot," which still had undertones of distaste from our original adventure together. "I'll take care of you." Again, I wondered if I had the wine to thank for her letting loose, but I lost my train of thought. She gripped me firmly, making me feel colossal in her small hand, then swirled her tongue around the head of my cock in a way that made my whole body twitch. She hummed in encouragement, and I fucked her hard with my tongue in protest. How and why did she get to unravel me so easily? I gripped her thighs before sneaking a finger into her, loving the way she clenched around it in unison with her working me. Every single whimper and sigh I could draw from her was a triumph, but as her own fingers explored my balls, lovingly cradling them and then giving them a firm tug, my heart raced faster and faster. She sucked and stroked me with one hand, then paused to reach across the bed. When she returned, the cool slickness of the glass toy slid between my cheeks in a hesitant teasing. Who was I to request that she do something I wasn't willing to do myself?

"Spit on it," I rasped, my own voice foreign to me. "Drool on it like you drool on my cock."

There was a pause before I heard her do as she was told, and I wondered what it would be like to watch her lick and suck the glass toy. I knew that spit wouldn't be enough, though, and had thankfully purchased some other accessories from Beatrice's shop, one of which had been lying next to the toy on the bed. I reached for it and shoved it down the bed toward Max's waiting hands.

"Use a lot."

The cork of a vial popped open from across the bed and I resumed my ministrations between her thighs, primarily because I loved it, but also because I needed a bit of a distraction. Sure, I was up for anything, but this was new. Exciting, but new. I licked her softly as she prepared the glass toy, but couldn't stop myself from gasping against her flesh when she slid a finger between the cheeks of my ass. It was slick with lube. I grunted against her skin.

"I… don't want to hurt you," she told me suddenly as she lazily circled her fingertip around the tight ring of muscle. I fought the urge to clench my legs together and force her out.

I kissed her cunt again before pulling away to speak. "You won't. Everything you do to me feels good," I confessed, kissing the outer lips of her pussy between statements. "You could break me and I'd beg for more." Ah, hell, it was true. It was in those moments that I realized the extent of my devotion to this woman; she could take me anywhere, and I'd follow without complaint, without hesitation… off the edge of a cliff, into the ocean, into the weird kinky back room of Beatrice's apothecary. I'd be there.

When Max pulled off of me and repositioned herself so that she sat between my legs, I almost protested at the lack of contact before I noticed the look in her eyes. Her gaze, dark and mysterious as ever, was glistening with… who knows? Perhaps desire that she'd reined in for months, I thought. I hoped. She crawled up my body, her hands exploring my abdomen, tracing my muscles as they tensed in response. When her fingers reached my chest, the rest of her followed suit so that she could look me in the eyes. "I've never seen this look before," I admitted, my mouth dry with anticipation of what might be next.

"I guess it's new." Max reached for the nightstand and took a hearty swig of her wine, then gripped my face with one hand. I opened my mouth obediently when she applied pressure on my jaw and to my surprise, she spit the liquid directly into it. "Swallow," she directed me. I didn't hesitate.

Then, she kissed me hard and deep, her tongue cold from the liquid as it explored the inside of my mouth. She trailed her lips down my jaw, my throat, to my chest where she bit my nipple playfully before returning to her space between my thighs. When she gripped my cock, not breaking eye contact, my whole body tensed. "Shit," I uttered with a grunt. She used her other hand to grab the vial of lube again and dripped it over her hand as she calmly stroked me. I shuddered as I felt it drip down my balls, but she didn't miss a beat and slid her other hand down to massage them, then work her way toward my ass again. She didn't stop stroking me as she pressed the pad of her finger against my entrance again, and I closed my eyes tight in an attempt to calm my racing heart, which was making it difficult to relax. I took a deep breath.

"Shh, I got you, babe," she purred, soothing me with her words.

"Ah, fuck, Max, you don't talk like that."

"Relax… it's okay," she said with a purr, and I breathed deeply again, just in time for her to slip the thin digit of her finger inside of me in one smooth motion. I gasped aloud as I adjusted to the intrusion, but Max was bold as ever and immediately sought out the spot within me that blinded me with sensation. I arched my back into the mattress, afraid that if she stroked me any more I'd explode without warning. "How's that feel?" she asked as if it weren't obvious. Tease.

"I'm sure—you can tell—" I said between strangled breaths.

Max let out a pleased sigh, and I forced my eyes open to see her staring down my straining body with a look of sheer wonderment on her beautiful face. Her soft, shapely lips were parted as she studied me. "Yeah…" She withdrew from me and nestled the toy between my cheeks once again, pressing the tapered end against the hole that she'd so thoroughly lubricated. I didn't know if I felt ready.

I couldn't help but ask, "You like seeing me like this?" I needed the reassurance that this was doing for her what it did for me.

"I love— Seeing you like this, yeah."

I groaned at her admission. "Suck my cock again, Nightshade," I told her finally. The eye contact was too overwhelming; I couldn't bring myself to be dominated by her while feeling so on the spot. She took me into her mouth willingly, occasionally glancing up at me while she slid my prick into the back of her throat, all while pressing the toy firmly up against me. She read me like a book, and whenever I relaxed a little more, she pushed a little further… that was how it always was with Max, though. Driving, nudging, sometimes shoving me to my limits. I panted, reaching down to tangle my fingers in her dark hair, and groaned as I felt the stretch of the widest part of the toy. She pulled her mouth off of me to sit back on her heels and watch what she was doing to me. I felt painfully on display for her.

"Baby, you're so close," she assured me, her voice soft but confident. I enjoyed shy, uncertain Max, but if I was seeing her true desires now, I didn't mind that one bit either. "Here it comes, okay?"

I pressed my head, already slick with sweat, back into the pillow and a guttural sound escaped my throat as the toy wedged its way inside of me just when it felt like it might be too much. "Oh god, oh shit, shit, Max."

"It's okay, it's okay, there you go. Oh, good boy… good job. You took that so good," she assured me. She ran her fingers over my cock, which was harder than I'd ever felt it, and squeezed the head, which caused a thick drop of precome to drip down the side of it. "Baby, you're leaking so much."

Goosebumps scattered across my flesh at Max's praise. If she called me a good boy again, I'd probably self-destruct. New kink unlocked. "You like that? Do you like how you make me drip, Nightshade?" I groaned, squeezing my eyes shut as the toy seated itself inside of me. I didn't have a second to adjust because it settled snugly against my prostate and, against my will, caused me to gasp. "Ah, fuck... it's always like this with you," I bit out, forcing myself to open my eyes and look down at her. "From the first time I watched you at the water-fall in the forest."

Max swiped a finger across the tip of my dick, then licked the precome from it while looking up at me. "Yeah? Did you almost come in your pants back then, baby?"

I gasped. "God, Max. Is this what's been bottled up inside of you all along? And all it took was a glass of wine?"

My goddess, my Nightshade, humored me with a laugh before climbing on top of me so that she was straddling my waist, the alcohol having no effect on her gracefulness. She lowered herself down, the damp folds of her cunt pressing against my cock. I felt like I could break through bricks at that point. Then, she ran her nails down my chest. "Why, is this how you like me?"

"I..." I must've tensed because the toy in my ass caused me to tremble again, my cock spasming against her flesh before I could get another word out. "Like you in every way... want you in every way. I can't get enough. Can't you tell?"

"Good boy. Now take me this way." Max shifted so that she could grip my dick and rub it against her pussy, which was slick now with both her juices and mine, before notching it against her entrance. She was teasing me, but she didn't realize just how close I'd been to the edge since the beginning of the evening. When she left me there, straining, desperate, I grabbed her hips and pulled her down onto me.

"This way?" I grunted, my fingertips digging into her bronze flesh.

She threw her head back with a delighted gasp. "Yes!"

"Are you going to ride me, or are you going to torture me more, Nightshade?" When she didn't reply right away, I added, "I thought I'd been good for you."

"You have," Max assured me, raking her nails down my chest again as she rose off my cock and then slid back down onto it. "So good. Just for me?" She was riding me now, taking me as deep as she could before pulling herself almost off of me and then slamming back down again in perfect rhythm. The way her body gripped mine, took me into it so willingly, made my head spin. My ass tightened as she bounced on me, causing jolts of electric pleasure to radiate through my already overstimulated body.

"Just for you, gods, only for you." I was barely holding it together when she slowed mid thrust and pulled off of me, hovering her cunt only inches from my straining cock. I groaned and pressed my head back into the mattress, my fingers twitching against her hips. "Please…" I gasped, like a man starved, tortured, crawling through the desert toward water.

"You want me? Fuck me, baby."

"You know what'll happen," I warned her through labored breaths, willing the toy in my ass to hold off its assault for as long as possible.

Max watched me through a heavily lidded gaze, her tongue darting out to wet her lower lip as she commanded, "You promised me a blubbering mess. *Fuck me.*"

When I gripped her hips tightly and hammered into her, the rush of blood in my ears blocked out my own panting and hers, aside from the occasional "good boy" that urged me on. My climax built inside of me, like a cauldron threatening to boil over; my balls tightened, my ass flexed, and I hammered into her like it was my only purpose in life. I was sweat-drenched and frantic when I finally came, every muscle in my body twitching as I emptied what felt like my biggest load of come into her. I was bleary-eyed, nearly delirious, but I stopped her from pulling herself off of me. "Where are you going?"

"I thought—"

"No, I'm still hard," I told her with a growl, my dick throbbing inside of her in response. I grasped at the nightstand for the open bottle of wine and downed it, then wiped my mouth with the back of my hand. "I'm going to fuck my come into you until you scream."

BLISS

AUGUST

I was in love. This was the beginning of forever for us.

PANIC

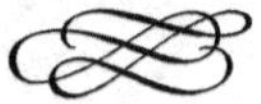

MAX

$\mathcal{I}$ was in love. It couldn't last. Good things never did.

POLITICAL DEALINGS

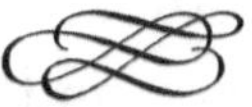

AUGUST

There's nothing I love more than banging Max. So when I was pulled out of bed by a sharp rap at the door of our shared chambers and shaken from my post-coital bliss, I was pretty annoyed. My new role in the kingdom of Barrien had taught me to be humble (as much as someone like me could) and to do a better job repressing some of my initial reactions, so when I opened the door, I did my best to keep a neutral expression.

Still, I couldn't help but remind the advisor of his poor planning. "It's past midnight, Olin." Olin was one of the last remaining advisors from my father's period of ruling and always seemed nervous. Part of it was probably because he had witnessed the downfall of my parents and the way they had been locked away, left to deteriorate in the basement prison of our castle, but the rest of it was just in his nature. He was constantly wringing his hands and glancing around like someone was out to get him. This demeanor alone was irritating to me, but I kept him around because he was a valuable resource for how things had always been done behind the scenes; despite the vast majority of Barrien's population being pleased with the change in rule, there were still some other members of royalty, however far removed, that were attached to the "old ways." Not only that, but he understood the laws of Barrien that I was still familiarizing myself with, and his nervousness meant that he was probably far too paranoid to do anything to jeopardize my plans or position, so I allowed him to stay.

He looked remorseful in addition to his paranoid nerves, but he persisted. "I'm aware, Your Grace, and I offer you my sincerest apologies, but we need to speak." True to Olin fashion, he had a handkerchief in his hands that he wrung as he spoke. It looked… damp.

"Can't this wait until morning?" I yawned, running a hand through my hair, which had grown unruly over the previous months. "I was quite comfortable before you arrived."

"No, I'm afraid not. It's best if we speak before Miss… er, my lady Maxine is awake."

"It's about Max?" I didn't like that one bit. I rubbed my eyes, then narrowed my gaze at my advisor before glancing back at our bed, where Max was sleeping soundly. I could see her frame rise and fall with slow, comfortable breaths in the candlelight. She was still naked, a sheet draped just barely over her hips while her chest remained exposed. My mouth watered again at the sight. Our empty wine glasses remained on the nightstand unbroken, and our clothes still littered the floor. When I looked back at Olin, I realized that I was standing in the doorway completely nude.

"Well, let me get dressed first, Olin, if you don't mind," I grumbled. One of the first rules of being in charge, I had learned, was not walking into advising meetings with your dick out. "Then I'll meet you in the study."

"Yes, Your Grace." He bowed quickly, then turned on his heel and shuffled down the hall away from our chambers. The click of his shoes echoed throughout the empty hall. It likely wasn't the first time the royal staff had seen me naked nor the last, but I realized that I should probably be more careful in case Danny came to our door in the middle of the night instead of an adult.

What I wasn't expecting in the study was to see Florian Featherfoot casually lounging by the fire, drink in hand, while my advisor sat nearby looking grim as ever. Would it kill him to smile? Or at least wear a neutral expression on occasion rather than looking like the world was about to end? And did Florian always have to pick my most expensive alcohol to "sample" during his visits?

"Florian," I addressed him, not completely comfortable with his presence and wondering what exactly he had to do with news about Max.

The elf hardly bothered to look up at me, just swished his drink around lazily and raised it maybe half an inch in acknowledgment. "August."

Olin piped up, his expression one of absolute shock and indignation. "You'll address him as—"

"Don't bother, Olin. We're on a first name basis," I assured him. Florian and I had an understanding. Would we ever be friends? No. But did we get along and agree on most things? Also no. But did I agree to work with him for the sake of our truce with Emynor? Yes, that one. "Well, spit it out. If there's some news relating to Max, I need to know now."

"How *is* Max?" Florian asked with a purr. I didn't even like hearing him say her name. It didn't sound right and reminded me of the way he'd been all over her at the Beast's Breath Tavern. Nothing like that had happened since, but I knew they had history, and I hated it.

I bit my tongue, though I was tempted to tell Florian just how well-fucked I'd left her upstairs, in *our* room… an experience which, I knew for a fact, he'd never had with her. "She's fine. Now tell me what's going on."

"Well, Y-Your Grace…" Olin began, the sweat-soaked handkerchief unfortunately still present. What the fuck was going on? "After the ordeal today in town, we've been hearing a lot of backlash from the people of Barrien about your arrangement with my lady Maxine."

"My arrangement?" I didn't fully understand. Sure, it wasn't traditional, but the laws of the land did not require the king to be married. Besides, up until that point, I'd had numerous arrangements with quite a variety of people, and no one in town seemed to have anything to say about it aside from "how do I get an invitation?"

Olin attempted to explain, parting his thin lips, the top of which was dotted with sweat. "You see—"

"They want to see the king of Barrien married," Florian declared finally before taking another sip of the drink in his hand. He looked unamused by the whole ordeal and was probably as annoyed by Olin as I was; at least we could agree on that.

"Married? Why?"

"I don't know, humans have some sort of fixation with these things, August. You would know better than I."

I rolled my eyes at Florian. "Olin?"

"Y-yes, Your Grace," Olin responded, now pacing behind one of the long, velvet couches in the sitting room. "They believe it demonstrates stability, you see. They want the leadership of their city to be solid, reliable, someone who can commit to another person for the entirety of their life rather than just living with their… er…"

"Mercenary girlfriend," Florian added.

"Uh huh." I nodded slowly, processing the information with my still-tired brain and found myself standing in front of the fireplace as I pondered aloud to our small group. "Marriage…"

"I assume it's not really your 'style,' is it, August? Kind of makes things difficult," Florian mused, a twinkle of amusement in his cold stare. He liked it when things didn't go to plan for me, but unfortunately for him, they often did.

"A year ago I would've agreed with that," I murmured. "And

maybe, in general, I do. But for the right person…" Marriage… What a concept. I was shocked to find that the idea didn't completely repulse me anymore, especially not paired with the idea of spending forever with Max. Would she wear a dress? I hadn't seen her in one since the ball. What might our vows be like? Hell, I'd never considered myself the type of person who would get married, and yet, the idea felt so refreshing and exciting, especially after the night we'd had together. This must've been it, to know that you've found "the one" that people are always talking about. It was nice.

"Oh dear, so you're willing, Your Grace?" Olin asked. "That *is* good news. The people of Barrien and surrounding cities will be so pleased to see you betrothed. They need that security, you know!" The excitement in Olin's voice was almost as nauseating as his handkerchief.

Florian sat up, his expression suddenly curious and almost optimistic. It was unpleasant to witness, like seeing a dog walk on its hind legs, but my mind was far enough away that I distracted myself quickly from the sight. "Well, since you're so open to it—I mean, I'm not sure how you'd tell Max, but I have a list of suitable elvish maidens who—"

Looking back, I definitely misheard that elfy asshole because I excitedly replied with, "I've got some ideas, don't you worry! Don't ruin the surprise for her!" I shot Florian a threatening glance before hurrying out of the study.

I stayed up all night to plan.

I'd need a ring.

FLORIAN FEATHERFOOT

MAX

I can sense Florian from a mile away, and it's not because I have a strong connection to him. No, it's more that I can *smell* him… Florian wears perfume that's more floral than any I've experienced and it's *strong*. Don't get me wrong, I don't hate Florian… in fact, our history would suggest quite the opposite. It's more like once I started seeing my relationship with him as less of a necessity to stay alive, I realized I didn't have to tolerate his nonsense quite as much. When I felt him approaching from behind, I addressed him before turning; I didn't want to give him the satisfaction of letting him think he'd snuck up on me.

"To what do I owe the displeasure, Florian?" I'd been standing by one of the windows high up in the castle, the tiny dragon friend that I'd acquired perched on the sill as well. I had no clue what to do with this dragon. It had followed me around since we returned back from that day at the market, despite me reminding it multiple times that it was free… I supposed I should feed it at some point, but what do you feed a dragon the size of a rat? Still, it seemed too weak to go hunt on its own. August thought he was cute, but we hadn't discussed him actually taking over ownership of the tiny creature, so I guessed he was mine for now. I stroked the creature's chin, and it hummed in delight, its throat warming in response as it rested its face on my fingertip.

"Is that any way to treat one of the royal advisors?" Florian asked, looking genuinely offended by my greeting. When I turned to face him, I found him with his hand splayed on his chest in utter shock. He'd been puttering around the castle, probably doing whatever August had hired him to do, until he unfortunately found me doing the same and cornered me in one of the halls.

"I thought you *liked* my honesty," I teased him, my tone mocking.

He huffed, blowing a strand of silky white hair from his face. Florian was thin, lithe, but despite his slight stature, he had enough height and skill on me to overpower me easily. Still, it was hard to be intimidated when I knew him as intimately as I did. "Still deciding," he told me coolly, then leaned on a hand against the wall above my head, effectively trapping me. "I'm here on business, of course."

I rolled my eyes and held my hand out for the little dragon to hop aboard. He huffed at Florian. Good taste in people already. "You're being intentionally vague for fun or… keeping a secret?"

The elf looked disappointed that I wasn't in the mood to play along. Honestly, I was in the midst of having some sort of internal crisis, so the last thing I needed was to deal with an elf's riddles. "A little bit of both, I guess."

"Well, get on with it or let me go."

"Since when are you so eager to get away from me?" Florian scoffed, removing his hand from the wall and folding it with his other in front of his waist. He looked genuinely hurt; I didn't have the capacity to care, so I turned on my heel and headed back down the hall without casting him a backward glance. The dragon skittered up my arm and settled into the collar of my shirt.

"Wait!" The elf caught me by the elbow, and much to my dismay, he was strong enough to stop me in my tracks. Old Max would've pulled out a dagger and dared him to touch me again without permission, would've cornered *him* and gotten the information from him without riddles, without games. But new Max, royal-life Max, could not be caught engaging in such behavior... The thought of those limitations alone made my blood boil and had me feeling even more torn than I had been in the past week. I gritted my teeth before turning to him, his ice-blue eyes catching mine when we were face-to-face. "Don't you want to know?"

I yanked my arm from his grip as discreetly as I could manage, jostling my dragon companion. A puff of smoke exited his snout. "Not necessarily, and certainly not if there are riddles involved, elf."

For a brief moment, something I'd never seen before flashed in Florian's gaze. Was it... concern? Real interest? A genuine desire to get my attention? It was fleeting and bizarre... so out of place that I was glad to see it go, but its existence in the first place had me doubting my judgment. "No more riddles," he said in earnest, that odd change lingering in his voice for just a second. Then, he switched back to his demanding self. "Let's go for a walk."

It wasn't enough to win me over. "I don't have time—"

"Really? What else have you got going on now that you're not hunting monsters? Are you going to be late for your pedicure?" He held up a finger to shush me before I could quip back. I wanted to break that finger. Besides, who was he to tease about pedicures when he probably had a standing appointment for them? I'd seen his feet; they were nicer than most women's.

"Believe me, you'll want to hear what I have to say," he continued. He was right, unfortunately. I did want to hear what he had to say... Not only that, but he was also right that I would've struggled to fill my time that day anyway. After the fiasco at the market, I was hesitant to venture too far or be too helpful, lest it backfire and get me completely disowned by the city of Barrien.

When we exited the castle walls, the first breath of autumn was there to greet us. It reminded me vividly of the night that August and I had first returned to Barrien together to confront his parents. It was perfectly reminiscent of the weather that evening: just slightly crisp, the air clean and fresh, the first shedding leaves beginning to grace the castle grounds. It would have been a sweet memory (aside from the obvious treason and heartbreak that followed his confrontation) had I not already been so torn internally about my belonging there. Florian offered me his arm, and I supposed that many royals might walk together like that, but if I wouldn't do it with August, I certainly couldn't bring myself to comply with tradition for anyone else's sake. I shook my head. "Walk, talk. That's it. What's the news? What business?"

Florian lowered his arm, looking ahead and avoiding my gaze. Just when I thought his pride was unbruisable, he continued to surprise me. A slight breeze blew by us, almost perfectly brushing his hair from his face. Hell, it might as well have tucked it behind one of his ears. He cleared his throat. "Well," he began, clasping his hands behind his back as we walked. "I came to bring news of something traveling through the continent… It's worrisome, to say the least." He nodded at a groundskeeper passing by, who looked surprised to see the likes of a pure-blooded elf on the property, despite the changes in leadership of Barrien. Florian was unfazed by his reaction. "Up your alley, though."

"If it's a monster, I don't want to hear about it," I confessed, showing my cards a bit more than I intended to with Florian. "My mercenary, monster-hunter, hired-hand days are… over. Or they should be, at least."

Florian smirked. I wasn't looking at him, but I could tell he was amused by my response. "Is that so? According to who?"

I narrowed my gaze at him. *"Me."* When another member of the castle staff walked by, I fixed my face enough to give them a neutral nod of acknowledgment. August would've smiled and made small talk; I wasn't quite there yet with my general people skills, let alone my participating-in-royal-life skills.

"I guess you're not interested in hearing about the werewolves then."

My eyes went wide against my will, and I stopped in my tracks. "*Werewolves?* Plural? There haven't been any in—"

"Decades, at least, by my count." Florian shrugged. "I mean, I haven't looked at the records, but it's been some time since I last heard about any being sighted."

"I guess our—*your* group would be the first to know." I started walking again, hoping that the movement would quell my interest in the topic. "Why should I be interested?"

Florian matched my pace, somehow staying exactly next to me despite the difference in the length of our strides. "A few reasons," he explained, speaking with less urgency than I expected when it came to the topic of werewolves. He was teasing me, drawing it out to see if I would lose what little patience I possessed and beg him for more information. I gritted my teeth as I waited for him to continue. "For one, they're spreading rapidly. You know how werewolves work." Florian gestured vaguely around himself. "They bite people, and then you get more werewolves, especially if there isn't anyone to handle them quickly."

"Uh huh."

"And cures, well, they're unheard of."

"Not true," I insisted. "We both know that the Isle of Wyrms—"

"Sure, but who is going to the Isle of Wyrms for a cure that may or may not exist? And once you've got a werewolf on your hands, who has the time to make that trip?" He was right; the time between werewolf bite and full transformation was shorter than one would think... especially if you didn't know that it was a werewolf bite making your loved one act sick and crazy. Even then, to go to the Isle of Wyrms... it was a big undertaking. That and werewolves had been gone for so long—by extermination, not healing—that no one living really knew if the cure actually existed. It may as well have been a fairy tale, much like werewolves had been for the past few decades.

I shrugged. "There are plenty of monster hunters out there, Florian. Enough to handle a werewolf infestation before it reaches too many big cities. Shouldn't you be organizing them yourself?"

Florian laughed. "First of all, monster hunters don't 'organize.' Second, you know better than anyone that I don't do anything for free."

"Not even for the greater good?"

He didn't need to reply.

"Yeah, stupid suggestion."

"Very. Third, this doesn't even affect me. You know elves can't turn into werewolves. It's like… we only get one magical affiliation." Florian laughed again, this time clearly amused by his own commentary. "Can you imagine a werewolf elf? The world would be over."

"Right… so there's really no reason for you to get into the werewolf fight. Why should I?"

"It's not just a werewolf fight now," Florian explained with a sigh. "Their return has led to a rise in the Covenant of United Neighbors for True Salvation—"

I tilted my head his direction quizzically. "CUNTS?"

"Right… they believe it's a sign of the end times. It's not, obviously. They're fear-mongering, and although it's mostly harmless, they're spreading out across the continent… and this whole situation needs to be handled appropriately." Florian stopped, grabbing me by the elbow once more, but this time his hand was a bit less demanding… more of a suggestion. "It's not my fight exactly," he told me, his icy blue gaze on mine once more. The intensity of it, especially considering he hadn't even ever looked me in the eye in the bedroom, was overwhelming. "But it could quickly become Barrien's… or anywhere else there are vulnerable humans."

I pulled my arm from his grasp again. "Then rally the monster hunters. They don't organize, but you could organize them."

Florian was exasperated now. "Who would I rally, Max? A bunch of assholes who don't know left from right? You know that you're—" He swallowed hard, as if he couldn't bear to give me a compliment, even if it meant saving the world. "The type of person who could handle a situation like this."

"Let me get this straight. You came here to ask me to leave Barrien, to save the world from werewolves… just because I'm the right 'type of person'?"

The elf closed his eyes and took a steadying breath. When he opened them again, he addressed me with a whisper of softness. He wasn't the flirty elf from our escapades in random taverns, nor was he the stern, pompous elf that interacted with the royalty of Barrien on a regular basis. That's not to say that he was sweet or even complimentary, but he was softer, somehow. It made me nervous. A person like Florian is only sweet when it benefits him. "Look, Max. You're probably the *only* person who could handle a werewolf infestation, okay? Well, not including me. But I'll get involved if you are."

"Why the hell would you do that?"

"Because you belong out there," Florian insisted, pointing a manicured finger out in the distance, over the walls of the castle grounds. It was vastly different out there, even from where I was standing; where one side had meticulously groomed shrubbery and pristine architecture, the other was wild and in some areas, dilapidated. Was that what August and I looked like next to each other? A sculpted hedge next to a blackberry bush, full of thorny brambles? How long before my spiked tendrils choked the life from his leaves?

I was starting to lose my temper with this elf. "Why? The world is fine without Max the Menace, Florian. It's time for me to put that life behind me. I have a new one here… with Danny… and August."

Florian threw his hands up and scoffed in indignation. "August? Really? How long do you think this whole charade is going to last? You're too different to stay here, and you know it. This isn't your world, Max. You're made for the road, for fighting, for taverns and bar fights, not *this*."

I set my jaw hard, willing his words to be a lie. I could make this work. I was trying. "This is my world. It could be. I'm trying to make it be." My brain flipped between both sides, seeming only to fight and defend my space in Barrien because Florian was questioning it. I couldn't let him see that my internal dialogue was more aligned with his words than he might think.

"Yeah? And when August realizes that the people of Barrien want a queen who is actual royalty and not one who was born in poverty and grew up in the woods killing Umbrals or burning down buildings with dragons, then what happens to your world?" Florian's nostrils flared with bottled-up rage. Was *this* the secret he had taunted me with? That he had heard about my mishap in the market? Had August complained to him about the public's perception of me? I told myself then that he wouldn't do that; August wouldn't complain about me, period, let alone to someone whom I had a history with. He had assured me that my mistake wasn't the end of the world, that it was the result of good intentions, that the people of Barrien would understand…

My mouth must've been hanging open because Florian lifted a gentle hand to press up under my chin, closing it. I clenched it shut in response before forcing out, "How did you—"

He ignored me, which was one of the first Florian-like things he'd done that morning. "Max… you're not meant to be here," he said, his fingers still on my chin, where they stroked my flesh as if I were an upset child. "You know, in your heart, that it's only a matter of time before August realizes it, too. This place…" Florian looked around as if evaluating his surroundings. "These people… you will keep trying to please them in the ways you know how, and they will never appreciate you for it like the rest of the world does… like *I* do." The elf looked down at me with a glint of mischief in his gaze, then tilted my chin up toward his face.

I tore away from him once I regained my senses. "Like you do? Florian, you don't know anything about me, least of all where I belong." I turned and left him in the courtyard, walking as quickly toward the castle as I could manage without running. The dragon on my shoulder dug his nails into my shirt to hang on.

"Come find me when your king kicks you to the curb for the next best political move!" Florian shouted after me. "I'll be waiting!" He lowered his voice. "I've got time."

I whirled around, suddenly not caring if he saw the redness of my cheeks or the sheer anger in my gaze. "Werewolves may not be able to turn elves, but they can definitely tear you a new asshole… and I won't be there to save you when they do!"

But deep down inside—hell, not really that deep, just under the surface, in fact—I knew he was right.

L-O-V-E

AUGUST

*L*ove is grand, don't you think?

I was deep in my planning stage when I looked out the window of one of the main halls of the castle and saw Max headed back toward the entrance... huh, and there was Florian, standing in the courtyard, looking as royally pompous as he usually did. I decided I couldn't be too annoyed with him since the proposal was technically his idea. It wasn't an idea I would've anticipated coming from him given his history with Max, but one I would take advantage of nonetheless. He and Olin had been right... It was time for me to settle down, and I thanked the heavens that I had the perfect person to do that with. Like I said earlier, things really did have a way of working out for me. I guess I'm just lucky.

"Your Grace, the florist has prepared some options for you," Olin piped up from behind me, drawing me away from the scene out of the window. Max looked furious, but Florian often had that effect on her. I only hoped he hadn't ruined the surprise.

"Great, I'll be right there." Before I turned to follow him, I knocked firmly on the glass panes in front of me in an attempt to get Max's attention, but she didn't hear me. It didn't matter; soon we would have all of the time in the world together… and I'd really get the chance to tell her how I felt. The more I thought about it, the more I realized that the truth had been aching to burst from me for so long. Yes, it was finally time. What a relief it would be to finally, truly bare my soul to her… especially after all she had done and continued to do for me. More than I deserved, but I supposed love felt like that sometimes.

"Which arrangement do you recommend?" I asked Mellia, a new florist that I'd met in the city during one of my outings to connect with the people of Barrien. The castle had had a longstanding florist for such events, but I had dismissed him when I realized that his views were much like that of the king and queen; they shone through in his arrangements, too, and brought the entire castle down in spirit. As much as I wanted to preserve some of the kingdom's history and keep the jobs of those who needed them, Barrien was in a new era, and there was no space for hatred within its walls. I liked this new florist; she was bright, curious, and not only did she assemble beautiful bouquets and fixtures like it was second nature to her, she grew them all in her own garden. I figured Max would appreciate her self-sufficiency as well; maybe I'd tell her all about it after the proposal.

"Hmm," the florist mused, putting her hand on her hip as she perused the options she'd filled the sitting room with. Bouquets covered every surface, including the armchairs and even the floor. Then she rattled off an onslaught of questions. "Tell me about her. What's she like? Does she have a favorite flower? Color? What's her *style* like, King August? What makes you think of her?"

I scanned the arrangements around me, but found nothing that could hold a candle to the way I felt about Max. They were beautiful, sure, vases bursting with a rainbow of colors and every shape imaginable, but none really spoke to me. "That's like asking me to describe the moon, Mellia." I swallowed hard at the realization that, if Max said yes, I'd have to stumble my way through vows at some point. It seemed an impossible feat when I really sat and thought about the intensity of my feelings for her and the ways in which she'd turned my entire life upside down for the better. Sweat beaded on my brow, and I wiped it hastily, the pressure of the event starting to eat at me… "Or the pull of the moon on the sea."

"Well, which one is she? The moon or the sea?"

"Both, in a way," I thought aloud, chewing my lip in each pause. "Silvery and ethereal, graceful, radiant like the moon, but with the depth and mystery of the sea. Though perhaps I'm the ocean, powerlessly drawn to her… and she embraces my turbulent undertow, wraps me in her glowing light, for reasons I can't fully comprehend." My mouth was dry when I finally looked at Mellia, and I found myself shamelessly in agreement with every sappy word that had tumbled out of me. "Does that help?"

The florist was smiling when she said, "That's perfect."

THOUGH I KNEW she was hesitant to explore beyond the kingdom walls given the outcome of her last two excursions, I was glad to find that Max had made her way out of the castle. Perhaps she'd get a ride in with Wraith or figure out what to feed that scrappy little dragon. I still wanted it for myself but admittedly did not have the time that day to research its diet. I was still mulling around the sitting room, finalizing a few of my ideas when Florian barged in. I couldn't place what that man wore, but hell, his perfume was strong.

"Your Grace… we need to discuss the movement of the Covenant—"

"Uh huh, not right now. There will be plenty of time for that later and…" I pulled him aside and spoke quietly out of Mellia's earshot. "I don't want anyone to overhear us and panic, Florian. Let's keep this under wraps until after the engagement, okay?"

"The engagement, right, you've already got plans for it? Shouldn't we look at—"

"Nothing to look at, I've got it all under control," I told him finally as I ushered him back toward the door.

"This is a nice change of pace, I admit. It's good to see you so excited about this next step for Barrien."

As excited as I was, I was grateful that Florian hit the road before the time came for me to propose. He was so caught up in how it would affect Barrien that all he did was bring an air of stress to the situation... not only that, but I didn't think that having Max's ex-lover around for a proposal was the most romantic gesture.

I tried hard to wait, but as days slipped by the weather continued to darken, grow cooler, and I knew I needed to take advantage of early fall before it was gone for the year. Max's behavior had changed a bit since her recovery of my mother's body and the catastrophe at the Dalcester Street Market. She was more reserved, quieter, except for when we were alone and out of the public eye. Then she'd let her walls down again. I figured it was a natural reaction to what we'd been through, both together and separately, in the preceding weeks and hoped that the proposal would be the ultimate display of my feelings for her; I wanted to lay all of her worries to rest.

HAPPY BIRTHDAY TO YOU

MAX

*E*ven when I was working on the road, I always made sure that I was home in time for Danny's birthday each year. I'd save up, take extra jobs, and pinch crystals leading up to the date so that I could bring him home a small cake for the celebration. The boy was open to trying most anything as long as it was sweet. But as his first birthday in Barrien approached, I found that I didn't quite know how to handle it. There were so many resources at hand now that I could make the event as big as I'd thought he'd like… and I found that I had no clue what that was.

I was puttering around the castle kitchen—creeping, really, because I felt like I shouldn't be there—to figure out the best way to get a birthday cake in the kingdom of Barrien. Going into Dalcester was out of the question, and ever since I'd decided to have an identity crisis, so was asking August for anything. The micro dragon, still unnamed, followed me as I looked through cupboard after cupboard of ingredients. They had everything, of course, but when you don't know what you're looking for, that doesn't really matter. One cabinet had an assortment of dried goods, a particular bag of which immediately caught the dragon's attention. He slid off of my shoulder and poked his pointed snout into the fabric of one of the bags, breathing so deeply I was shocked by the volume.

"Find something good?" I asked him before picking up the bag and loosening the drawstring. "Aha!" The dragon perched itself on my arm as I examined the contents of the bag: some sort of dried animal meat that admittedly did smell quite good. I gave him a piece, which he took gratefully, and popped one in my mouth as well before replacing the bag. "Not half bad," I mused aloud as I chewed. It was salty, a little sweet… I couldn't quite place the meat, though. With my luck, it was probably the meat of some exotic animal on the verge of extinction. "What do you think?"

The dragon had just chittered at me in what I assumed was agreement when another sound interrupted us. "My, my, what do we have here? A mercenary and her dragon raiding the castle kitchen?" August's voice was rich and smooth, as always, and I felt hesitant when I turned to face him, almost as if I were actually in trouble. When I found his face graced with a charming smile, I quietly sighed in relief.

"Caught red-handed, I'm afraid," I told him, swallowing my last bite of food. The dragon clung to my shoulder as it chewed the remainder of its treat. I put up my hands, unsure of whether I was joking or not.

When August closed the gap between us, he took both of my hands in his and brought them to his face to kiss my palms before telling me, "Don't worry, you'll find I'm quite a benevolent ruler… I'll let it slide this time." He held on to both of my hands as he spoke to me, and I let myself relax under his gaze. That man's eyes held all the love in the world. "Did you find a snack for your little friend?"

"I think so," I told him. Then, with a sigh, I let myself rest my cheek on his chest. He released my fingers only to stroke my hair with his.

"What's got you rummaging around in the kitchen at this hour?"

"Danny's birthday…"

"Oh? Is it soon?" He sounded disappointed.

"Yes," I told him, feeling small and lost and a little out of control of my own life. "Normally I'd get him a cake somewhere on the road, but, um…"

"But everything is different now," August said, completing my thought. When I looked up at him, he wasn't upset. Instead, he seemed curious, interested to understand what it meant to be in our unique position. He brushed a thumb against my cheek as he held my gaze and pressed his forehead against mine. His brows were furrowed in concern, and I reached up to smooth the space between them with my fingertip. If only it were that easy to actually release stress.

"Yes." The dragon wiggled between us, then lay across my chest like a scarf.

The king of Barrien smirked at the small creature's antics, but returned his attention to me quickly with the corners of his eyes still creased in amusement. "While I hope the differences are mostly positive, I want to hear about all of them…" he told me before pulling away to look me in the eyes. Then, he turned toward the counter near us with his hand on his chin as if he were searching the area. "Perhaps while we figure out how to make a cake for Danny." I must've looked shocked because he laughed immediately. "What?"

"You *bake*? I didn't know that."

"Oh, gods, no. I'd like to say yes and that I'm full of surprises, but we both know that you read me like a book," August told me, scanning the cabinets now. Eventually he must've found what he was looking for because he grinned widely, then held up a thick, leatherbound cookbook as if to say "ta-da!" "As for baking, how hard could it be?"

The kitchen had been fully decorated in misplaced flour, bowls of reject batter, and a hearty scattering of sprinkles and chocolate chips when I stood back with my hands on my hips. We had gotten one promising cake into the oven after hours of meddling, and boy, were the kitchen staff in for a rude awakening when they came to work in the morning. As we worked, he delicately attempted to get me to open up about how life had changed for me.

I tried my best to put it into words, but it was a challenging feat to do so without sounding ungrateful. "It's just… different." I sighed in frustration at my lack of grace. "When you spend most of your life finding a way to survive, it's hard to move away from that, especially when it means…"

"Not working as hard?"

"Right… If anything, it's easier for me to put in more effort, to find ways to adapt to challenging situations. Letting myself relax, it feels impossible, August."

"You know that you deserve to relax, right? You've had enough work in your years to last a lifetime and then some. It's okay to bask in a life that's uncomplicated and undemanding. It's okay to rest. It's time to stop telling yourself you don't deserve that." August stood nearby, leaning on the counter to take a break with a dishtowel flung over his shoulder; his clothing was as messy as the remaining surfaces in the kitchen. His gaze was intent, serious, and he never looked away from me when he spoke. "Sometimes I fear you're punishing yourself for some crime you didn't commit. You have nothing to repent for."

"Why are you doing all of this?" I asked suddenly before I could think twice.

"That's easy, Nightshade," August said with a laugh. He looked lighter than I'd seen in months, as if there had been some grand development inside of him that had allowed him to shed the crushing weight of the year prior. "I love you."

I was frozen in silent stupor when a bit of smoke streamed from the oven, effectively interrupting us. The little dragon was spooked by the sight and scurried back onto my shoulder from his place on the flour-dusted countertop. Without hesitation, August pulled the dish towel from his shoulder and used it to remove our cake from the oven. "Don't worry," he told me as he replaced the towel and set the cake on top of the stove. "You don't need to say it back." The king stroked his chin in thought again, a faint smile on his lips, and added under his breath, *"I guess that's how I know it's real."* When his attention turned to me again, he shrugged. "Shall we try our final concoction?"

I didn't say it back that evening. I wanted to. Though I was restrained still by my own shock, my insides were rolling with mixed emotion.

"What is it?"

"I don't… I'm not sure how to respond."

August nodded, digesting my statement. I couldn't help but wonder if he'd imagined the moment going a lot differently. I would have. "Well," he began before closing the gap between us. He hooked an arm around my waist and hoisted me up onto the messy counter, effectively turning my black pants white. "Was it nice, hearing me say that?" My lover's gaze was so hopeful that it broke my heart.

I wrapped my arms around his neck. "Yes."

"Then just enjoy it. Enjoy me," he said softly, his gaze shifting to my mouth. "You're allowed to, you know."

I kissed him then, and all of my worries dissipated within the softness of his lips and the eagerness of his tongue as it explored mine. It was easy to enjoy August, king of Barrien. The rest was difficult. The future was heavy. But for that moment, for that evening, I could try to forget everything but him… his tender heart, his valiant spirit.

When we broke apart, he reached behind me to stick a fork into our experiment and bring a piece of chocolate cake to my mouth between us. "Eat."

I did as I was told, a little hesitant considering the lack of baking skill between us. He took a bite as well, then kissed me again, the faint

taste of chocolate still lingering on him. "Shockingly delicious," I
told him.

August laughed. "Great, then we'll make this for his birthday. Now
that that's handled… I'm still a bit hungry."

"What's for dinner?"

The king was already on his knees in front of me, his fingers deftly
undoing the laces of my pants when he said with a smirk, "Guess."
Both his stubble and my bare ass ended the night covered in sprinkles
and flour.

At Danny's birthday party, an event that was far too extravagant for
the likes of myself and my brother, August asked me, "I hate to admit
this, but we haven't celebrated one of your birthdays together yet.
When is it?"

"It's—"

Danny must've overheard us. "Max doesn't have a birthday."

I turned red immediately.

"Everyone has a birthday, my boy," August told my brother,
ruffling his hair before sending him off for another piece of cake. I
could tell when he turned back to me that he wasn't going to let me
dismiss the topic.

I shrugged. "I don't remember. It's been a long time since I've celebrated my own birthday… not since my mother was still alive." How
old was I now? Twenty… five? Twenty-seven?

August's brows knitted in concern again, as they often did when
he was speaking with me. "Pick a day, Nightshade… and we'll celebrate you. Your existence is worth celebrating."

Later that day, once the excessive festivities had winded down, I
caught August and Danny playing with a set of wooden swords that
August had given him as a gift. They were beautiful, carved by an

artisan woodworker in Dalcester and painted to look realistic. I watched them from afar, in awe at the way that August kept on his feet for so long, even with how tired his leg must've been. He took the time to show Danny a few moves that I, myself, had only shown him months before, and he even let my brother get in a "fatal blow," which caused August to fall to the ground dramatically. While he was down, Danny chucked his own sword to the side before tackling the king, his bright laughter filling the air. "Best. Birthday. Ever!"

THE PROPOSAL

AUGUST

It was early one evening when I asked for Olin to fetch Max, a task that he approached more shakily than usual. The man was afraid of her, and honestly, I didn't know that I blamed him. Nevertheless, he followed through, and some time later she emerged into the courtyard, where I was waiting for her. The sun had just started to set, and the sky was beginning to turn a brilliant shade of orange as she stepped out. I hadn't asked for her to dress up for the occasion because I didn't want to give anything away or lead her to believe I wanted anything but "just Max," so when she walked down the cobblestone path toward the courtyard in a loose white blouse and the same worn leather pants she loved, my breath hitched in my throat. A light breeze caught her hair, pulling it from her neck, the bronze flesh of which might as well have shimmered as she walked. She was stunning.

The path between the two of us had been decorated with vases of arrangements created by Mellia based on my description of our relationship... She had delivered. Each pot exploded with massive white lilies in the center of a sea of blue hydrangeas and delphinium, which was speckled with black hellebore and tulips. The lilies were accented by pale yellow zinnias. I could see her vision… a massive, all-consuming moon, surrounded by stars and the turbulent, dark ocean that was pulled to it.

As she walked, looking slightly hesitant but otherwise hard to read as ever, the musicians behind me began playing. I imagined what she might look like walking down the aisle to our wedding. The music was soft and sweet, a piece I'd picked because of the way it reminded me of her touch, and it managed to keep my heart from crawling up into my throat. Wraith, too, had joined in the festivities and begrudgingly allowed an attendant to weave matching flowers into her mane. The dragon, still unnamed, sat atop her back and surveyed the event with curious black eyes.

"Nightshade," I addressed her as she approached, reaching out to take her hands in mine. "How was your day?"

Her hands were clammy, and she seemed just as nervous as I was, though I imagined it was for different reasons. She had probably guessed what I was planning by now, hadn't she? Maybe she was nervous about how she would react when I finally asked. I could understand that it would be stressful to be put on the spot, so I had ensured that only those who really needed to be included—like the musicians and the animals—were present. I had no control over which of our advisors or attendants were anxiously watching from the castle windows. Olin, in particular, had seemed extra uneasy once the decor was arranged…

Max gave my hands a squeeze. "It was fine," she told me finally, offering me a small smile when our eyes met. "What's going on, August?"

"W-well, I…" My mind went blank, the days of practice I'd poured into fine-tuning my speech completely vanishing on the spot. I took a deep breath, then smiled at her again. Fuck. "Ah, shit." I ran a hand through my hair in flustered overwhelm before deciding to pour my heart out in the least eloquent way imaginable. I'd get points for honesty, right? "I can't live without you, Max. You know that, right? The world meant nothing to me until you dragged my half-naked ass out of the castle and showed it to me through your eyes. I want to spend the rest of my days seeing it that way, the only way that matters."

Determined to carry the proposal out before my nerves got the better of me, I let go of one of Max's hands to grab the ring from my pocket. It had been specially crafted for her because there were no family heirlooms for me to pass down, not that I would have wanted them, and I had measured the size of Max's finger with a string while she slept. The piece was thin, delicate, a band of yellow gold vines accented with small diamonds that culminated around the largest emerald this side of the continent. I held on to it while lowering myself onto one knee as gracefully as I could manage with my leg, before asking, "Max... my Nightshade... would you do me the immense honor of marrying me?"

NOPE

MAX

The words slipped out of my mouth before I had time to think about them, to craft them into something delicate and gentle, into a response worthy of the effort that August had clearly put into this moment: "August, I... no."

The worst part was that I wanted to say yes.

More than anything.

I wanted to say yes, to scream it, to go with the flow, to listen to what my heart was telling me instead of every other outside force. I wanted to be the type of person who let themselves be happy.

But as I stood there, surrounded by musicians and flowers and my dressed-up horse, all while our attendants looked on, I was reminded just how out of place I was in the kingdom of Barrien... and how right Florian had been. I was not meant for this world, for August; I couldn't give him or his people what they needed. They deserved someone fit to be queen... who would fill the role easily and not with the great effort I had to put in just to walk through the courtyard. August deserved someone adventurous in the ways that *he* was: in the bedroom, in his taste in cuisine, but not in the monster-hunting sense.

And though my heart shattered when I rejected him, each splinter piercing my insides, I still had to. Florian's talk had left me bracing for separation and—Florian. My desperate sadness took a quick turn toward rage when I realized that Florian had manipulated both of us. It wasn't so much his scheming that angered me, however. Instead, I was upset with the fact that he knew me well enough to do so. He understood the inner workings of my mind enough, knew my buttons and exactly how to push them, while August didn't. I didn't know if he ever would. I gritted my teeth. "I can't."

I tore my gaze away from the pots of honey he called irises and tried to steady myself as the courtyard spun around me. The world as I knew it, the world I'd struggled to remain in but was growing to love, was over.

WHAT DO YOU MEAN, "NO"?

AUGUST

"**G**ood one." I laughed. I laughed because I'm a big idiot, just like Max always says. But then again, she hadn't called me that in a long time… Maybe that should've been my first clue that something was awry. I didn't assume she was joking because it was a joke to think she would reject me, but more so that I had been so sure about her… I hadn't imagined that things could pan out any other way than pure bliss… "You're joking."

When she turned and took off back into the castle, I followed her as quickly as I could without running. "You're joking, right? Max!" Then, I started to run… because she was running. Oh hell, why was she running? "Max, please tell me you're joking!" I shouted after her, dropping the flowers from my hand and pocketing the ring as quickly as I could. I couldn't keep up with her; my leg wouldn't let me… and knowing Max, if she was running somewhere I couldn't, it was for good reason. "Did I do something wrong?" I asked, already breathless and knowing full well that we weren't going to converse while I was pursuing her. My pursuit of her turned into a full-on chase into the castle, and panic coursed through my veins so severely that I thought I might be dying. "Max! Please…"

I found myself at the base of the stairs with so much anxious energy that I was trembling, but couldn't move to start the walk up. Day after day, I had denied the toll that the staircase had taken on me and my damaged leg, but now… I knew that once she got to the stairs, I'd lost her. If I tried to chase her now, I'd fail or fall… two things that could certainly make this nightmarish situation worse; I wasn't sure my pride could take any more of a beating. My foot had barely graced the first step when I heard a door upstairs slam, but I knew the sounds of the castle enough to know that it wasn't *our* door. She was hiding from me.

"Not the sexy kind of hide-and-seek either," I muttered to myself as I finally gripped the handrail, determined to begin my ascent no matter the cost.

Olin had just appeared in the entryway. "Your Grace? How did it—"

"Tear it down."

"Sir?" Olin wrung his usual handkerchief, and I wanted to rip it from his clammy hands.

"There will be no engagement," I told him firmly, gritting my teeth as I scaled the stairs. Pain seared through my leg. "Tear down the decorations, call off the remaining events for the day. I don't want to hear from anyone." I didn't know *why* there would be no engagement or how I'd missed her cues so blatantly, but all I wanted was to get to Max and figure out where I'd gone wrong. If my "surprise" had made her run from me, then I wanted to destroy all of it.

Sometime later I made my way to Danny's room and knocked on the door. "Max, are you in there?"

All I could make out was a sniffle and a whisper. *"Don't you think you should talk—— ow! Hey! I'm just trying to help!"* Another sniffle. I'd made her cry. How had I managed that? The last time I'd made her cry, I had shut her out after she'd torn down my walls at the End of the Road Inn. I'd vowed to never do that again.

"Danny, what's going on? Is she okay?" My voice was pathetic and pleading, but I didn't care. I was ready to beg.

Danny spoke up through the door. "Uh… she's alright. What did you do to her?"

I pressed my forehead against the wood of the door and sighed. "I asked her to marry me."

"You did *what*?" The boy sounded as shocked as I had when I first considered the proposal.

"Danny, can you just—ugh, Max, please talk to me. I'm sorry. Just tell me what I did, and I'll fix it. Is… is it… maybe marriage isn't your thing, I don't know, but please. We can figure it out." I pressed myself up against the door as if I could will my body through it and onto the other side, but in reality I just wanted to see her, see her face, be close enough to her to know that I hadn't completely sabotaged our relationship.

"There's nothing to figure out!" Max's voice finally broke through the thick wood of the door, and it was strained, sadder than I'd ever heard it. She was speaking between choked sobs. The sound tore at my heart. "I can't marry you."

"That's okay!" I blurted out. It hurt, and I wanted to know why more than anything, but… "I don't need marriage, I just need you."

Danny grumbled. "Gross."

The hall was eventually silent, and neither of them humored me with another response, not even Danny with his childish commentary or attempts to be a middle man for us. I was selfish to wish that he would keep her talking to me, but I didn't care. As the silence crept on, I wanted to bargain with him for his help. Alas, there was no shuffling on the other side of the door. I rested my back against the wall near his bedroom, from which I could see the entrance to our own chambers, and wondered if this was the beginning of the end.

"Is this what you meant when you asked if you had ruined us, Max?" I asked no one in particular as I let myself slide down the wall and sit on the cool marble floor of the hallway. "Because it feels like that right now, like I've destroyed the best part of my life... and I need you to tell me that's not what's happening." I fought the urge to beg again, though I may as well have been already. I would've done anything to rewind the day with the knowledge I had then; if we could just go back to that morning, when everything had been fine, I would forget marriage.

I would tell the kingdom of Barrien, tell my advisors, tell Florian that they could shove engagement and marriage up their asses. I would have done anything to escape the lonesome silence of the hallway, where I didn't know where I stood with the one person in my life that truly mattered. To have her hide from me was a pain I didn't know existed, and I had been through a lot of pain in my short life already. This felt reminiscent of my mistake following the first time we'd made love, only magnified by a million.

The light in the hall eventually dimmed as the sun finally went down, setting earlier and earlier as we shifted toward winter. My heart felt the frigid emptiness of the changing seasons, too. The castle staff came through to light sconces in the hall, and again, I was left in the silence of the empty walkway with nothing but my thoughts to accompany me. Occasionally there was a shuffling behind the door, something shifting here or there, but if they were speaking to each other I couldn't make it out. I stretched my injured leg out in front of me and stifled a groan at the way it ached when I moved it, but soon exhaustion overtook me, and I fell asleep in the hallway, sitting across from my bedroom door... I couldn't go there because the bed smelled like Max, and she wasn't in it. Maybe tomorrow.

But tomorrow came, the blinding light of morning filling the hall again in a pale yellow assault. When I knocked on the door, there was no shuffling. No whispering. I pounded. Again, nothing. I grabbed a member of the castle staff and implored them to unlock it before I realized I could simply command it.

"Now."

"Your Grace, you always insisted that we give young master Danny the utmost privacy…"

I shook my head, telling myself that it was about safety now, not just my own needs. "Open it."

The room was empty, aside from everything I'd ever given them both and a small, black dragon sitting on Danny's desk, with a note that read: *I'm sorry*. It fluttered in the light fall breeze coming in from the open window. I approached the scene hesitantly, as if interacting with it would make it more real. The dragon came to me, curious about the intruder in the room, and let me scratch it under the chin. When he moved, I realized that he had been sitting on a small object: A cord with Max's tooth hung on the end of it. It was like she had predicted her departure long ago.

TIME AND SPACE

MAX

I was a ball of unbridled rage when I tore into the woods on Wraith's back, Danny hanging on for dear life behind me. I was moping, feeling sorrier for myself than I even thought possible. My internal dialogue just kept reminding me that I wasn't made for royal life, that I was out of place… that I was destined to live a life full of struggle. Wasn't made for Barrien, or August, or comfort and consistency. Nor safety. I said a silent prayer for any creature or man who encountered us wherever we went next because there was no way in hell I knew how to be anything but my real, feral self now that I was no longer with August.

Hell, I was no longer with August, but had we ever really, officially been "with" each other? Did it matter? If what we had wasn't real or official, then I would have no way of knowing what actually was…

"Max, watch out!" Danny cried from behind me, his grip on my waist tightening as I narrowly avoided guiding Wraith directly into a tree.

"I got it!" I hissed at him, silently grateful that he'd said something but too volatile to acknowledge that he'd saved us from crashing. A few branches hit me in the face as we swerved. Apparently, I did not have it.

WE SLUNK into town for one last time under the cover of nightfall and found ourselves in the dingy streets of Barrien once again. Despite all that August had done for the town, it still smelled like pee. I knocked on a door that I had been at not so long before and found the exhausted face of Ermaline on the other side.

"Max?"

"I know it's late," I told her, pulling a sleepy Danny against my side in the doorframe. "But I promised I'd stop by."

"That's alright, dear, come on in." Ermaline ushered us into the house, the warmth of which I was surprised by, and closed the door behind us. "The girls are already asleep."

We entered quietly, and Ermaline served us glasses of milk and stale cookies, a generous gift from someone like her, and I elbowed Danny in the ribs when he started to complain. He had gotten too comfortable with royal life. Thankfully he sat quietly for the remainder of the trip. I would've liked to have left him with Wraith, but the town at night wasn't a safe place for a young boy, and I needed to get used to keeping him close again.

Ermaline wrung her hands as she waited for me to spit out whatever I was going to tell her, but we both already knew what it was.

I swallowed a piece of cookie, washed it down with some milk, and then wiped my mouth on my sleeve. "I, um…" Hell, the last time I'd told someone I'd found the dead body of their relative, it hadn't gone very well. "Found your husband's body… at the Invisible Cliffs." When she said nothing, just stared at me with her teary gaze, I forced myself to continue. "He had, um, a drawing of your family with him. I thought about bringing it back to you, but I—"

"No, no… you did the right thing, leaving it for him to rest with." She dabbed at her eyes with a dirty handkerchief. It had been so long since her husband had last left for work and not returned… I wondered if it was a relief to know that he hadn't run off or been captured and instead had simply succumbed to the hazards of his job at the time. It was a shame he hadn't lived to see the closure of the Invisible Cliffs, but then again, it had been his livelihood. Though the disappearance of every monster on the continent might have provided its other inhabitants with more safety, I surely would have mourned my loss of income as well.

The rest of our visit went by in silence, until we exited and Ermaline pulled me back through the doorway into a tight hug that I hadn't been expecting.

I DIDN'T KNOW where we were going, so the following few days felt aimless and exhausting; it's amazing how quickly you can forget all of the things you'd learned to survive, like how to get from one part of the continent to the other. I'd only taken enough crystals to get us through the first week if I was careful, and I'd only gathered enough supplies to fit in Wraith's saddlebags. I had prioritized the essentials, like clothing we would need for the upcoming winter, but Danny had huffed until I grabbed the sword August had gifted him on my way out the window. I suppose I owed him at least one small pleasure given that I was now dragging him back on the road and away from comfort. Why couldn't I just suck it up and fit myself into royal life like I was meant to? We'd had *everything,* and my own fucked-up feelings of belonging had driven me away. "Was it that?" I mused aloud as Wraith carried us down a back road past Dalcester.

"Huh?" Danny stirred from a nap against my back.

"Nothing. Go back to sleep."

Was it that? I asked myself again, this time internally. Was it really that I was afraid of not fitting in, or was it the fear that I might actually get everything I ever wanted—love, stability, family—that had caused me to sabotage my own happy ending? Couldn't I have sucked it up and prioritized my brother's sense of belonging instead?

The crunch of footfall on shriveled leaves caught my attention, and both Wraith and I perked up at the noise. I steered to the side of the road and off the path. Danny had fallen back asleep and was silently resting against me, so we stopped and waited, looking out onto the road from behind a thick group of trees.

Approaching were two soldiers, one on horseback while the other walked beside him on foot. They both looked tired and dirty, but what really caught my eye was the symbol on their armor: the buzzard of Barrien. They must have been returning from the land of the elves, but it had been months since August had pulled back his forces from Emynor.

"Can't believe that bastard had the balls to make us stay and help those damned elves, after all of the work we put into keeping them in line," one of them said as he walked, spitting on the ground at the mention of who I could only imagine was August. "Felt like we were just undoing everything… savages." He grunted.

"An actual bastard, though, eh? Never thought we'd find out he was the illegitimate kid of the real king and some elvish trash." The soldier speaking picked at his teeth, flicking something from his finger away from him as he rode leisurely atop his horse. Ever classy, those soldiers of Barrien.

"No?" the other one asked with a laugh. "I dunno, Bruce, I'd've given it to summa those gals. They're not half bad once you get past the ears. Those things are as creepy as they come."

The man on foot laughed, a loud, ugly sound, and my blood boiled. "I *did* give it to some of them!" he added, making a lewd gesture with his hands. When he stopped, he reached down and scratched at the front of his pants. "Not sure what they gave me, though."

I peeked through the foliage to get a better look at the men as they passed, which turned out to be more than just the two, and I was grateful for Wraith's almost-silent breathing. I was able to slide Danny off of me so that he slumped forward on Wraith's back, then I climbed onto one of the trees we were hiding behind and scaled it quickly so that I was above the group of men. My horse knew to wait for me, and hopefully, my little excursion would be quick enough that Danny wouldn't notice me missing.

"As for the ears," the same man continued, unhooking something from his belt loop in front of him. It was almost too far away for me to see. "I got an easy solution for that!"

The man on the horse chuckled again. "Ah, yes, forgot about your little… collection."

As the men passed directly underneath me, I got a closer look at what he was holding up; it was a leather cord, on which multiple pointed pieces of flesh of varying shades were hanging. They were tips of ears… elf ears. Each one had a hole punched in it so that they could be threaded onto the cord and kept, apparently.

I tried to calm my impulsive thoughts. *Punish them.* You're not being paid, save your energy for tasks that involve money. *Just kill them. The world is better off without those men.* Do you really want Danny to see you murder someone in cold blood? *Is it cold if they deserve it? They raped and mutilated elves. Shouldn't he know justice?* My own personal dialogue went on for what seemed like forever but in reality was a split-second, and the devious part of me won, hands down. My fingers twitched for the blades on my thigh as I stepped carefully, silently, from one tree to the next until I was above them again.

My entire body trembled at the thought of these men cutting the ears from their victims and keeping them as trophies, so much so that I couldn't allow them to return to Barrien like this. What if… what if

August saw them? What if they treated him like that just because he was part elf? They didn't have the right, but that wouldn't stop them from slandering him behind his back… and if I knew anything about the way that people worked, it was that beliefs like that spread quickly. I willed myself to be calm, to be steady, lest I ruin any chance I had to make this situation right… well, as right as a group of soldiers with body-part trophies could be made… and when I decided to drop down on their group, I leaped and landed on my ankle, causing myself to stumble and roll into the group.

That had not been the plan.

The soldiers stopped as I gathered my wits, and the man with the trophies was grinning at me through rotten teeth when I finally looked up. I could smell his breath from my spot on the ground. "Well, whadda we have here, gentlemen? A little lady eavesdropping on our conversation?"

"You like soldiers, little miss?"

My stomach turned as the man with the trophies held his hand out to me and helped me onto my feet. I'd have to wash that hand. Normally, I would've told him to go fuck himself, but I needed them to see me as harmless as they apparently did… because the second he grabbed my hand, I managed to pull him to his knees in front of me, unsheathe one of my daggers, and press it to his neck while his friend looked on.

This didn't faze the trophy man at all. In fact, he laughed. "Oh, I like 'em feisty!" He stunk even more up close.

"Oh yeah?" I pressed the blade against his flesh a little harder.

"Now, now," the man on the horse started, sucking his teeth as he leaned over the front of his saddle to get a closer look at me. "What are you doing? You trying to rob us? We ain't got any crystals… Hell, we're humble servants of the kingdom of Barrien."

I rolled my eyes. "Is that so? And was it the order of the kingdom of Barrien to do whatever you did to those elven women?"

The man on the horse sat back in his saddle with a bewildered look on his face. I couldn't tell what my hostage was doing. "What're you, some vigilante workin' for the elves?"

"No, I'm—" *Just someone who loves an elf, okay?* Oh, gods, had I really just admitted that to myself? "Someone who can't stand injustice."

Both men laughed, and I decided that it wasn't really my style to converse with my victims. It hadn't been in the past, and even though I was clearly having difficulty easing back into my life as a mercenary, I should stick to my tried and true methods. I didn't wait for the other man to respond, instead gesturing for him to get off the horse. "Get down, or I'll slit your friend's throat right now."

When he then rolled his eyes in response, I pressed the blade into the trophy man's neck until a steady flow of blood leaked out of a small cut in his flesh. He changed his tune quickly. "Help me out here, Bruce. This bitch is crazy."

The man on the horse complied and hopped down with his hands raised. Even the horse looked uneasy.

"Now, I need you to listen very closely, alright?" I instructed the men.

"Yeah, sure, sure," the man from the horse agreed, but when I saw his fingers twitch toward his own sword, I sighed and dragged the dagger across his partner's throat.

"See, look what you made me do," I scolded him. "So sloppy," I said with a groan, then turned my blade toward the other man before kneeling next to his partner, who was quickly bleeding out. He had his hands around his throat and was blubbering some sort of nonsense as crimson leaked from between his fingers. Then he was silent. "Toss your weapons over there," I told him, jerking my chin toward a row of bushes on the side of the road. "Now."

He did as he was told, then looked at me with uncertainty and a bit of disbelief. "Don't do anything hasty, miss," he said, putting his hands up again. "You don't know the penalty for killing a soldier of Barrien, let alone two."

"Something tells me I can handle the penalty," I muttered to myself. A tiny, unreasonable (and likely unstable) part of me enjoyed the idea of being captured and taken back to Barrien to stand trial in front of August. When I looked up at the soldier again, I told him firmly, "Do not try to leave. I will catch you. And don't scream, okay? My baby brother is taking a nap, and it's a whole thing if you wake him up, you know? I'm trying not to expose him to too much gore… it's *hard* raising kids these days." I caught myself rambling again, then cleared my throat. "If you want to live, you're going to stand right there until I say you can go. Got it?"

He nodded shakily, and I had to suppress a laugh. Was I the ghost of all of the women he'd wronged?

"Good." Then, still on one knee and with the horse rider in my peripheral vision, I leaned over to the dead man and began my work. It took me only a few seconds to unclip the leather cord with the elf ears and pocket it. That was mine now. What I'd do with it, I wasn't sure, but they would be handled correctly from then on out. Then, I grabbed the man by his hair so that I could take a closer look at his own ears. There wasn't much to cut, I thought, but enough to make a point… so I grabbed the top of one of his ears and sawed it away with my blade, leaving nothing but a bloody stump and lobe on one side. Then, I did the other. The cartilage crunched and blood gushed over my fingers as I worked, annoyed at how messy this little side job was. Normally, I'd demand pay for such strenuous and filthy work.

"You want these trophies?" I asked, holding my palm up to the other man with his friend's bloodied cartilage in it. They looked like trimmings from a butcher shop. Maybe this was what micro dragons like to eat. When the man shook his head again, I opened his dead partner's mouth and stuffed the ear tips inside, then shut it. His jaw snapped closed with a satisfying click. "Good," I said to no one in particular, groaning a little as I stood from the ground. Nights of sleeping in the dirt had not been kind to my body. "Now, listen very closely, okay?"

The soldier's eyes were wet with tears.

"No, no," I told him firmly, reaching up to pat his cheek with a bloodied hand. I left a small, red handprint on his flesh. The air smelled metallic. "None of that. You're going to take your friend here and load him up on your horse… are you following?" When he didn't meet my gaze and was stuck staring at his partner on the ground, I yanked his chin toward me. "Are you following?"

"Y-yes."

"Okay, good. Load him up and take him back to Barrien. When your fellow soldiers ask what he did to deserve this, you tell them, okay? So they know that anyone else caught disrespecting the king of Barrien or the elves of Emynor will meet a similar fate. You know," I said, squeezing his jaw again, "I should do the same to you, but I really need a messenger."

He stared at me for longer than I liked.

"Hop to it."

When I returned to Wraith, Danny was still asleep. I slid the ear tips into the saddlebag after wrapping them in a scarf I had packed and got back into the saddle, not moving until I saw the soldier take off with his friend loaded up behind him. All I could smell was the copper tang of blood, which had now soiled one of my very few sets of clothing. I had missed that smell.

THE MOON'S PULL

AUGUST

"Your Grace, you requested an audience with the entire army of Barrien?" Olin's voice was obnoxious any time of day, but especially when he felt the need to verify requests that I had very clearly made. One day I'd slap him with that sweaty handkerchief of his.

"Yes, that sounds right."

"Your Grace, have you slept? It's been—"

"Olin, respectfully," I said, rubbing my eyes before looking at the advisor again, "please shut up. I requested an audience with the army. Where are they?" I had been up and ready for hours, waiting for Olin to wake so that I could put in said request, only to have him questioning me instead. I needed him to comply, not advise, this time.

"They'll be here shortly, sir, but only the captains. Er, the entire army will not fit inside the castle, Your Grace." Olin bowed his head a little, as if he were afraid that I'd be angry at this news.

Perhaps I should've known more about the size of my own army. Whatever. "Fine. Escort them into the room when they arrive. I don't have time to waste."

Olin blotted his brow with his handkerchief. "Sir, are we going to war?"

I rolled my eyes, the near year of work I'd done on myself as a decent human being and ruler vanishing in an instant. I was ready to be an absolutely insufferable tyrant again. "Don't you think you'd know if we were going to war, Olin? This is personal."

Olin deflated immediately, clearly having been worried that the world was ending without his knowledge. He left without another word and returned fifteen minutes later with the entire leadership of the Barrien army in tow. Embarrassingly enough, I had never met a single one of these men, even when I was involved in my father's dealings. They were an impressive group of men, and back in my days as a philanderer, I would've probably liked to share a bed with most of them. It was a shame I hadn't known about them before I'd gone and fallen in love with a single person who had ruined me for anyone else. The group was young, each one of them my age or younger, and fit; most of them were lean and muscled, while a couple were a bit bulkier. All wore immaculate armor that suggested they hadn't seen battle and were clean-cut and clean-shaven.

"Gentlemen," I addressed them. "Stand down, we're not going to war like my friend Olin here believes. I've called you here for reasons that are beyond the needs of the kingdom. In fact, this may be your most important assignment yet."

The group looked at me attentively, searching for additional information as they stood perfectly still.

"I need two of your best soldiers—*the* best soldiers we have to offer. Perhaps that's one of you, or maybe it's one of your charge, but I need you to identify these men immediately. They will be working closely with myself and another hired expert: a witch."

One of the bulkier men who looked to be my age piped up. He had short, dirty-blond hair and dark eyes. "What will they be doing for you, Your Grace?"

"I need someone to be followed, um, closely," I explained. I met the man's gaze first before speaking to the entire group, but as I struggled to find the words I realized I hadn't fully explained this plan out loud yet. It was a lot more suspicious sounding than I had expected. "They mustn't know you're following them, and you must not intervene in anything that happens to them unless you're certain not doing so would result in their death. We'll utilize my dragon, Magnus, to transport messages and updates while they're following this... individual." The dragon in question stayed by my side, following my gaze whenever I looked at a different man or adjusted my position. He was highly in tune with every move I made. In fact, he'd hardly gone anywhere else since Max had left... and as a result, he was fed every chance I stumbled upon food that I didn't want to eat myself. He was growing more than I'd expected for a creature labeled "micro."

"How long will this assignment be for?" another man asked. They were valid questions, but each one made me doubt my planning a little more. I had to be resolute in my instructions.

"As long as I say," I told them firmly, unwilling to face the fact that this person may never return to me and the group may be following her forever. "I will pay handsomely for this work," I suggested, unsure of how else to entice them. In reality, they were obligated to do as they were told, but I knew that people worked better when they were motivated. "Three times your current wages."

"We don't... typically work with witches... o-or dragons, Your Grace."

"Well, there's a first time for everything then, isn't there?" I set my jaw hard, determined not to let them talk me out of this plan. "Your first step will be getting in contact with the witch herself. She's not aware of this project, but I am certain that we can convince her. Start by speaking to Beatrice the apothecary." Beatrice knew Juniper. Juniper knew Sidney. Sidney knew Max. Or at least I thought I had remembered that correctly based on what Max had told me following her retrieval of my mother's body.

"And the dragon, sir?"

"Keep him fed, and you'll have nothing to worry about," I told them, reaching down to stroke Magnus behind the ear. He purred, much like a cat but at a magnitude that caused the floor of the weapons room to vibrate, and rubbed against my fingers; already his power was greater than one would assume for his size. "You'll give him messages to return to me. You must wait for him to come back to you before you move again. I won't have him lost." When the dragon rubbed against my hand again, his mouth parted as if he was about to pant, and a small stream of black smoke billowed out from it instead; he was content. Magnus had grown quite a bit since Max had brought him home and now resembled a medium-sized dog in stature, but was heavily muscled. His thick body was lined with dark green scales, which shimmered when he moved. Some of them had a silver quality to them. As for his claws, they were so long and sharp that balancing on a human's shoulder was no longer an option, and they left divots in the hardwood flooring of some of the castle rooms. "He'll be a useful resource if you run into any trouble, but remember… do not intervene unless your target appears to be in immediate danger… and whatever you think danger is, multiply it by ten before stepping in. She can handle a lot more than it seems."

The soldier who responded looked surprised. "*She*, my lord?"

"You'll be following a mercenary named M-M…" I struggled to say her name, then pinched the bridge of my nose in irritation. I hadn't said it aloud in days. My stomach turned, and the group of soldiers eyed me curiously, glancing at each other to see if they should step in and offer me assistance… They probably thought I was having a stroke. I closed my eyes and took a steadying breath.

Olin piped up, unfortunately filling in the blank for me. He clearly didn't approve of my plan. I didn't give a shit. "Maxine, Your Grace?"

"Yes, *thank you, Olin*. She rides a massive horse, black. She'll be on the road now, probably taking on odd jobs, monster hunting, to get by, especially with the spike in werewolf sightings. She'll have a young boy with her." Fuck, I missed that kid.

The soldier who had been doing most of the conversing with me swallowed hard. Clearly, he'd heard of her. "Yes, Your Grace. Doesn't she go by… Max the Menace?"

"That's the one," I told him with a nod. I loved that she had a reputation.

"And… if she notices us?" The soldier rubbed his neck as if concerned. Not very brave in the face of danger, apparently.

"Don't let her," I said simply. Some deranged part of me enjoyed the idea of Max chasing down the soldiers I sent to follow her. What would she do when she realized I'd sent them? I suppressed a pleased shudder.

"Yes, sir… but *if*—"

"What's your name?" I asked him suddenly, still half in some sick daydream of my ex-lover toying with a group of soldiers as punishment for me trying to keep tabs on her.

"Thorne, Your Grace."

"If she notices you, Thorne," I warned him, "you won't see the light of the next day, let alone your tripled salary."

The soldier pulled at his collar, attempting to be discreet in his nervousness, but it was obvious and warranted. "Yes, Your Grace."

"Anything else?"

"If she's been on the road, where should we expect to find her first?"

I sighed and scrubbed my face with my fingertips. "I wish I could tell you, but that's where the witch comes in. She's an expert in finding people who can't be found… or who don't want to be," I explained. "She's met… the mercenary before, so she'll have a reference point to work with. Follow her lead from there. If she refuses, increase the offering until she agrees."

~

IT WASN'T long before the soldiers were back. Well, two of them—Thorne and another that I later learned was named Aldric—but they weren't alone. They had a young woman with them, and it didn't take much for me to surmise that *this* was Sidney the witch. Seeing her stirred up memories of the day that Max had brought my mother's body home after working with this woman to find her, and all I could think was that she must see me as a monster… After all that Max had done for me, I couldn't even keep her happy in return. She'd traversed treacherous terrain, and I'd driven her away to live back on the road with only a few crystals to her name. It hardly seemed right that I should not attempt to use one of her connections to find her.

"What's the meaning of this?" Sidney demanded with a hiss, yanking her arms free from the men who were escorting her. She whirled around to point a gloved finger in one of their faces, coming dangerously close to Aldric's eyeball. Pointy. "You should know better than to mess with someone like me, big boy!" She was scrappy for someone so small, I'd give her that; I seemed to have an affinity for that type of woman.

"We either got ahold of you or faced the dragon," Thorne explained, gesturing to Magnus, who had perked up since their entrance. He stretched like a massive cat. The soldiers had gotten my demands slightly wrong; I didn't really care to meet Sidney, but if it was crucial to getting her to agree to the assignment, then I'd suffer through conversing with the witch. "King's orders."

"King, huh?" Sidney turned away from the soldiers to eye me with a hesitant irritation. "King of *what*?"

I stood from my seat, quite enjoying the fire that this woman brought into my home. This was not how Max had described her. Her recounting of their interaction had made *Max* out to be the fiery, hot-headed one, and Sidney to be calm and cool, but I supposed that kidnapping someone might change their tune. "Barrien," I answered plainly, approaching the group. In reality, I didn't feel like the king of anything special anymore. I snapped my fingers, and Magnus appeared next to me as I walked, a slithering, scaled shadow of a creature that I'd grown used to having by my side.

"I don't answer to the king of Barrien or any king," Sidney declared.

I couldn't help the faint whisper of a smile that crept onto my face. "So I've heard…"

"Yeah, from who?"

"Max…"

"Max… is she okay? I haven't seen her since… ah," Sidney mused aloud, a light sparking in her potent gaze. "You're the half-elf. I see." She eyed me for a moment, perhaps wondering just how the rest of that evening had panned out. I didn't want to talk about my mother's dead body, though. "Where *is* Max?"

"That's what I need your help with."

Sidney searched my expression. "She's lost? I find that hard to believe. I can't imagine a person like Max ever gets lost." As far as I knew, they had only met once, but the look on the young woman's face was enough to express concern. Despite being a self-proclaimed introvert and steel trap, Max had always had the ability to leave a mark on people, one way or another. I felt her worry whether she wanted to or not and hoped that it was enough for her to help me. The thought of Max and Danny together on the road with winter around the corner and the werewolf contagion spreading mortified me more than I cared to admit, and if I had to pay people to track her for the rest of our lives just to make sure she was safe, I would do that. I would do that in a heartbeat. I would spend every crystal the kingdom had, then work to earn more, just to fund the work that would keep her from death's door. I didn't want to live in a world where Max the Menace wasn't alive and beating the ever-loving shit out of people.

I cleared my throat, unsure of how to describe the situation without either oversharing (I probably would) or making myself seem like a lovesick stalker (I might as well be). "Not exactly, but *I* don't know where she is, and I need to. That's all I can tell you."

Sidney looked bored by my explanation. "If she doesn't want to be found by you, why would I help you find her?"

"Everyone has a price."

Sidney chuckled a little, and I immediately felt like I had no leverage with her. "Not necessarily," she said coolly, glaring at the guards once more before approaching me. When she stepped closer, Magnus's body tensed… but then she reached out, and he pushed his snout against the palm of her hand before relaxing. Well, there was one of my tools, completely gone to the likes of Sidney the witch. Useless. "Shouldn't she be allowed to hide from you, if she wants? I mean, I don't know why, but I imagine she'd be here if she wanted to be, *king* of Barrien."

I watched her interact with my dragon, not stupid enough to argue any of her points, before clearing my throat nervously. "I don't need you to bring her to me. I just need to know that she's safe. She has her younger brother with her, too, and they're on the road. Surely you can imagine that it's not the safest place for both of them."

Sidney's gaze met mine again—she was a tiny thing, but the air about her was massive—and she reached out to pet Magnus once more, to the shock of the soldiers behind her. "Him," she offered finally, scratching beneath his chin.

"What?"

"I'll take him as payment," she said simply, gazing into the drag-on's eyes. He melted under her touch.

My mouth went dry. "No," I said firmly.

"Why not?"

"I can give you anything else," I offered.

"An answer, first, then I'll consider an alternative."

"He's the last thing Max gave me." I also had no clue where I'd find another like him. He wasn't a micro dragon like the rest at the salesman's stall, but he had to have come from somewhere. In the end, all that mattered was that I wasn't losing my last tie to Max.

The witch's eyes glittered with amusement. "Fine, then I'll take one like him."

MEMORIES IN SMELL

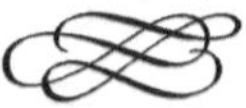

AUGUST

*D*ays later, I came across some of the soldiers of Barrien again, but in a completely different context. Olin called me to the stables, a place which I'd avoided since Wraith's own stall had become vacant. Heckle had probably forgotten my face. I was still in a dressing robe, the cold ground crunching under boots that I'd hastily pulled on, when Olin met me there with a frazzled-looking soldier that I'd never seen before.

"Your Grace—"

"What is it, Olin?" I asked the attendant, once again annoyed by his existence. I gave the soldier a once-over before I realized that the horse behind him had another person flung over its back. The last time I'd seen that arrangement, I'd come face-to-face with my mother's dead body. The man on the horse, however, sported a bloody face and head. "What happened here?"

"W-well," Olin began again, never deterred by the fact that no one wanted to hear him speak. "Some of our soldiers were on their way back from Emynor, as you know. It seems these two encountered someone peculiar on the road… and were told to bring a message back to Barrien."

"Spit it out."

The living soldier was as pale as his deceased counterpart when he attempted to explain himself. "Y-Your Grace, w-we… I…"

"What did you see out there, a ghost?"

The man burst into tears as if I'd just threatened him before going over to the body on the horse and pulling its mouth open. It didn't appear to take much effort, which made me think the body was no longer stiff. He had to have been traveling with a dead partner on his horse for a good while. No wonder he was frazzled. When he moved out of the way, he revealed the two chunks of meat that had fallen out of the dead man's mouth and onto the dirt of the stables. Even his finger trembled as he pointed at them.

"What are those?"

The soldier's response was unintelligible.

"Speak up," I directed him, but part of me knew what I was looking at.

"Ears."

Time slowed as I approached the body, getting close enough to pull the man's head up by his hair. Sure enough, there they were: butchered ears that had their outer rim of cartilage sawed off. They looked noticeably more brutal than my own, but it was very clear that this message was intended for me to see. The body stunk.

"Who did this?" I knew. Who else could have? And why would they?

"I d-don't know her name, but she… she said to bring his body back as a warning."

I glanced from the body back to the living soldier. "A warning for what?"

"A warning that anyone who… disrespects the king of Barrien or…

the elves of Emynor will…" The man looked like he might faint. "…m-meet a similar fate."

I stood from the spot where I'd crouched next to the body. "And this man," I said, gesturing to the dead soldier, "he did those things?"

"Y-yes, he—"

"I don't need the details. Do as you were told, and make sure your fellow soldiers get the message."

The soldier's eyes widened. "Your Grace, d-don't you want to know more about… the woman?"

I was already on my way out of the stables. "No need." Who else could it have been? No one but Max would punish someone so brutally in the name of myself or my people. My cock was hard at the thought.

It was ten minutes until seven in the morning when I banged on the wooden door of Beatrice's apothecary. The wooden "closed" sign clanged against the small window, mocking me, so I banged again, despite the way that it made my head pound even more.

"Beatrice," I groaned, leaning forward on the door when my hand began to ache. I pressed my face against the glass in exhaustion. I was alone this time, having left Magnus back at the castle… It wasn't a good look for the king to walk around with the same fire-breathing monster that had taken out a bakery only weeks before, let alone one that had grown exponentially in size. I felt naked without him and lonely. "Let me in." Ugh, gods, is that what my voice sounded like? Whiny and pitiful… I was spiraling into a pit of self-despair… soon Magnus wouldn't even want to join me there.

Morgan opened the door. I didn't want to see Morgan. Their demeanor reminded me of Max. Oh, fuck, maybe I did want to see

Morgan. When they opened the door, we locked eyes for a moment, and then they turned to let me in, shaking their head as they did so.

Never mind. I didn't really care for Morgan.

I did notice, however, that they locked the door behind me and left the sign on "closed." I guess I could be appreciative of a bit of privacy. It would've been easy for them to open the store early now that I was there and let the public keep me from bothering them too much.

Beatrice ambled down the steps at the far end of the apothecary, probably from a small apartment that they shared above, and yawned before greeting me. "Kinda early, isn't it, King August? We don't usually open until nine."

"It's an emergency." I was still whining.

The shopkeeper's eyes immediately went wide, and she hurried down the last few steps to the landing. "What is it? Is everyone okay?"

"My bed doesn't smell like her anymore." Before I could elaborate, I choked back a sob and leaned forward on the shop counter. I couldn't face them. We had just been here not too long ago, perusing the wares for sale like we were any old couple. Now she wasn't even in the same city as me, let alone our shared bedroom.

Beatrice pulled her glasses off and set them on the counter between us so that she could rub her eyes. "I'm sorry, what? You're talking about Max? Just ask her for some of her perfume. There's no way she's gone through it all that quickly, knowing her unbathed self," she told me, starting to trail off in her rambling as she replaced the thick glasses on her button nose. "That little bottle ought to last her the rest of her life."

"I can't ask her," I forced out, looking up at the woman from my spot, face pressed to the countertop. It felt cool against my skin. Didn't she know that Max was gone? Wouldn't Max have told her, stopped by to stock up on potions before taking off? Had she really left in such a hurry? I couldn't imagine her heading out into the wilderness unprepared. My heart sank at the thought and then upset overtook me. It didn't matter how worried I was, she was gone. The soldiers would follow her, sure, but that was just to keep an eye on her. It wasn't like they would eventually lead me to her. Besides, Max was an expert at remaining untracked, and I was… "I'm a big idiot," I said with a trembling sob again.

I wasn't prepared for the way Beatrice came around the counter and pulled me into her arms, cradling me against her bosom. She was almost a foot shorter than me, but I let myself be held by her as we stood there in her shop, in the silence of early morning, and I cried about the fact that Max had left. I didn't tell her much, just that I'd made the mistake of proposing, and it had gone sideways… and that Max had left with no warning, taking Danny with her. That I was worried for her, that I was lost without her… gods, okay, I told her a lot. "Oh, sugar," she hushed me, stroking my hair. She avoided my ears, her stroking halting as she approached them and then resuming once she'd moved her hair around them. I didn't open my eyes because I was certain I'd find Morgan standing there with their arms crossed in judgment that I probably deserved. It was a long while before Beatrice tried to talk to me again, but she did so gently. "Are you sure you want her perfume, August? Don't you think that'll just make it hurt more?"

"I know it will," I replied after a brief moment of silence. "And I need it." I needed to feel that pain, the sting of familiarity, so that I knew I was still living. I had done nothing productive since she had left, aside from rallying the group to search for her, hadn't answered the door despite the begging of my advisors, and I feared it would only get worse if I didn't have some small comfort to rely on. I couldn't sleep. Food was unappealing. "I need this, I need one last whisper of her in my life. It's the only thing keeping me hanging on."

I left the shop with twelve bottles of the perfume that Beatrice had given Max on the night of the Autumn Equinox ball, and I had paid her extra to ensure she wouldn't make the same scent for anyone else.

Most homes in Barrien and the surrounding cities don't have baths. They're lucky if they have a washbasin with hot water and washcloths that are occasionally clean. Meanwhile, the castle of Barrien has a bath that is itself the size of most homes. That evening found me calling for an attendant to fill the bath for me, and Magnus followed me into the room as if he'd missed me all day. I had avoided washing, had avoided really caring for myself since Max had left. The fear of washing away any reminders of her was strong… but at the same time, their presence frequently left me depleted. Whether it was the drawers full of her clothing or the door to Danny's room, the fact that she had existed in this space and was no longer there tore at my heart. The only reason I'd relented and agreed (with myself) to bathe that evening was the promise of reapplying Max's perfume. I let the staff change my bedsheets as well.

Of course, there were painful memories in that room of the castle, too.

"I'm sorry, what were you saying? It's hard to focus when you're…." I gestured to Max's naked body as she lowered herself into the bathtub across from me. I wanted to travel the soft curves of her hips, the valley between her breasts… I would've lapped the bathwater from her flesh if she'd let me.

She laughed, and the sound made me instantly hard, like most things about her did. *"I said…* what do you know about werewolves?"

I leaned back against the edge of the tub and tilted my head back to stare at the ceiling of the bathroom, partly in thought and partly so that I wouldn't get distracted again mid-sentence. "The basics, I suppose…" I mused aloud, my voice echoing off the tiled walls. "Werewolf bites man, man turns into werewolf at the full moon, becomes a destructive, unpredictable killing machine... kind of like you, just hairier."

"*Me?*" Max asked with an exaggerated gasp. "Destructive and unpredictable? Killing machine I can deal with."

I chuckled. "Fine, fine. Not destructive. Definitely unpredictable, but I like it that way, Nightshade."

"Good. Now, how do you kill a werewolf?"

"Silver?"

"Sure, that's handy... but the foolproof way is beheading." I must've cringed because she added, "Hard to keep attacking people if you don't have a head."

"Good to know... but why do I need to know this?"

"I'm assuming Florian already told you there's an outbreak of them across the continent. I'd be more concerned about the cultists who think it's a sign of the end of the world rather than just monsters doing what they do best."

I let my chin fall so I could look at her again. "And what's that?"

"Mmm, being unpredictable and destructive, I guess." Max stroked her chin in mock contemplation.

"Great. Lesson complete. Come here." I gestured to her across the tub, and she complied, having to practically swim her way over to me before she settled into my lap. The water was hot and smelled divine, and when she wrapped her arms around my neck, I thought I might've died and gone to heaven.

WHEN MAGNUS and I returned to our room, it had been cleaned. The bed was made with fresh sheets and blankets, piled high with warm linens that looked nothing like the last set. I had given the staff permission to do this, yes, but when I actually *saw* it, my stomach dropped. Magnus stayed closer to me than normal, sensing my stress.

I forced myself into clean clothing and into the bed, Magnus settling at the foot. I had just turned to the side to face the door when my eyes settled on the nightstand on my side of the bed. I still slept on my side. But it had been cleaned, too, and the surface was bare.

Panic exploded in my chest, and I leaped from the bed so quickly that the dragon on it was on high alert, hissing as if there was an invisible intruder to protect me from.

"Where is it?"

I scanned every surface in the room to find them bare as well. Everything had been cleaned up, put away. It was missing. I rushed to the door, where the speaker for the castle attendants was posted. I rang the bell. I rang it again.

"Your Grace? Is everything alright?"

"Where is it?" I spat, accusing the person who had responded as if they had any clue what I was talking about.

"Your Grace, where is what?" The panic in the attendant's voice was palpable.

"The necklace, where is the necklace I had on the nightstand?"

"Your nightstand, sir?"

I pressed my face into the speaker as if it would make me any clearer. "I need…" My voice cracked, the sheer desperation I'd been hiding with anger slipping through momentarily. "I need whoever was in charge of cleaning my chambers here immediately. Please."

"I believe they're—"

"Now." I cleared my throat. "I don't care where they are," I told them firmly. "Wake them. Call them. Get them here, now."

When the attendant who had cleaned my bedroom finally arrived, I found that I didn't recognize him, and that alone set my worries further on edge. The young man was short and chubby, and his cheeks were already red with anxiousness when I called him into my chambers. Olin stood in the hallway behind him, as if he were keeping an eye on the interaction; whether he was more concerned for his staff or me was unclear. I didn't care.

"Tell me where the necklace is," I told him firmly, unable to temper my frustration. "Did you take it? It's not worth any—"

"N-no, sir, I don't recall. I must have—"

Olin piped up from the hall. "Your Grace, I'm certain whatever you're looking for must be—"

"Olin, I swear to the gods, if you don't find what I'm looking for or shut the hell up, I will strangle you with your own handkerchief," I told him, my tone venomous. Magnus skittered to the doorframe as if he had understood me and postured in a way that caused my assistant to raise his hands in surrender. When I turned back to the young man in my room, I was seething. "Find it, now."

I stood in the doorframe while the young man searched through the bedroom, clearly retracing his steps by going through each and every drawer he may have placed something in earlier. The more time passed, the higher the tension in the room became; the kid was clearly concerned that I would have him killed for stealing, meanwhile, I just needed him to find that fucking necklace. I felt I might drop dead without it. My hands began to tremble as I watched him. "Well?" I snipped in frustration when a few moments of silence went by.

"I'm sorry, Your Grace, I haven't found it yet. It must be some-where…" he told me apologetically as he closed another drawer. I could see sweat seeping through his shirt as he worked.

After a few more seconds, I could no longer restrain myself. I grabbed the young man by his collar and pulled him away from the nightstand just as he held up the object of my desire: a thin black cord with a small pearlescent bud of a molar hanging from the end of it. I was too distracted by his discovery to notice how much I was terri-fying the attendant and instead snatched the piece from his hand before shoving him and Olin out of my room.

Olin attempted to speak, but I shut them both out by slamming the door.

I was paralyzed by my own panic when I found myself alone and fell onto the bed, the necklace still clutched in my hand, before letting myself cry. Ever since Max had left, I'd put off wearing the piece because to do so felt like resignation… it felt like admitting defeat, like admitting that Max had been right when she called it something to "remember" her by. But now that it had almost been taken from me, I realized I couldn't leave it on my nightstand any longer. I pulled the piece over my head, tucked it into my shirt, then doused my pillow in Max's perfume before burying my face in it. I'd almost lost the last piece I had of her; I wouldn't let it leave my sight again.

THE LEAST I CAN DO

AUGUST

I was staring at the fireplace, like I often did, when Florian walked into the sitting room of my castle. "If it isn't my second least favorite elf."

"I pride myself at being first at everything, August," he said simply. "Who is my competition?"

"Me."

"Oh dear, you really have gone off the deep end," Florian said with a chuckle, his perfectly manicured hand spread out in front of him for inspection. "I expected you to be a bit more hardy after all you'd been through."

"Do you have news to report, or are you here for pleasure?" I asked, glowering at him over my drink. I swirled the glass in my hand, not even remembering the alcohol that I'd filled it with moments prior… anything to take the edge off. That was for everyone else's sake, not mine; I'd been insufferable since Max left, but it was my duty to remain cordial and professional with the people of the castle, lest I become a replica of my miserable father. I gave the glass a sniff and realized it was brandy.

"Little bit of both," Florian confessed before draping himself over the armchair opposite me. The man moved like he was made of liquid. "You know I love to see you glum like this, but yes, I do have some news. First and foremost, the Covenant has moved through the Wild Open. Werewolves continue to spread, which is only urging on their mission. We need a plan of action if they're to approach Barrien, which is likely their next stop. They haven't gone as far as Emynor, and I doubt they will with the elves being immune to werewolf venom… not worth their time, even to recruit us for their purposes. The Emynorian elves have too much going on to be dragged in by their propaganda."

I was about to respond to him with a delegation when a familiar noise made its way into the room and its maker landed on the edge of my armchair, effectively tearing a hole in the fabric with his claws. Magnus. I unrolled the scrap of parchment the dragon had brought in, read it, and then pocketed it. "The Wild Open, you say? Any sign of them going further west?" It took great effort to keep my tone even, but I didn't have the energy to give Florian any additional arsenal.

"Not that I've heard, no."

"Very well." Magnus's claws dug into my arm before I remembered the small dish of preserved fish I'd started keeping for his trips. I plucked one from the side table next to us and tossed it into the air, where he caught it with great ease before scuttling off to lie by the fire. He had grown even stronger and bigger from eating well and flying long distances to communicate between myself, Sidney, Thorne, and Aldric. Had I not been avoiding the market as if it had the power to kill me, I might've purchased the remaining micro dragons just to feed them and set them free. I'd have to go there eventually, but I was dreading that day. "Speak to Thorne's second in command…" I gestured at Florian, who was curiously observing the dragon, to continue.

"Right, well, there is still the matter of your engagement." He held up a finger. "And before you protest, consider this. Soon, the Covenant will approach Barrien, one way or another. Perhaps the werewolves will even break in through the city somehow. You want your people to feel united and supported, not fearful that their reclusive king will vanish in their time of need; marriage to the right person will solidify this."

"Reclusive?" I took a sip of my drink. "You're an ass."

"A bit off topic, don't you think?" He looked at the dragon by the fire once more before adding, "You know it's going to get bigger, right? A lot bigger. I'm not sure *what* you people market those as, but I've seen a few of them in the Wild Open, and they're menaces. They'll eat all of your horses." He turned back to me, and in that moment, I prayed that Magnus would one day be big enough to set the elf on fire. Wishful thinking, perhaps.

"It's supposed to be a micro dragon. This one doesn't seem to be."

Florian eyed him curiously. "Nope. Not this one." He shrugged. "In any case, I have a proposal." Then, Florian laughed at his own cruelty; he really was heartless. "Oops, wrong phrasing, I suppose."

I polished off the remainder of my drink and set the glass down harder than I had intended to. The sound caused Magnus to turn and hiss. "Spit it out, elf," I said hoarsely.

"I believe you should be wed to one of *your people*—not a Barrien citizen, but an elf. Listen, the people of Emynor still don't fully believe that Barrien wants to make things right after your father's rule. They haven't seen you since you returned with Max, and ever since she left, well, your presence even in your own kingdom has been scarce."

A chill ran through my body at that name, *her* name. It sickened me to hear it in his voice. He shouldn't have been allowed to utter it. The suggestion that, after everything that had happened, I would attempt to marry again, and to someone I didn't even know, was atrocious… sickening, unreal, and a stretch even for someone like Florian Featherfoot. Sure, he was my advisor, but this seemed needlessly personal and cruel. "Florian, why would I—"

"A union—a real union, not just talk—between the two kingdoms would solidify Barrien's credibility and demonstrate your commitment to repaying the elves for their misfortunes at the hands of your parents and their army." When I didn't respond, he added, "It's the least you, as the king of Barrien, can do, and you know that."

We sat in silence, as I did often lately, and I watched the flames of the fireplace flicker in the reflection of Florian's rings. What more did I have to lose now? What harm could come from marrying someone simply to keep the peace between two warring nations, one of which I'd been practically stolen from as a baby? Truthfully, I did want peace with Emynor, especially after seeing what my people had done there. I had vowed that no harm would come to another Emynorian child on my watch, and if marrying someone for the sake of appearances, of commitment to my agreements, would ensure that, then I should do it. It had nothing to do with love. It was a political deal like any other. Even Max would understand that. Besides, she was the one who first gave up our love for the "greater good," or whatever version of that lived in her head. The notion of marriage for love had been forever tarnished for me.

"It's the least I can do," I agreed. I made a mental note to acquire steaks for Magnus.

CRYSTALS CAN'T BUY HAPPINESS

MAX

*W*inter crept in quicker than it had the previous year, but being out in the wilderness meant that every change in the weather was amplified. The air smelled different the night before the first snow: bitter, hollow, like the earth was sucking in a deep, frosty breath that it was about to unleash on anyone unlucky enough to be in the elements.

"I'm cold, Max," Danny chirped from behind me as Wraith walked us through piles of crunching grass and leaves. He was shivering against my back already, despite me having given him almost all of the layers I'd packed for myself on top of his own. We'd gotten by so far on small change that I could earn from jobs here and there; admittedly, it was harder to find work with Danny along for the ride. I couldn't accept anything too dangerous unless I already had a place to tuck him away for the duration of the job, and since we weren't near our home in the Wild Open (and even if we were, the location was no longer secret), that left us with very few options. As the cold crept in, everything slowed... even work... and the pouch on my hip was running dangerously low on crystals. There was no longer any heft to it, and the remaining few knocked around sadly when I moved.

"I know," I told him. "We need to get you a winter coat." I had a list running in my mind of all the things I needed to provide for him, things that had come without asking when we were in Barrien. Clothing. Food. At least a few nights' rest somewhere warm. He was missing out on schooling, too, so I'd need to figure out a way to ease us back into this nomadic life while still teaching him things. "We need to find a place to stop by nightfall, too…" I murmured to myself. Wraith huffed in response, as if I could forget that she hadn't been eating much lately either.

"I miss my bed," Danny said after a few moments of traveling in silence. Guilt snuck up on me again so quickly that I almost snapped at him, but it wasn't his fault. He was allowed to miss all of the comforts I had torn him away from.

Thankfully, sometimes the universe provides. Never in the easy way—no crystals falling from the sky—but with opportunities.

Off in the distance, there was a screech. We halted, and Wraith's ears perked up as I turned toward the sounds. A screech didn't mean much unless there was a person being bothered by the screecher. Then I could—

"Help!"

"Follow that call, Wraith."

"What was that?" Danny asked, tightening his grip around my waist.

Wraith did as she was told and led us toward the screech and the call for help, but she didn't run. Instead, she approached cautiously. Smart girl. "I have an idea of what it *could* be," I told Danny as we approached. "But I don't want to speak too soon. No time to find you a hiding spot, though… especially if this is going to be a paid job."

We came upon a small home in a clearing, where the screaming of whatever creature was assaulting the residents became infinitely louder. As the scene came into view, the perpetrator was made clear: a beast that looked like the white version of Wraith, but this one had a horn protruding from its forehead that must've been three feet long. It was sharp, I could tell even from a distance, and glistened red with blood. It reared up on its hind legs and let out a whinny that sounded straight from hell. Nearby, several wounded—or dead, hard to say from the distance between us—bodies lay around the property, no doubt having been impaled by the mystical beast.

"Is that… a unicorn?" Danny peeked under my arm to get a better view.

"Uh, yeah. That's a unicorn. Not like they make them out to be in fairy tales…"

Wraith snorted, digging a hoof into the ground as if to brace herself. It would be a shame to kill a unicorn, I thought, but it was obviously feral and agitated, especially this far away from wherever its home was. There would be no safe way to relocate it.

The man keeping the unicorn at bay with a flaming stick looked over to us. "Help me!"

"I can!" I yelled from afar, not wanting to intrude on the situation until we had an agreement. "For a hundred crystals!"

"Wha—" The man looked bewildered that I was attempting to negotiate in the midst of chaos, but I'd found that was often the best time. "A hundred?"

"And the horn! And… some blood!" I thought to add, knowing that we'd need other ways to capitalize off of this kill.

"F-fine! Just help me! There are others inside, but we can't keep this beast at bay! Please, it's already killed all of our stable hands!"

"Hold on!" I told the man before sliding off of Wraith's back. I looked up at Danny, who was still on her back. "I need your help, Danny."

"*Mine?*" My brother's eyes were wide with terror, any previous notion of being cold or tired immediately gone.

"Yes," I told him, grabbing his hand and giving it a firm squeeze. "You always say you want to be part of this. Now is your chance. Take the reins and use Wraith to distract the unicorn. Keep its back to the house. She won't let you get hurt, just keep moving."

"But Max—"

"Come on, Danny. Winter coat. Bed. Warm food. It'll be quick." I patted Wraith on the butt before I took off toward the house, praying that I was right to place my faith in the horse that carried my brother. If I was the reason he got injured or killed, I'd never be able to live with myself. I sprinted for the home in the distance and felt assured that I hadn't overcharged the man when I realized that the house was rather nice, better than most in the area, and the people cowering inside were well-dressed. They could afford a unicorn extermination fee. I gave the people inside a nod of reassurance and scaled the side of the house, hoping to get onto the roof so that I could have a better vantage point over the unicorn. How had it gotten here in the first place?

The side of the house was riddled with thick moss due to its location in the woods, which made scaling it easier than most slick-sided castle walls. After realizing that the moss would indeed pull off if I grabbed the wrong spot, I got the hang of climbing it and scaled the far side of the house easily.

As I watched the creature, enraged and rearing up repeatedly, its once-white mane and horn streaked with red, I couldn't help but see myself in it. It wasn't the beast's fault that it had been transported away from its home; it just didn't belong there. Of course it felt rabid, hostile, and feral. When the blaze of the fire caught my eye and the unicorn reared up again, I realized just how close Danny and Wraith were getting to keep it distracted. My heart went out to the beast in silence as I poised myself above it, determining how to put it out of its misery quickly and efficiently. It was very angry, and while I couldn't blame it, I did wish it would calm down enough for me to land on it...

Even though I'd practiced jumping off of things to land on a horse, the horse in question was usually standing perfectly still. I said a silent prayer for my joints and leaped.

Danny screamed from the distance, "Max!"

My aim hadn't been ideal, and I nearly missed the unicorn, only managing to grab it by its mane to avoid hitting the ground and being trampled. As expected, the creature was not pleased. I struggled to hang on as it thrashed, turning its head frantically, trying to shake me off. It tossed and screeched that loud, piercing screech that made me almost let go in order to hold my ears. Instead, I was able to leverage one of its frantic movements and use it to propel myself up and onto the creature's neck, where it continued to attempt to throw me off of it. "Shit, shit, shit." I managed to cling to it, bracing myself against the beast's thick neck with my legs clamped firmly around it, before reaching for my weapons. "Danny! Look away!" I managed to yell as I was continually tossed around.

I dropped one dagger, then fumbled for the other, and in a brief second of stillness, I managed to plunge it directly into the unicorn's eye. It froze for a moment, then collapsed, taking me with it. We hit the ground hard, the beast's mass landing on one of my legs as it pinned me beneath its muscular neck. The next thing I knew, Danny was dismounting Wraith and making a run toward me as I watched through a sideways view from the ground. "I'm alright!" I told him as he approached. "I'm okay!" I wiggled my foot underneath the unicorn. "Nothing's broken." Sore, bruised, battered, sure. But I hadn't broken any bones, by some miracle.

The owner of the house stood by in complete and utter shock at how his interaction with a unicorn had gone sideways so quickly. His torch hung limply from his hand, and I snapped my fingers to gain his attention. "Do you mind? I don't think either of us can lift this thing alone."

Once I'd been freed, Danny hugged me like he'd been certain he was going to witness my death, and I realized that even though he knew what I did for work, he didn't really know. Not until recently. He'd never seen me take a life or almost lose mine. I reassured him multiple times and sent him back to Wraith for a breather, insisting that a warm bed and food were only moments away. I just had to finish the job.

"It's a shame to kill such a beautiful beast," I pondered aloud, the scent of blood and gore thick in my nostrils. I wondered if Danny was looking on and being scarred by the sight before him or if he'd decided to focus elsewhere as I dug around in the unicorn's skull to dislodge the base of its horn. "How did she end up here?"

The man wiped his forehead with a cloth from his pocket and looked away. "We had her brought in…"

I paused my work, realizing that this had been self-inflicted for the man… and had led to the death of several people and the unicorn itself. I couldn't help myself when I added, "Poor judgment on your part, then." I didn't want to know for what purpose they'd had her captured and delivered to his home, though I had some guesses. However, being able to take the most valuable parts of her body satis-fied me. I finished removing the horn and stashed it in one of our saddlebags, making sure to wrap the pointed tip in cloth to avoid it snapping. Once I had collected several small vials of blood—what I'd do with them, I didn't know—I took our pay and led Danny and Wraith away from the unfortunate massacre.

Battered and bruised, we mounted Wraith one last time that evening and pulled back onto the dirt path that led north of the Grim-maker Woods. Despite there being no more Umbrals to chase us, I'd had enough negative associations with the woods to last me a lifetime, so I chose to venture somewhere new to me. I could do this. *We* could do this. Danny and I could take care of ourselves, and a new begin-ning was somewhere on the horizon.

It had been dark for a few hours when we came upon a light in the distance, and the warm glow of a tavern gave me another burst of hope. The swinging wooden sign above the entrance read "The Last Straw." Danny was yet again asleep against my back when I led Wraith toward the stables. I woke him, and we slid off of her back in exhaustion, but I made sure to give the horse an extra scratch behind the ears before we left, as if to say it would be okay and that things were finally looking up again. I plunked down a few crystals for her boarding and feed with the stable hand before entering the tavern.

The tavern was warm—a welcome change from the outside world—and clean enough, I supposed, to have a young kid with me. It looked older, though, and I was surprised that I hadn't stumbled upon it before, but if my map was right, this path didn't go all the way over the Grimmaker Woods, just narrowly avoided them for a bit longer. I didn't know where we'd go next, but I approached the innkeeper at the front desk and found myself longing for a familiar face. I needed a Juniper… or a Seymour. Just someone warm and familiar that would scold me for not taking better care of myself. Instead, the front desk was manned by an ogre who towered over the tiny countertop and looked at me like the fact that I'd walked in was inconvenient to him. I approached, keeping Danny just a bit behind me, and looked up at the ogre expectantly.

He didn't say anything.

I didn't want to say anything on principle. Where was the customer service? But it was late, and I relented. "We'd like a room for the night."

The ogre grunted. "Ten crystals."

"That's steep for one night's stay."

"Boutique experience," he grumbled.

"Yeah?"

The ogre turned away from us to grab something from the counter behind him, and I noticed that he was wearing pressed slacks and suspenders in addition to his crisp white dress shirt. When he turned back around, he placed a basket on the countertop. "Yeah."

I peered over the edge of the basket.

"Clean sheets, lavender bath oils, local chocolates, eye masks." He looked over the edge of his thick rimmed glasses and pushed the basket toward me. "Boutique. Ten crystals."

I stifled a groan of annoyance and dropped the payment on the countertop, but once the ogre gathered up the pieces, he held out an empty hand, his blue-green flesh willing me to place something else into it.

"What?"

"Tip."

"Oh, for fuck's—" I was about to argue when Danny elbowed me in the ribs, so I dutifully plopped one more crystal in his massive paw. "How much for dinner for the kid?"

"Included."

"Lovely."

That night, we fell asleep under clean, warm blankets to the smell of lavender—the scented oil of which I'd dumped into our washbasin, having no time for an actual bath—and with full bellies. Danny ate all of our chocolates. I had to admit, whatever this boutique tavern experience was going for wasn't half bad. The cook had given us two bowls of beef stew and a biscuit, and I'd even sprung for a pint of beer. I found, though, that all I could think about when I drifted off to sleep was the taste of sparkling wine on August's lips.

THE COVENANT OF UNITED NEIGHBORS FOR TRUE SALVATION

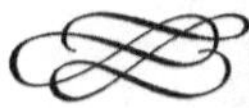

AUGUST

The cult of anti-werewolf doomsday conspiracy theorists was rapidly expanding across the continent, along with the population of actual werewolves, apparently. How did I know? Well, they showed up at my door. Not only that, but they were positively harassing my staff when I walked by and decided to see what all the fuss was about.

"I'm sorry, who are you with?"

"The Covenant of United Neighbors for True Salvation," the representative said proudly, handing me a scroll of parchment, which, no doubt, outlined the extent of their insanity.

The fact that my tact had been gone for quite some time was solidified when I asked, "You're aware of the acronym, I assume?"

He scowled. "We prefer to go by 'the Covenant' if one is looking for a shortened way to refer to our group."

"That's good because otherwise it's—"

"Yes, I'm aware."

"Because otherwise it's CUNTS," I told him, leaning against the doorframe to my castle.

The man on the other side of the door narrowed his gaze at me, clearly unimpressed with my inability to be serious about his very real, very important cause. The person traveling with him seemed a little more amused, however, and stifled a chuckle.

Before they could continue, Olin popped up behind me. "Your Grace, do you require my assistance?"

"No, that won't be necessary, Olin. I'm just speaking with these CUNTS—"

Olin gasped.

"—about… what was it again, fellas?"

"Er, the rise in the werewolf population as a sign of the end of the world."

I looked over my shoulder at Olin and jerked a thumb at our guests. "That."

Olin excused himself, clearly in no mood to watch me torment seemingly innocent guests, but I had no filter to be found.

"And what are we doing about said infestation and the consequent end of the world?"

The man on the other side of the door looked uncomfortable, but was clearly committed to his spiel. "Well, we're identifying those who may be harboring werewolves in their midst."

I stifled a laugh; you can't harbor a werewolf.

"And we are repenting. We encourage all who wish to survive these end times to do the same."

"Repenting for what, exactly?"

"Why, our sins, of course."

I laughed. "I don't know that we have enough time for that, gentlemen."

AMRYS OF EMYNOR

AUGUST

*A*mrys of Emynor arrived in Barrien on the coldest, darkest day of winter, escorted by a slew of royal guards who were sent to ensure her safety, because despite us being promised to each other in marriage, Emynor still had absolutely no reason to trust me or my kingdom. Florian rode at the front of the group, regal as ever on Stratus, and somehow his pompous ass looked younger than the last time I had seen him. The air was frigid and smelled like snow would fall at any moment. The elf wore a coat, the collar of which was made of some sort of white fur. Perhaps he was fueled by my misery or the thought that somewhere out there, Max the Menace was single and available. As I watched the group stream into the courtyard, a carriage drawn by Emynorian steeds pulling the woman who was to be my bride, I mulled over the idea of a single Max. I couldn't tell if that was better or worse than the idea of her being with someone permanently. Was there a man out there whose proposal she would have accepted? I died a little inside at the thought.

"Your Grace, may I introduce to you Princess Amrys of Emynor," Florian announced as he stood next to the carriage door, waiting for the other elven escorts to open it. When they did, a young woman exited. She was tall, probably just a couple of inches shorter than me, and slender, as all elves seemed to be. She wore a coat similar to Florian's, but more form-fitting, and it cascaded down to the ground. Beyond that, she didn't look much like Florian; her flesh was pale with a slight blush from the cold, but her hair cascaded down her shoulders in a tumbling chestnut waterfall. Her eyes, a brilliant green, lit up as she met my gaze. I knew then that this woman was warm, unlike her dark elf counterpart, and was already attempting to form some sort of connection with me despite the awkwardness of our arrangement.

I didn't like it.

I bowed.

I took her hand.

I kissed the back of it.

I welcomed her into the castle.

"Olin will show you to your chambers."

"My chambers, Your Grace?" Amrys asked, her voice lilty and warm, just like her expression.

"Yes," I said, clearing my throat as we entered the castle. Lately I didn't speak much unless I needed to or unless I was tormenting petulant cult members that felt the need to bother me in my own home. "I imagine they'll be to your liking. If there's anything else you require, please let the castle attendants know. There's a, um, bell in your room."

Olin escorted Amrys up the stairs, and the second she was out of earshot, Florian pounced. "You're not going to sleep in the same room as your bride-to-be?"

I sneered, turning with enthusiasm to face him. The words came more easily now that I was warmed up from speaking with the princess. "There was a moment in time, Florian, that I believed we were on the same side," I told him. It had been Max that helped us work together. "The more you twist the blade, however, the more I realize that you're a sadistic asshole who enjoys suffering wherever he can get it, especially if it has to do with you having the upper hand."

Florian shrugged, the fur collar of his coat bunching up around his neck as he did so. "That may be true in general, but when it comes to you, I only care about suffering related to Max."

"What do you know about that?" I sneered.

"I know that neither of us have her and both of us wish we did."

I gritted my teeth, unwilling to listen to him profess his love for Max. It felt wrong that he would confirm my fears now, when he'd just escorted an elven princess to my home for an arranged marriage. If he came across Max again, what would he say to her? Would he tell her that I'd moved on and married? My stomach turned at the thought. "I won't be sleeping in the same room as anyone else, Florian. I hope your elven princess isn't offended."

"She will be, August," Florian said with a sneer, closing the gap between us. "And she'll ensure that her people know she was snubbed by her betrothed. Perhaps they'll label you a traitor to your own race. What's the problem? Do you not find elven women attractive?" If not for the context around our relationship, one might've thought that Florian was simply doing his job as an ambassador between two previously warring kingdoms.

In that moment, I wished more than anything that Magnus was by my side. I would've snapped my fingers and set this pompous fuck alight. What would Emynor say about *that*? Probably not much, considering he wasn't even Emynorian. He just acted as a middle man between Barrien and the elves… and a nuisance in general. Because I was without my dragon companion, I resorted to physicality instead and grabbed Florian by the lapel of his cloak, crushing the fur between my fingers without hesitation.

Florian was relentless in his teasing, however. He looked me straight in the eyes, those soulless, empty clouds of irises locked on to mine when he said through struggling breaths, "It would be beyond disappointing if their elven princess didn't appeal to the king of Barrien, a known womanizer who has fucked everyone in a hundred-mile radius, don't you think?"

"I'd crush the air from your lungs right now if I didn't need you," I told him honestly. "Don't forget that, okay?" Part of me wanted to hurt him, to really hurt him, just to limit the chances of him spreading some rumor that I was still living in my promiscuous ways, but I knew that not much beyond death would stop Florian from running his mouth. When I released his cloak, he tried to hide the way he gasped for breath as he flattened out the fabric of his clothing. The potential damage to his attire, I was sure, was his biggest concern.

I RETIRED to my room shortly after Princess Amrys's arrival. Meanwhile, the king and queen's old quarters had been prepared for her residence; Olin and the housekeeping team had ensured that she would long for nothing during her time in Barrien, which, much to my dismay, was intended to be the rest of her life. They'd spared no expense when it came to outfitting her room with silk sheets, plush pillows, concoctions of all sorts for body care and perfumery, as well as filling a dresser and closet with the finest clothing they could source. Florian had suggested pieces that blended Emynorian style, which was returning now that they were no longer under tyrant rule, with the style of those of Barrien, of which there was very little. Back when I'd been more enthusiastic about the rebirth of my city, I had daydreamed about the uprising of the people's style and interests once they were no longer struggling to survive. It was a nice thought, but it hadn't crossed my mind in a long time. Perhaps Amrys would bring to Barrien what I could no longer.

The window in our bedroom was open, its curtains swaying ever so slightly in the cold night air. They had remained open ever since I'd sent Magnus and the soldiers out to follow Max; I wanted to be reach-able if there was ever a note coming for me. I had just lain down, still fully dressed in the day's formal attire, when there was a knock at the door.

"Your Grace?" The voice of one of the castle attendants came through the thick wood of the entrance.

"What is it?" I asked, barely lifting my head to respond. "Olin is available should Princess Amrys require anything."

"Erm, well… she requires your presence, Your Grace."

"What for?"

"Dinner."

I sat up in confusion, then stumbled through a response. "Surely she's… exhausted from her travels and prefers to eat in her room?"

"I'm certain she will appreciate your consideration. However, she's already dressed for dinner with the king and awaits your company. The chefs are putting the final touches on your first course now, including some Emynorian specialties, suggestions courtesy of Sir Florian." I could tell the man on the other side of the door was nervous about hosting guests from another land, let alone a guest from the land we had stolen and ruled over wrongly for so long. The way he shuffled his feet caused the hallway lighting to shift through the crack beneath the door.

Fuck. I groaned internally at the thought of choking down lichen-covered mung bean patties or butterfly nectar in the name of formality. I wanted to drink, jerk off, and go to sleep.

"Sir?" the voice asked when I didn't respond quickly enough.

"Yes, sure, I'll be down shortly."

The man who faced me in the small mirror on my dresser was not someone I recognized. I'd avoided looking at him for so long that I wondered why I'd even given him a second glance this time. My hair was longer than it had been since Max and I had returned to Barrien; something about being with her had caused me to neglect the complex self-maintenance routines that I had once had. With Max, there were more important things to focus on than the length of my hair or the shape of my eyebrows. I ran a hand through my curls, but flinched when I inadvertently touched the top of one of my ears. I never touched those; that was her domain. It took a few seconds, but I managed to adjust my hair so that it covered my ears and vowed to forget the way she had tenderly caressed them almost every time she kissed me. Forget, forget, forget. If she never touched me again, it would be okay, as long as she was alive and well… and I had to tell myself that she would never touch me again.

3… 2… 1…

I gave myself three seconds to straighten my collar and then look away. Just dinner, I told myself. Just dinner, and then you'll be done for the day. Perhaps there will be an update about Max when you return to your room. That would have to be enough to get me through.

Amrys was, indeed, awaiting my arrival at dinner. When the butler announced my entrance, I attempted to wave him off, but the elven princess was already standing.

"Your Grace," she said, curtseying as I entered the dining room.

"Please." I took my seat without looking her in the eye. "There's no need to stand on ceremony; it's not like that here." One of that evening's servers poured me a glass of bourbon, a recent favorite of mine, and I raised it briefly in the direction of my new housemate. I don't know that I would have ever been able to think of her as my fiancée or wife. The glass in front of her place setting was filled with something warm and steaming, with a sprig of some plant sticking out of it. Right, per Florian's suggestions. "Eat, drink. You must be tired from your travels."

She offered me a soft smile, but I don't think it reached her eyes. I didn't look long enough to care and instead, helped myself to a bit of food from the spread before us. I wasn't really hungry.

"Thank you. That's very kind," she replied.

Ugh, the formality of it all was atrociously boring. Was it kind of me to offer someone food after they had spent days on end in a carriage, likely marinating in their own sweat on numerous bumpy roads? Or was it just common decency? "Sure."

We ate in silence.

Painful, dead, empty silence. All that filled the air was the occasional clink of our silverware and the shuffling of the waitstaff as they swapped our plates and filled our glasses.

I was startled when Amrys spoke again, about the same time that the familiar beating of leathery wings met my ears. "Shall we... talk?"

"No, I don't think so," I said bluntly before wiping my mouth with my napkin and standing from the table. "If you'll excuse me..." Unfortunately for me, Amrys was seated near the exit of the dining room, and as I passed by her, she caught my forearm. I froze in place, realizing then just how long it had been since I'd let someone touch me, let alone a *woman*. But I hadn't let her... she'd just done it, and it had fully incapacitated me.

"Your Grace," Amrys addressed me, her grip on my arm gentle but all powerful. The room spun. "Will you meet me in our chambers once you're finished with whatever business is pulling you away from me?"

I cleared my throat and slid from her grasp, managing the most minute semblance of a nod before slipping out of the room. Florian's warnings rang in my head.

THE ONLY THING that kept me walking toward the sitting room was the promise of a message about Max, but the second I slipped from the dining room, I was lightheaded. I staggered and leaned against a wall, unable to comprehend how the touch of a woman—a sensation I had experienced a million times over—could render me so defenseless. It made me want to scream. That interaction from someone other than the person I wanted it from, needed it from, desperately longed for it from, felt *wrong*… Furthermore, the fact that I was expected to make it part of my daily routine, to uphold the facade of being married to an elven princess, made my stomach roll.

It was Magnus's snort and huff from the other room that snapped me from my trance, however temporarily. "Magnus, my boy," I greeted him, grabbing a dried side of fish from the platter that had been left in the sitting room specifically for him. He took it gratefully, then pressed against my side and nearly knocked me over. "You've grown." It had only been a few days, and yet, he looked bigger. "How long before Max notices her little micro dragon following her?" I rubbed between his eyes, and he closed them in contentment. I, too, felt calm settle over me; he was in for the night, and for now, I had a tie to Max. At least until morning.

The note read:

> Moving west. Noticing more werewolf sightings, but what's worse are the Covenant cultists that follow their paths. Both are okay… seem healthy. No imminent danger. Can't wait for my own dragon. Feed that boy extra treats for me.
>
> - Sid

I read the note as many times as my tired eyes would let me, then folded it carefully to place in my breast pocket. Magnus and I climbed the stairs together, his frame supporting mine as I convinced my injured leg to go one step at a time. The door to our bedroom was so close… when I remembered that I had promised to visit Amrys in what was once my parents' chambers.

"Go on," I told the dragon, who looked at me through narrowed eyes. "I'll be right there."

He huffed.

"Nothing's going to happen," I told him.

Another.

"What're you, the protector of my fidelity? Don't you think I can manage that on my own?" I waved him off with a grunt, then whispered harshly at him, "Why am I arguing with you anyway! Go to bed, I'll be right there. Leave some space for me this time!"

THE WALK from the top of the stairs to the royal chambers felt like miles, much like it had when I was a little kid and I had stood there debating whether to bug my parents. Almost every time, I would turn the opposite way and go to my own bedroom, the one I still slept in, instead. I wanted to do that this time, but Florian's threats echoed in my head. I decided then that, if I wasn't going to at least *try* to commit to the charade, there had been no point in agreeing to it in the first place. Maybe I could go in there and talk to her. Maybe it would be completely innocent. Or maybe I would just have to get it out of the way for the sake of this union. I could do that. I'd done it before, slept with people I'd only just met or whose names I hadn't yet learned. If that was what it would take, then...

Amrys's door swung open before I could even knock on it.

And there she was, swimming into my vision like the embodiment of poise, like most elves were. Not me, of course. But my mother had probably been a lot like that. Oh, hell, why was I thinking about my *mother* during a time like this? I shook my head a little as if to reset my thoughts and stepped into the room, closing the door behind me.

"Your Grace," she addressed me, again.

I backed myself up against the door, then cleared my throat. "No need for formality," I reminded her. "Now, how about that talk?"

In the dim light of the room, Amrys looked like an entirely different person from the one who had joined me for dinner earlier. Her gaze was heavy lidded, perhaps due to the alcohol from our meal, and she looked at me with almost predatory interest as she approached. Her walk was smooth, silky, much like the emerald dressing gown she wore, and I found myself praying that she had other garments beneath the thin fabric. "I've heard that there are other activities you might prefer, King—"

"August, just August is fine," I choked out. "But—"

"August," she addressed me again, my name smooth and natural on her tongue. Nope, I hated the way that sounded, too. I tried to distract myself and wondered what my name might've been if I had grown up in Emynor and not Barrien. Probably something flowery like Florian. Aster. Oleander. Catkin. When my focus shifted again, I realized that she had nearly closed the gap between us, and the dressing gown had slid itself off of her shoulders and was resting in the crook of each arm, the hands of which were folded in front of her. Her shoulders were smooth and pale, almost as if made of marble, and the candlelight cast dancing shadows across her flesh. "You seem stressed," she told me, unlacing her fingers to place her hands on my chest. My heart leaped into my throat. "I would like to ease some of that for you, if I may."

Amrys had undone two of the buttons of my shirt before I caught her wrist, and the fact that I let her get that far had me questioning myself greatly. "No," I managed, my lip tingling from where I had bitten it. I moved her hands back to her sides and released them, unable to step away because I had cornered myself from the get-go.

"Are you not… interested?" Amrys's voice was concerned. "I promise, I'll be able to please you." Before I could protest again—and gods did it feel like a cruel prank to put me in this situation—she'd shrugged her way fully out of her dressing gown, revealing the rest of her form. The silk slid off of her frame and puddled around her feet, where I had forced my attention in order to avoid her brazen nudity. "Don't you see… anything that you like, August?" My name sounded foreign on her tongue, and it *was*. It was new to her. I was new to her, and yet here she stood, naked and trying to seduce me. I forced myself to look up and consumed her body in a way that any man would have: with objective appreciation. Her hips were slight, slender, her pubic hair cut short into a precise triangle. Her breasts were full and round, somehow perfectly symmetrical to the eye, with nipples of a light pink that reminded me of a kitten's tongue. The elf's hair, chestnut brown and golden with the reflection of the room's lighting, tumbled over her shoulder in waves so smooth she must never have laid her head on a pillow. She was, by all accounts, beautiful.

But she was not my person.

Perhaps she was another beautiful planet, with its own endless pull. But she was not my moon, and I was not her ocean, nor could I ever be. Not with time, not ever. However many tales there are of arranged marriages that lead to true love, this would not be one of them.

It was then that I realized that I could never do this. Not really, not fully, of course; I had known that since the arrangement had been proposed, but I realized that I also couldn't commit to it halfway. If marriage meant consummation, I could not fulfill the suggestions of my advisors.

"Kiss me, August," Amrys said suddenly, as I was deep in internal turmoil.

I put up my hands as if to block an assault and managed to catch her gently by the shoulders before she leaned in. "I can't."

She looked alarmed. She'd probably never been denied before, and I hated to be the one to give her that experience. "What? Why not?"

"Please, put your clothes back on," I pleaded, looking over her head so that I didn't have to see her naked body.

She squatted quickly to grab her robe, then pulled it back up around her shoulders as if she'd been scandalized. "Have I done something wrong, Your Grace?"

"No, I just…" I put my hands up to indicate that I needed her to back away. She did so, and I slid to the side from the door so that I was no longer a captive audience. "It's not you."

Amrys backed away, hugging the gown around her body despite the warmth of the room; the fire had been lit by the house staff, and the window was shut tight, unlike mine. That and the intensity of our interaction had me sweating.

"That's hard to believe," she commented, crossing the room to sit on the edge of the bed. That was my parents' bed. I wondered then what they would think from their prison cell if they knew what was happening in their bedroom.

I remained standing and rebuttoned my shirt, securing it around my throat as if to cover as much of my flesh as possible. "I mean it," I muttered, unsure of what to do with myself. I couldn't just turn and leave; sex or not, this woman was meant to *marry* me and live out the rest of her days in this castle. "It's me," I said finally. "And before you assume that's some sort of line that I give people I reject, it's not. I—"

"Well, what is it then?"

My mouth opened and I attempted to reassure her, but what came out was nearly incoherent rambling. "This will purely be a marriage of convenience… and I don't intend on fulfilling any part of it other than the legalities. I understand that it's necessary for the union of our two kingdoms… and while you're here, I promise you'll be treated as nothing but royalty and have access to anything you could ever wish for, aside from an actual romantic relationship with me. You're more than welcome to have relationships with whomever you might like.

I'm not concerned with my line being carried on, in fact, I don't care if Barrien burns to the ground, and I'm sure you came here expecting more from me, but—"

"Oh, thank *gods*," Amrys blurted out suddenly, almost as if all of the decorum had left her repertoire in a hurry.

"I know, wait, excuse me?" I dropped my hands from my collar and found Amrys still seated on the bed, a look of relief across her fair face, and was she... smiling? "Did I miss something? Not to suggest that you should've come here with nothing but the desire for romance, but..."

Amrys ran a hand through her dusky mane and crossed her legs. "You first. Why don't you want to, well, you know..." Suddenly, she looked shy, almost as if she hadn't just come at me in the nude.

I was baffled. "First of all, I think I'm still in charge here. So how about *you* go first, and if I like your answer, I'll give you mine over breakfast."

The elf shrugged. "I like women. I have no interest in marrying a man for love or sex, August. But if it's what my kingdom needs, then so be it."

We remained in silence for longer than I liked. I was still bewildered by our predicament.

"Well, does that satisfy you?"

Suddenly, a sigh of relief escaped me. "More than you'll ever know," I admitted. Sometimes things just work out for me. "I need to go back to my room before my dragon roasts me alive."

"That is sound logic. Are you sure you and your dragon don't want to sleep in here? It is the king's chambers, after all. I'm happy to relocate."

"That's quite alright."

"Breakfast?"

"Yes."

That night, with Magnus consuming the majority of my bed, I dreamt of Max peacefully, knowing that I would be able to keep every promise I'd ever made about loving her and only her.

AN UNLIKELY FRIENDSHIP

AUGUST

*M*agnus departed the next morning, much like he always did following a check-in, and I felt the hole in my heart deepen with loneliness.

When I arrived downstairs for breakfast, a meal I had been skipping for a few weeks prior, I found the dining room table filled with a spread large enough for a small army. This was new. Perhaps Amrys liked to eat more than I had anticipated, or we were just pulling out all of the stops for her. Neither was wrong, per se, but if our conversation from the night before had actually happened, she may have been easier to please in this relationship than previously anticipated.

Along the table were several foods I had never seen before, and I assumed that they were our Barrien chef's attempt at making Amrys feel at home: a loaf of bread that looked as light as air, the top of which was sprinkled with a shimmery silver dust; jams and spreads of every shade of pink and blue; strips of some sort of mystery meat that I imagined must have been faerie thighs or tree bark turned meat-alternative. There were, of course, plates of more familiar food as well. From where I sat, I could see bacon, eggs, and a stack of normal-looking toast with a plate of butter. It all seemed quite bland in comparison. I let the server pour me a cup of coffee with a hearty glug of whiskey.

"Do you mind?" the elven princess asked once I had seated myself. She was eyeing the spread hungrily.

"Of course not," I told her with a nod. "Help yourself."

When she didn't immediately dive into either the food or conversation, I got the message and turned to the wait staff that was patiently hovering in order to refill beverages or provide additional cutlery. "Some space, please. We'll call if we need you." They cleared the room immediately, probably assuming that we would be banging on every surface imaginable as part of Amrys's initiation into Barrien royal life.

Once we were alone, Amrys helped herself to the food on the table. It was clear that she had left some of the pomp and circumstance behind following our conversation, but she was still polite, neat, and graceful, wiping her lips between bites and never speaking with her mouth full. Unlike the night before, however, she actually ate, and for that, I was glad.

"Well," she said finally after swallowing a bite of the tree-bark looking concoction. "We had a deal. Are you going to tell me why you're against going all-in on this arranged marriage?"

I had been mid-sip of orange juice when she dropped the question. I should've been expecting it, but I choked a little anyway. "Straight to the point, huh?"

"Based on our conversation last night, I feel as though that approach might serve us best, *husband-to-be*."

The title made my skin crawl. It wasn't cute or funny. I hated it. We'd need to address that at a later date. "Uh, well…"

"Wait, wait, let me guess."

Oh, gods, please no.

"You only like men?"

"No, not exactly. I mean, I *do* like both men and women, but that's not it."

"Hmm, oh… do you have… *groin goblins*[1]? I've heard some horror stories."

"What? No!" I dropped my fork in shock. Me? A venereal disease? Amrys of Emynor was truly turning out to be the opposite of what I expected from an elven princess. "What a strange thing to say. Do you go around asking people personal questions like that?"

Amrys laughed. It was a sweet, light sound, completely unbothered by my reaction. "No," she said with a shrug. "But I also don't get shipped off to foreign kingdoms after basically being sold for marriage, so… I suppose there's a first time for everything."

"Well, it has nothing to do with my sexuality nor my… cleanliness," I said finally, shoving a bite of toast into my mouth so that I wouldn't have to speak for a few seconds.

The elf chewed thoughtfully across the table from me. "I'd rather not keep guessing, if you don't mind. The last thing we need is for me to guess something else completely outlandish and ruin this working relationship we're building."

I nodded once I finished my bite and set my silverware down with a resigned sigh. I *had* promised her, and so far this arranged marriage thing *was* working out in my favor. "I'm in love with someone else," I said plainly, admitting it out loud for the first time ever. "And to give myself to anyone else that way wouldn't be… right to me."

"Oh."

I chewed my next bite for longer than I needed to, cringing as I swallowed the overprocessed mush after a few moments. "Yeah."

"What happened to them?" Amrys asked, spearing another piece of food with her fork.

"She's alive, just not with me." I cleared my throat as I began to feel choked up. "I proposed. She said no… and then she left."

Amrys sucked in a breath, as if she could feel my pain. "So even if you never see her again, you still wouldn't... move on?"

"There isn't really any 'moving on' for me." I nodded as if in agreement with my own statement, then looked down at my plate to realize I wasn't really hungry anymore. I pushed my food around with the tines of my fork before setting it down and wiping my hands. "On that note." I attempted to conclude the conversation by downing the rest of my drink and standing to push my chair in. "Thank you for joining me for breakfast. I imagine we will have many more opportunities like this, but for now, I have business to attend to."

"Wait!" Amrys said a little louder, catching me by the forearm again as I headed for the exit of the room. I flinched, and she let go. To her credit, we never spoke about touch again, and she never tried to touch me again. Then she asked, "Aren't you going to tell me about the dragon? And the guards?"

"How much time do you have?"

Amrys looked off into the distance as if to truly contemplate my question, a fork still hanging loosely from her fingers as she did the math on an invisible parchment in midair. "Well, if we're wed... and it's for the greater good of our kingdoms, then... forever, I suppose."

"Then you'll hear all about it eventually, I'm sure. A story for a story, though."

----

1. Groin Goblins: slang for pubic lice.

NO SHAME IN HELP

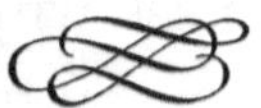

AUGUST

$\mathcal{A}$nd so it continued like that each morning. We gathered for breakfast, dismissed the staff, and shared one story each.

~

"IT'S SUPPOSED to be a *micro* dragon?" Amrys balked one morning when Magnus joined us, scarfing down an entire plate of bacon on his own. He had continued to grow.

I laughed a little. "I'm guessing he got mixed in with the wrong batch somehow," I commented, tossing him a piece of toast from my plate, which he downed immediately. "I have no idea how large he'll get."

~

"FLORIAN *IS* OBNOXIOUS, I AGREE."

~

"I was a nightmare at the start of that trip."

"I'm sure you weren't *that* bad," Amrys argued from across the table.

"You'd be wrong, then, as kind as you're trying to be," I told her. To recall the first interactions of Max and myself was embarrassing, but it also made me smile a little. "I was obsessed with my own comfort. I didn't even bother to ask why I was being held captive and instead fixated on the chafing of my nipples… and the style of coat she'd purchased to keep me warm on the road." I chewed a bit of my breakfast before adding, "Not sure how she didn't kill me the moment I started talking. She did knock me out, though."

Amrys chuckled.

"You know, she pulled out one of her own teeth to save some little kids from an infestation of tooth faeries."

"Sounds like a good woman," Amrys said with a soft smile. "Maybe a little rough around the edges, but I suppose we all are in some way."

I was heading upstairs to my chambers when I stopped midway to breathe through the pain that inevitably came with transporting myself on my injured leg. Most days, I was used to it; I didn't have to be anywhere too quickly, so it was just a matter of taking my time. I was running my fingers along the banister, thinking about the fact that so many generations of Theodorics had run their hands over that exact piece of wood before, when Amrys's voice came from the top of the stairs, at the entrance of her own room. "August?"

"Huh?" I looked up suddenly, startled out of my daze. "Yes?"

"Why do you put yourself through that every day?" She exited her doorway, the door closing behind her, and approached the top of the stairs. It appeared she was already ready for bed, her long hair in a loose braid over one shoulder, and she'd changed into loose slacks and a blouse that matched. It was a stark difference from the elf who had tried to seduce me weeks prior, and I enjoyed the fact that she felt comfortable enough to, well, let herself be comfortable. That was all I could ask given the circumstances. She came down the stairs to meet me, her bare feet padding quietly across the marble floor.

"What do you mean?" Honestly, she could have been talking about anything. At this point simply existing each day often felt like a chore.

Before I could argue, she'd hooked one of her arms through mine and was guiding me the rest of the way up the stairs, pulling me a bit toward her so I would lean more weight on her than my leg. "Walking up these stairs each day, multiple times a day," she mused aloud, walking with ease unlike myself. She hadn't even broken a sweat. "Surely there's an easier way."

I laughed a little, surprised at her help but trying not to be ungrateful. "Like what?"

"Like… moving your bedroom to the main floor," she offered gently.

I halted, my body tensing against my will, and shook my head. "No."

"Story for another day, I suppose," she said with a knowing smile, then urged me to keep walking. "Well, how about having the staff rig up some sort of platform… with a pulley to get you up to the next floor? Machines or magic, there has to be a way. Certainly you have the resources, King August." She glanced sideways at me and winked.

We arrived at the landing, and she released me immediately, knowing that I would have preferred not to be touched altogether. My leg ached, but not nearly as much as it would have had I walked alone. Then, she spoke again, "And—"

"There's more?"

Amrys waved me off. "Yes, there's more. *And* a cane for flat surfaces."

"Why would I do that?"

The elf's gaze was deep and curious, much like the way she looked at me when we were sharing our daily stories. "Why *wouldn't* you? Why suffer for the sake of suffering? There's no shame in receiving help, August." Before I could argue with her, she bid me goodnight, then turned and left, her footsteps quick and quiet. The door to my parents' chambers closed behind her, and she was gone again until breakfast time. I didn't know if I agreed with her. Florian would laugh, and so would anyone else who could see into my pitiful moping mind, but part of the reason I dealt with the pain of scaling the stairs was because it reminded me of the greatest adventure of my life. It was okay that I was injured, that I was hurt, because I'd gotten that way from being on the road with Max… and that was an experience I knew I might never encounter again. If pain was my only reminder, then I'd cling to it.

A few days later, I was late to breakfast and found the dining room table covered in scrolls of parchment with drawings that I couldn't quite make out when I entered. They were intricate and looked like the work of an architect, perhaps, but I didn't recall having one on our staff.

"No time for stories today, my friend," Amrys announced when I walked in, still rubbing the sleep from my eyes. She leaned over the table to move the rolls of parchment around as if arranging them in a particular order. "These are the plans that the architect dropped off after I sent him my ideas." She hadn't even looked up at me, but pushed some of the paper out of the way to reveal several wooden sticks beneath them, almost overlapping our usual spread of breakfast foods. "And I have canes for you to try. They're not completely done yet, but they've been roughed out to a general shape, and you should be able to get a good feel for which one suits you best."

When our eyes met, she added, "Don't worry, you can try them out on your own. I won't watch. Now, grab a plate, and let's look at your options." I must not have moved an inch because she clapped her hands softly. "Come on now, make haste. If I'm going to spend your money, I'd at least like a bit of your input."

AFTER AMRYS excitedly showed me the plans for the platform that would travel between each floor of the castle, she left me on my own to inspect the canes. The idea of relying on a cane for support was a strange concept to begin with, not to mention having to select one that would best suit my style. It felt like admitting defeat… No, it felt like broadcasting my defeat, just like putting Max's necklace on had felt. Nevertheless, I couldn't deny that it hurt to walk and that I couldn't stand the idea of Amrys coming to my side to "help" me again; it was more stressful, more humiliating than relying on an inanimate object.

I ran my hand over each of the pieces of wood lying across the dining room table, admiring the way that the woodworker had left the natural grain and knots of each piece of lumber intact and visible. The detail reminded me of being in the woods with Max. I took a steadying breath and gave them each a try. Of course they were immediately useful.

"Dammit, Amrys."

When all was said and done, I settled on one that was elegant in its simplicity, made of a dark wood that I didn't recognize with a flat handle. I tore a small piece of the parchment the plans had been drawn on and left Amrys a note: *This one. Thank you.*

When it was returned to me days later, the handle had been encased in gold with an intricate filigree design. When Amrys delivered the final product to me, she held up a finger. "Hang on, I had them add a little surprise." She gave the handle a small jiggle and removed it from the rest of the cane, revealing a shockingly sharp dagger that had been nested inside the tool.

I didn't want to, but I loved it.

CALLAHAN

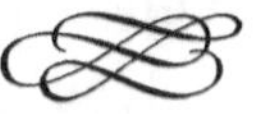

MAX

The sun was just beginning to set when we arrived at another stop on the road—a tavern whose name I hadn't bothered to look at upon our arrival—and I had no clue if they would let me bring a kid inside, nor did I know if I'd want to risk it either way. It wasn't like there were posted rules or anything. It's just you didn't see a lot of eleven-year-olds in taverns unless they were kids of the barkeep or were slaving away behind the counter… or trying to steal from the patrons. Mostly, everyone felt like kids ruined the fun, so they weren't exactly welcome. Not only that, but I'd kept Danny a secret from pretty much everyone until recently, so I wasn't looking forward to the fact that I was reintroducing myself as the mercenary with a young sidekick. Not very menacing of me at all. I was exhausted, dirty, hungry… and thankfully tired enough that I couldn't really think of much else besides our basic needs. But when I hopped off Wraith, a rowdy group of bar patrons stumbled out of the front door of the tavern, nearly taking us down with them. I pulled Wraith aside as quickly and quietly as possible without waking Danny, who was slumped forward on her back. I'd thrown an extra cloak over him to keep him warm.

Before I could tie Wraith up and get Danny down, the front doors of the tavern burst open as if someone had been thrown through them, and another crowd of maybe ten patrons stumbled out. Just my luck, they were arguing loudly.

"I'm tellin' ya," one patron yelled, clearly drunk by his belligerent commentary. "There're werewolves out there! And if you"—he belched loudly—"if you don't watch yerself, you'll get gobbled right up!"

"Or worse!" another chimed in. "You'll get turned into one yourself!"

"The end is near!" a third, equally sloshed man added.

"That's enough. We're sick of hearing your doomsday nonsense," a more level-headed patron chimed in, and when I got a better look at him in the group, I realized that he and several others were ushering those spouting werewolf propaganda out and away from the tavern. "Go on then, ya CUNTS." They stuck around outside long enough to see the Covenant members leave the premises (presumably into a forest full of werewolves) before returning inside. I hoped that meant the rest of the coast was clear of troublemakers and that we could get ourselves some food and rest without a fight. I turned toward Wraith in time to see Danny sitting upright, apparently having watched the entire scene unfold.

My brother looked mortified. "What do they mean by that, Max? Are we gonna get eaten up by some damn werewolf?"

"No," I whispered harshly. "And watch your mouth."

Danny folded his arms over his chest in defiance. Sometimes I forgot he was an eleven-year-old boy. "Why? We ain't in Barrien anymore," he argued. I knew he was just saying it to drive a point home now; we *weren't* in Barrien. Hadn't been for a long time. Would never be again. And adjusting to life on the road again had been challenging for both of us, most of all him. He'd never had to adapt to life on the road before. In fact, he'd led quite a comfortable life in the Wild Open, with me providing for him… Sure, he probably got lonely sometimes, but his belly was always full, the fire was always going, and he never had to worry about being eaten by monsters. What a life. "Besides, shouldn't we be worryin' about the werewolves and not my grammar?"

I groaned, too exhausted to go on fighting with him. "Get your ass down and let's go inside." Danny complied, but not without muttering under his breath. As we approached the doors of the tavern ourselves, however, my fears about it being the wrong place for a young kid were confirmed. Even through the door, it was loud… and stunk of cheap beer and cigars. One table was full of a group of rowdy travelers drinking Hippity Hops, a beer made with frog legs, as indicated by their loud belching that mimicked a frog's croak.

I tried to keep my chin up as we entered and slid us into a booth in the back of the tavern near the bar, hoping I could feed the kid and then sneak us up to a remaining room. But before I had only squeezed him past swaths of people and into a seat, I realized that the group from earlier had only been a small portion of the Covenant members from the tavern that night. The rooms were undoubtedly all booked by the doomsday morons, and staying any longer only meant more propaganda to fill Danny's head. We needed to find somewhere to sleep. Hell, it was getting so late that I wasn't sure where we'd find a vacancy… "Get up, we gotta go."

"Why? We just got here! Is it 'cause of the werewolves?"

I grabbed him by the arm to get him standing and out of the booth, but pulled him close enough so that I could whisper in his ear. "Danny, if you don't shut up about the werewolves, I will find one for you and feed you to it myself." The last person who needed to worry about monsters was the kid brother of the continent's best monster hunter, especially when he'd already gotten pretty proficient with his own little blade and would be able to take care of himself if needed. But that was the thing about brothers; they tease you no matter what. Older, younger, trusting or not.

We were halfway through the crowd again when someone stepped in front of me and blocked our path.

"You! Young lady! Have you repented for your sins? Have you begged for forgiveness, or are you the cause of the infestation this great continent is facing now?" one Covenant member asked, getting up in my face as I attempted to steer Danny out of the tavern. I pushed our way past them.

"What do they mean by 'sins,' Max?" Danny asked.

"Ignore them."

They followed. "Missy, I'm talkin' to you! The time to repent is now, lest we all be eaten up by the great beasts… or worse, turned into them to do the devil's bidding!"

I rolled my eyes, then whirled on one of the speakers, putting Danny behind me to shield him from the onlookers. "Lady, if there is a devil, I've already met and made peace with him."

Okay, this wasn't going to work. I could hold my own in that group, but the last thing I needed was my eleven-year-old brother getting hurt in the middle of some drunken brawl… and there was no way he'd listen to me if I tried to lock him away in our room for the night. I mentally cursed my baby brother's stubbornness, as if it weren't the same as my own, and pulled Wraith back toward the road without mounting her again once we were outside.

She snorted and nipped at the back of my sleeve. She wanted to rest, just like all of us did, and yet I had her up and moving again after miles and miles of travel.

"I know," I muttered in frustration. "I'm tired, too. But we can't stay there… and we need to find some place with food. You're hungry, right? Or is the spirit of adventure enough to keep you full and happy?"

Huff.

"That's what I thought." I reached up to stroke the side of her face as we walked, determined to find a stopping point close enough that she wouldn't have to carry me again that night; I could only imagine the physical toll that hauling both Danny and myself for so many miles was taking on her. When she nudged me with her head, I sighed. "Bet you're missing Barrien right about now, huh?"

Snort.

"Those stables were nice," I mused. "And don't think I didn't see all those apples they were sneaking you… they were all going to your ass, Wraith. It's good to keep moving." I was lying to both of us now, and Wraith knew it. She bit me. "Hey!" I liked the fat, comfortable Wraith… the predictability of knowing when and where each meal would be coming from, the warmth of the same bed each night… familiar faces. I missed all of those things… some more than others. We walked in silence for a while before I admitted, "Fine. I miss Barrien, too."

She nudged me again.

"And—"

I was just about to confess the deep desires we all knew I'd been holding on to when Wraith halted.

"Callahan. I mean, I don't miss Callahan. But doesn't he live around here?" Wraith didn't respond. "It's been a long time, but I think if we turn down there," I explained to no one in particular, gesturing down the road, "he's around the corner." I let out a sigh of relief when the small cottage I remembered came into view. It was a bit more run down than the building in my memories, but I wasn't in a place to judge. Smoke trailed out from the chimney in a twirling wisp; he was home, and the fire was going. It was my lucky day. I kept one hand poised to grab a weapon because, well, that's what you do when you're on the road, and I let Wraith go to the trough full of water at the front of the cottage. I shook Danny awake as gently as I could and helped him off the horse before knocking on the door.

No answer. I knocked again.

Callahan's voice, gruff and guarded, came from the other side. "Who's out there? Whaddya want? Explain yourself!"

"Cal, it's Max."

"Max?" The door creaked open a little, the warm glow of the fire illuminating the gap. A slice of the man's face appeared, and one of his gray-blue eyes peered through at me. He cleared his throat. "What're ya doin' out here, Max?"

"Yeah, hey, I'm passing through with my brother," I explained, the cold of the evening finally getting to me. I began to shiver. "We need a place to stay for the night. Some food. I've got crystals or—"

"Uh, yeah, yeah," Callahan replied after a brief pause. "Let me just…" He grunted a little behind the door, then the sound of multiple locks being undone followed. There were… a lot. Just when I thought the door was about to open, more locks clicked and rattled. I hadn't been inside Callahan's house in a very, very long time but I didn't recall him having that many locks on his front door. Maybe the area was even less safe than before. All the more reason to get ourselves inside before the sun went down completely. I left Wraith to graze wherever she could find food, trusting her to stay close. There were likely a few fruit trees nearby; Callahan took pride in being self-sufficient and rarely needed anything from others. The last time I'd visited him, he was setting up a beekeeping operation on his property and had offered me a taste of the sweetest honey I'd ever had. I didn't hear any bees buzzing nearby this time.

"Come on in, I'll get you somethin' to eat."

Callahan's home was small and neat, exactly the type of place I was used to keeping for myself and Danny. In fact, I had instilled a sense of ownership in my younger brother when it came to our place in the Wild Open, and every time I returned home, I found it cleaner and more orderly than one would expect a ten-year-old capable of maintaining. One thing seemed out of place, though, as I set my bag down.

"Hang on," Callahan grumbled as he laid a blanket down on the floor for Danny and me.

"Thanks." I pushed my bag to the head of the makeshift bed and laid Danny down gently, then looked around the room while I sat next to him. He stirred a little, then settled again; the boy was tired. On the small table near the fire, there was a single mess to be found: a pile of bloodied bandages near a bowl of water. There were also a few strands of thread strewn about the table and a bloodied needle. "You alright, Cal?"

"Eh?"

I gestured to his arm, which he was obviously favoring as he ladled some mystery liquid from a cauldron over the fire into a wooden bowl for us. The sleeve of his shirt was torn over his forearm and stained with blood that looked surprisingly fresh. "Don't bleed in my soup, Callahan," I told him, half teasing and half warning. If I hadn't been so tired, I would've been more put on edge by his strange behavior.

He waved me off, setting the bowl down so that he could fill another. "Just a scratch," he said with a grunt. I could appreciate that he was a man of few words.

"You want me to help you stitch it?" It was clear he'd tried and failed, which seemed odd given how self-sufficient he usually was. I wasn't an expert at suturing wounds and relied on Savers Salve more often than not due to its ease, but I knew firsthand how hard it was to mend an injury on your dominant arm. I wondered what he'd scratched himself on bad enough that it needed stitches.

He shook his head. "Just need to rest it." He set the two bowls down on the floor next to our makeshift bed for the night and turned away before I could get a good look at him. "Eat up and sleep. The sun'll be up before you know it."

The contents of that soup remain a mystery to this day, but I ate it without question and left the other bowl next to Danny for when he woke. Callahan puttered around the cabin for a bit before going to the opposite side of the room to lie down as well, and I put my body between him and Danny on instinct. I thought nothing of the way that he secured all six of the locks on the door again before lying down; if anything, it seemed like he was just keeping us extra safe. Callahan was one of us, after all; he was rough around the edges, but only because he knew just how hard life could be. Beyond that, he was a good guy. He always had been… and I was so, so tired. The floor was hard and cold, aside from the whisper of warmth that radiated from the fireplace across the room. The food had been questionable, which also seemed odd for Callahan; he normally took pride in what he grew and butchered and harvested and cooked. Food was food, though, and I knew better than to complain about free food. I fished a bit of too-rare meat from between my teeth as I closed my eyes. Sleep was so close, and my body ached for it. Not only that, but I longed for the escape of a dream… I had so few, but sometimes they were a reprieve from the life that I'd let myself drag us back into.

There, in the darkness of my dream state, I heard him.

"Nightshade, where are you?" The nickname alone tugged at my heart, pulled me toward him, but I didn't know where that was. Hell, I didn't know where I was. I found myself in a passageway, much like the winding corridors of the castle, but different enough that I knew it wasn't the castle of Barrien. August's voice bounced off the stone walls.

"I'm here!" I called out, taking a tentative step down the hall. It split off in two different directions.

"Well, come on then!" August laughed despite the panic that the situation was filling me with. No matter how hard I listened, I couldn't quite pinpoint where the sound was coming from. I took a chance and picked the hall to the left, then sprinted down it as if time was against me. I caught sight of the edge of August's boot as he turned the corner, and just as I was able to call out for him again, relieved that I was going the right way, the dream flitted away, crumbling into darkness once more.

I woke in such a disoriented state that I could hardly recall where I was or who was with me. It wasn't right. It wasn't like me. Had I, in my privileged months as a resident of Barrien, become too soft for the road? I'd been asking myself that for weeks now. I gasped and sat upright when my brain finally shook me from my sleep and realized what was happening around me… not a full picture, but fragmented pieces.

There was screaming.

"Max!"

I shook my head to shake some of the smog from it only to find that I was surrounded by actual smoke. The room was on fire.

"Get back!" Danny waved something bright and burning—a flaming broom—at a dark figure in front of him.

Where was Callahan?

The figure snarled, almost in response to my thoughts.

"Max! Help me!"

I grabbed my weapons, knocking over Danny's uneaten bowl of soup as I did so, and clambered to my feet toward my brother, who was fending off a shadowed attacker with what seemed like very little success. It closed in on him. I hurled myself toward the figure and landed on its back, digging my fingers into its flesh to find it dense and furry. It stunk. The beast threw me off of it with a growl. "Get out, Danny!" I screamed. He bolted for the door before I realized my mistake; we didn't have the keys to all of the locks.

"It's locked!" Danny screamed as I waved my blade at the beast, managing to nick it enough to elicit a howl.

"The window!" There was only one, right above where we'd been sleeping, so I guarded Danny as he made a run for it. If he could just get out of the building, we could trap this creature inside and leave it to burn with the rest of the structure. I'd figure out how to deal with destroying Callahan's house after the fact.

All of the dagger skills and exposure to monsters in the world couldn't make Danny anything other than what he was: an eleven-year-old boy. So, as he scrambled toward the window, climbing onto a stack of precariously balanced crates, he started to cry. "Max, I don't want to die!"

"You're not going to die!" I told him, grabbing the flaming broom from him and using it to push the wolf creature back away from us. It yowled and snarled as its fur singed and gave us enough time for me to boost Danny up onto the windowsill. "Break it and get out!"

"What about you?" he screamed, his voice frantic; I could tell by the sound of it that snot was already streaming down his face.

"I'll see you out—" I had turned to reassure him but was cut short when the werewolf came directly for me, knocking me down with a swift swipe of its claws. I hit the ground hard and groaned, my arm in searing pain. "Get out, Danny!" I screamed again, scrambling to my feet. The swipe had tossed me to the far wall, but I could see that Danny had managed to knock the window loose and was squeezing his body through the opening. He was going to get out. He could get to Wraith, and I would meet him outside. We'd be okay. Danny would be okay.

I was seconds away from reaching the beast myself when it noticed that Danny had broken free; all that was still inside the cabin was his bottom half, which he was frantically wiggling to get through the small window.

Then the room filled with a cry I'd never heard before because I'd never let Danny get really, truly hurt before. No broken bones, no sprained ankles, he'd never even hit his head that hard.

But this time, he screamed.

He sobbed.

He was pulled back into the flaming cabin by his leg, which was in the werewolf's mouth. "Max!" he screeched, writhing against what must have been agonizing pain. Then, he went silent.

The following moments were a blur. I clawed my way across piles of discarded and broken furniture to leap onto the beast's back and sunk my blade into the back of its neck, which caused it to release my brother and wail in pain. Only when I had it firmly on the ground and at my mercy did I make eye contact with its human gaze. Callahan had been a friend, but this wasn't Callahan anymore… at least that was what I told myself as I steadied my hand to put the beast out of its misery. Despite all of Florian's warnings and the fearmongering from the Covenant, I hadn't bothered to equip myself with any silver weapons. Instead, I'd have to decapitate him. Even if I could detach myself from the idea that this was once a man, a friend, someone I had bonded with, I didn't like the idea of removing any creature's entire head. It was dirty work, visceral and gory. I needed to make it quick, though, and get back to my brother.

I let out a tremendous yell as I plunged my dagger deeper into Callahan's neck, then pulled it across to slit his throat. That wasn't enough, I knew. "I'm sorry," I choked out; if the Covenant was right, if the werewolves were punishment for our sins, they had targeted the right sinner by putting me in this position. Blood squished through my fingers as I sawed at the wolf's spinal column long enough to snap it. When I stood, shoving its head away from the body with the toe of my boot, flames rising around me, the beast's body changed. The last thing I saw as I forced my way out of the shattered window was Callahan's lifeless stare as his head returned to its original form.

The building continued to burn, eating up my bag and the supplies we'd brought inside with us, but also tearing a flaming hole in one of the walls. Outside, Wraith was inconsolable, squealing and pacing as if her enthusiasm alone would put out the fire. I dragged Danny's body behind me and loaded him up on the horse's back once I'd confirmed that he was still breathing. My own body was beaten, burned, scraped, and torn in places, but there was no time to waste.

"Wraith, go home!"

A TOAST TO SETTLING

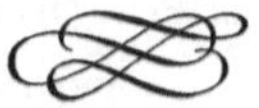

AUGUST

Saw them at a tavern on the outskirts of the Grim-maker Woods, lost track of them in a Covenant scuffle, and not sure where they went. I'm sorry. We'll keep looking.

-Thorne

"Well, I've decided to say fuck it," Amrys announced into the quiet emptiness of the sitting room, where I had just folded the last bit of parchment Magnus had delivered. Magnus seemed anxious upon his arrival and had fled after I took the paper from him. They were gone. Vanished. The group I had hired for their expertise and paid handsomely had lost track of a tiny mercenary and her kid brother following a… scuffle? Wasn't this the exact type of thing I'd hired them to prevent?

"Yeah, fuck it," I agreed, leaning my head back against my

armchair in defeat. I perked back up again a second later. "Wait, what? That's not very ladylike."

"First of all, how dare you," Amrys said with a scowl and then a warm laugh, reminding me painfully of the way that Max might've responded to such a comment. But Amrys wasn't Max, not even a little bit, outside of that comment. She flopped down in another chair across from me and rested her cheek on her hand with a sigh. "Second, if this is the hand we're dealt, we may as well embrace it, don't you think?"

"How do you mean?" I scrubbed my face with my fingertips, trying to distract myself with Amrys's commentary.

"We're both going to die without the loves of our lives—me because I haven't had a chance to find them and you because... well... you know—and we're serving the greater good, so we might as well have a little fun with our suffering. Let's get drunk."

I must've mulled it over for too long, something I'd rarely done in response to such a proposal in the past, because Amrys then added, "What is it? The king of Barrien doesn't like to drink anymore or... Barrien doesn't have anything good to get drunk off of?"

"Nope, incorrect on all counts," I told her, still unable to muster much more than a general air of agreement in my response. I didn't want to get drunk, not with her or anyone, but it couldn't have been any worse than the silent torture I'd been putting myself through all this time. "We have plenty to get drunk off of."

"And..."

"And I wouldn't mind a moment of mind-numbing drunkenness." Of all the vices I had considered using as a distraction, I'd only been using alcohol for a steady buzz, which had gotten harder and harder to maintain with how regularly I'd been drinking. I had been trying to keep my wits about me, to be the ever vigilant ruler of the land, and all for what? It wasn't like it had gotten me anywhere yet.

Amrys popped up from her seat and headed out of the room,

returning later once she'd found someone to provide us with refreshments. Moments later, Olin and another attendant entered the room with… an array of alcohol carried on multiple trays, as well as some food, the smell of which immediately caught my attention.

"Is that… bacon?" I asked, slightly confused by the plan for the evening.

Once she was back in the armchair, draped over it in the same way that Florian often did, she nodded and plucked a piece of bacon from one of the silver platters that had been laid out for us. "Sure is," she commented, eyeing the strip of meat curiously. "I've never tried it, but since we're saying 'fuck it' to everything, I figured now's the time."

I couldn't help but laugh at her approach and sat up to pour us both a glass of what I thought might go best with her snack of choice. I handed the drink to her across the gap between our seats.

Amrys took the glass and raised it in my direction. "A toast to settling and embracing our suffering. May we…"

"May we always have enough Riesling and bacon to ever so slightly dull the pain," I finished before clinking my glass against hers.

"Hear! Hear!" Amrys exclaimed before taking a good-sized bite of the meat. Her eyes widened in enjoyment before she sampled the wine.

I emptied my drink in an instant, then refilled my glass. We sat in silence for a bit, the crackling of the fireplace filling the space between us. Amrys reached over for another strip of bacon, and I smiled a little. Just a little. "You know, and I'm not just saying this because I'm about to be blitzed out of my mind, but you really are lovely."

"You're not so bad yourself."

We were silent for a moment as we sipped our drinks. In another universe, maybe, this could've been a different arrangement. "Why does it feel like betrayal to even consider baring my soul to someone else, Amrys?" I asked suddenly, even surprising myself with my directness. Since when did I share thoughts like that? I shook my head as if to erase the thought, then filled my glass for the third time.

"Whoa, maybe that's enough mind-numbing indulgence for one night," Amrys commented. "Wouldn't want you getting too deep in your feelings." She was teasing, though, because she sat up and looked over the fire at me after finishing the last piece of bacon. She shrugged. "Really, though... I'm guessing love is like that sometimes. You're keeping your soul for her, whether or not she's here to receive it."

I DIDN'T KNOW WHERE ELSE TO GO

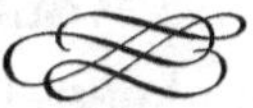

MAX

*W*hen my fist collided with the massive front door of the castle of Barrien, uncertainty coursed through my veins. It didn't stop me from pounding on the wooden barrier so hard I was certain my knuckles would bleed, but with each knock, I thought "turn around" and "this isn't worth it, you can find someone else" and "are you really ready to see his face again?" The only one of those thoughts that made any sense was looking for someone else, but that would've taken so much longer. I didn't know where Florian was, and he was probably my second-best bet, but even so, how could he take care of Danny? Behind me, slumped over Wraith's panting form was my brother, who would soon be writhing in pain once he regained consciousness again, and I had no way to keep him safe if I didn't get him into the castle. I could hide him away in the Wild Open again, but without anyone to care for him while I searched for an antidote, he would die before he had the chance to turn. I hadn't really thought of where I'd been going until we'd gotten there; in fact, I'd actively ignored it, even when Wraith gave me judgmental glances and huffs along the way. She never stopped, though, hurling toward Barrien at a breakneck pace despite having to push herself to her limits to do so. She knew that Danny was our responsibility and that nothing else came before his safety and well-being. If I had to sacrifice my own safety, I would. If I had to grovel, I told myself, I would. It didn't matter how embarrassing, how uncomfortable, how indescribably painful it would be to see August again, I would do it for Danny. I would be indebted to him if I had to, I just needed someone to keep him safe so I could get him medicine.

I'd been racing against the clock to get Danny somewhere safe before the unthinkable happened, but also running from the dark, winged cloud that seemed to be following us over the past few days. The continent wasn't known for housing full-size dragons, but I had seen several—or the same one over and over again—recently, and it had me on edge. The world was in ruins, with werewolves and dragons running loose. Unexpectedly, I saw it circle above us again as we entered the grounds, and it landed on top of the castle, no doubt eyeing us curiously as we approached the front door.

As if the universe knew to set the tone for my pleading return to my ex-boyfriend, it began to rain, and when the door swung open, I was drenched and bloodied. Frozen. I hadn't slept, hadn't stopped moving since the attack, and despite narrowly avoiding a bite myself, I bore the battle wounds from facing off against the werewolf formerly known as my friend Callahan. Now my right hand, my good hand, was scuffed and bleeding as well. Never mind the fact that I hadn't rested or showered or eaten well in weeks. It was shameful that I gave my appearance a second thought, but when I came face-to-face with the king of the castle, the contrast between us was stark.

August was red-cheeked in hearty laughter, a glass of alcohol in his hand, when his gaze met mine. He looked good. Happy, aside from the way that his smile faded immediately upon seeing me. Healthy. Bright. He leaned against a cane, the likes of which I'd never seen before. The warm light of the castle filtered behind him, illuminating the man. I looked like a wet rat who'd clawed its way out of the sewer.

"August," I sputtered, droplets of water spilling into my mouth as I spoke. The rain came down hard, drenching our party and chilling me to the bone.

"*Nightshade.*" August's voice was barely audible, but I'd know that word by the shape of his lips anytime. If it had been dark, and all I had was my sense of touch, I would've traced his mouth and known he was saying his name for me.

We stood in silence, and I cursed myself mentally for not getting to the point, but I wanted to run to him. God, I wanted to run to him so badly that my muscles ached as I forced myself to disobey my gut; they strained, they pulled me to him, but I fought back. It wasn't until Danny groaned behind me that I found my words again. "I didn't know where else to go, I'm sorry."

August didn't speak immediately, but shook his head as if to dismiss my apology. He turned away to set his drink down and call for his staff: "Olin, I need everyone here! Now, please!" His voice was harsh, demanding, and I was surprised that he somehow managed to add pleasantries. It was a stark contrast from the man who had been slowly growing into his role as a leader. "I need towels, blankets, and fetch the doctor." Before I could protest, the castle staff were swarming us at once, ushering me in against my will.

"My brother—" I protested, reaching back toward Danny as a maid attempted to pull me inside, out of the rain.

"I've got him." And then August was out in the rain, his fine clothes soaking immediately as he pulled Danny gingerly off of Wraith's back. He'd left his cane inside so that he could use both hands to hold the boy. The horse regarded him with a snort that reminded me a lot of a sigh of relief, and August nodded back to her as if to say that it was nice to see his old friend. August pulled Danny into his arms, letting the boy's head rest on his shoulder, and I couldn't help but think that my brother looked like such a small child and August… looked like more of an adult than I'd ever seen him. He gestured to one of the staff and instructed them, "Take Wraith to the stables to dry off and eat. Send the doctor up to Danny's room when he arrives."

Danny's room? It had been… months, and Danny still had a room here?

I slumped into the maid's arms a little and let her direct me inside, but watched until August came in behind me with Danny.

"What happened?"

I was breathless, exasperated. "Werewolf attack," was all I managed, completely unable to meet August's gaze.

"Let's get him upstairs."

I headed to the staircase as if it were second nature—and it had been, when I'd lived there—but was surprised to see August heading a different route. No matter how much I trusted him, I didn't have it in me to leave Danny alone with anyone, especially since his current affliction was due to my misjudgment. "Where are you—"

I turned the corner and found that August was heading for an intricate door of wrought iron, which one of the housekeepers opened for him; the young man assisting us held August's cane under his arm as he pulled the door open. "Get in," he said roughly, still holding Danny as if he weighed nothing. "It's faster." I complied in silence, hurrying onto the platform as the housekeeper closed the gate in front of us. Then, the sound of whirring gears filled the air, and we were being lifted up, traveling up the floors of the castle with ease. How many times had I watched August struggle to scale the stairs, which must have felt like climbing a mountain after the Umbral attack? And why hadn't *I* thought of something like this before? We stood in silence, both of our quickened breathing filling the small space around us for the duration of the trip. It was brief, but I was acutely aware of him next to me, even if I didn't look at him. His figure was large, looming, protective... and he smelled like soap and liquor and a little bit like the perfume I'd worn to the ball over a year ago, but that couldn't be.

When the gate opened again, he waited for me to step out before following, then immediately took Danny into the room that was once his.

Nothing in it had changed. Perhaps the bed had been made and some toys returned to shelves, but beyond that it was clear that nothing had been taken from or added to this space. I was stuck in the doorway, taking in my surroundings when some of the house staff pushed by me.

"Excuse me, pardon me, miss—" One of them stopped to look at me, then bowed their head in recognition. He looked surprised to see my face. "Miss Maxine, please."

I moved out of the way and let them in, where they removed Danny's torn clothing and attempted to clean his wounds while he drifted in and out of consciousness. His groans tore at my heart, and I found myself gripping the doorframe in response. Moments later, a doctor arrived and shoved past me as well. I was glued, stuck in a trance as I watched them work. They were making him comfortable, sure, but anyone who knew anything knew that a werewolf bite wouldn't be fixed with medication and bandages. Unable to collect my thoughts while watching them, I stepped out into the hall and tried to breathe. It was impossible. This place, I shouldn't have been there... It felt so familiar and so foreign at the same time. It smelled like *him,* and there *he* was, leaning on his cane as he supervised the care of my brother. His gaze was intense, watching every move the professionals helping Danny made, ready to step in at any moment, it seemed. He'd let us in without a second thought...

When he stepped out into the hallway as well, all I could manage was a quiet "thank you."

"Nightshade," he addressed me, his voice gruff, no doubt from the drinking. He looked me over in a way that suggested we had all the time in the world. My heart thundered. "What have you done to yourself?"

"I didn't, I don't—"

August reached out absentmindedly—as if an invisible force was pulling him toward me—his fingertips brushing my shoulder, where my shirt had been torn and was hanging off me by a few ragged threads.

I was about to respond… maybe… when we were interrupted by a voice I didn't recognize: "August, what's happening?"

A RUDE AWAKENING

AUGUST

Amrys's voice snapped me from my reverie almost immediately and the previous months came flooding back to me. This was not just any other day with Max, no. She'd been *gone*, and she was here only due to a life-threatening emergency.

"Ah, Amrys," I addressed her, withdrawing my hand from Max's shoulder as if I'd been caught doing something scandalous. In a way, the touch had been obscene because of its effect on me. Heat rose in my cheeks, and I willed it to dissipate so that I could be a normal human again. I looked at Amrys as if I couldn't fathom actually saying the next words that were about to come out of my mouth. I'd dreamt of this moment, but in my dreams, Max had returned under different circumstances; in my dreams, it was her undying love that had drawn her back to me. "This is… Max. She's here because her brother's been injured, and they need some help."

Amrys's brows knitted in concern immediately, and knowing her, I knew it was genuine. But also knowing that she had the full picture of my history of Max, I couldn't imagine what she would say once we had a moment alone again. "I'm so sorry to hear that," she said, holding out a hand to the tiny mercenary. "It's a pleasure to meet you, however, even under such unfortunate circumstances. I'm certain we'll do everything we can to help."

When Max looked from me to Amrys in confusion, I added, "This is Amrys, my…"

"…fiancée," Amrys finished, knowing that I wouldn't be able to.

Max shook her hand, tentatively at first, but then cleared her throat. "I appreciate that more than you know." If I had seen her face at that moment, I wasn't sure what I'd find. Relief? Disgust? Jealousy? No. I chastised myself for even considering the latter and instead watched the way her jaw tensed as she looked at Amrys. We stood in the hall as the doctor and nurses continued to clean Danny up and make him comfortable, Max filling both of us in. I didn't realize it until after, but I spent the entirety of the conversation standing next to her rather than Amrys and focusing intently on how she relayed the story of Danny's injury. Max was injured, too, and deserved medical care, but I knew she would have refused it, especially with her brother in such critical condition. Perhaps I would ask the doctor to hang back once he'd tended to Danny.

"There isn't… a cure for this, is there?" Amrys asked once Max was finished.

Max rubbed the back of her neck. "There might be, but it's only a story at this point. We need Florian; he's heard more about it than I have."

"I'll get ahold of him," Amrys offered, helpful as ever. "You should rest, if you can. I'm certain he won't be here until morning, even if Magnus is able to catch him right now."

Max didn't ask any questions, just nodded and said a thank-you to her before she turned to leave. But before Amrys left the hall, she turned to me with a gentle smile. "I'll see you shortly, darling?"

My mouth went dry, and I struggled to speak, gripping the head of my cane as if my life depended on it. "Y-yes, of course." The hall was silent once she left, and when I looked at Max again, she wouldn't meet my gaze. The air was thick with tension. My body ached. "Ah, there's a… spare bedroom available there," I told her, pointing at the door next to Danny's. I avoided looking at the door to our old shared room, even though I had been in it just earlier that day. "And a bathroom there, as you know. I'll have the maids bring up some clean towels and, um, some new clothing for you." We had plenty of clothing that would fit Max. In fact, it was all still in the dressers she'd left it in months ago.

"Thank you," she said softly, finally looking up at me. My chest constricted, burned like it was engulfed in flames, when I looked into those dark pools of near-black. "I'll probably, um, stay with Danny, but thank you." She glanced down the hall toward Amrys's room. "She seems… lovely. I appreciate both of you being so willing to help."

~

"You're going to have to explain yourself."

"Listen, August," Amrys began, sitting gracefully on the edge of my parents' bed. "I know you still love her… and I know that tomorrow, whatever Florian tells us needs to be done, you will find a way to do it for her. That's who you are, that's what she means to you…." She twiddled with her fingers in her lap, looking just the slightest bit nervous to tell me what she was thinking. That was new. "I just don't think that she needs to know the extent of all that… She's already seen Danny's room. Does she need to see you retire to your old shared bedroom, too? Does she deserve to know she has that power over you after she took off?"

Truthfully, I didn't know. How much does one deserve after completely destroying your heart?

"All I'm saying is… maybe just wait until everyone's asleep to go back to your room if you really need to. There's no need to pour your heart out now when you don't know what her intentions are. I just… don't want to see my friend hurt."

I listened. I listened because Amrys was wise and because Max's return had just proven that I was an absolute wreck when it came to her. It was late when I slid off the chaise in Amrys's chambers and snuck out of the large door; she had already been asleep for some time. I made my way back to my own room as quietly as I could manage with my cane and slid inside in silence, knowing that Max was only feet away from me for the first time in forever. Despite the sobering events of the evening, I was still buzzed when I shed my clothing, Danny's blood staining the chest and shoulder of my shirt. Nothing in our room had changed since Max had left. I lay down on the bed, her scent long gone, aside from what I'd put there artificially thanks to my perfume supplier, and closed my eyes. All I could hear was the way she'd said my name when she arrived at the entrance of the castle. Magnus's note had said they'd lost her, but there she was.

AN UNLIKELY TRIO

MAX

"There's supposed to be a cure on the Isle of Wyrms."

"That's what they say, Max," Florian told me with a nod as we all gathered in the sitting room early the next morning; the sun hadn't even come up yet. A fire was going in the corner of the room, but I still found myself freezing. "And how are you going to get to this place? By the time you travel there on horse, it'll be too late. Danny has a few days at best before the next full moon." Florian had unrolled a map that was propped up on a holder in the sitting room and was gesturing to the distance between Barrien and our proposed destination; it was far past the Grimmaker Woods and the Wild Open, farther than we had time to go.

Amrys piped up suddenly. "There's a portal to the isle."

"Where?" I asked, a burst of hope flooding my chest. I'd spent the night imagining my kid brother's death, so I was feeling fragile. I got to my feet to peer at the map next to the group that had gathered around it.

"Right..." Amrys searched the map, then pointed to a spot on it. "Here."

"In the… Gardens of Wysterum? I've never been there." Hell, I'd never even heard of it. There must not have been much work for monster hunters there.

"Me neither, but how bad could a garden be?" Those sounded like famous last words the second they left Amrys's lips.

"There's only one issue with that idea, *ladies*," Florian interjected. "The Isle of Wyrms only has one ally—Emynor, you know, Barrien's adversary until very recently—and they're not going to let some mongrel mercenary use the portal, let alone take a resource from their island, without an elven representative. It's not like they just hand out wyrm fangs as souvenirs for visiting!"

"A fang? We need a fang?" I asked, ignoring the most important part of his statement. "Wyrm" really made the creatures sound less dangerous than they actually were, and I was starting to feel burnt out on things with massive claws and fangs. Why couldn't the cure be in the garden from the map? Perhaps it was grown in the center of a giant flower? That would be nice.

"They're big, too," Florian added, a glimmer of mischief in his gaze.

Amrys looked at me with an eye roll and then back at Florian. "How is the elf thing an issue? Obviously I'm going with them."

"Them?" Florian asked, appalled at her attitude. I, on the other hand, loved it. I wasn't sure if I was supposed to like her, what with her being August's fiancée, but something about her fire spoke to the flame in me; besides, anyone who could keep Florian in his place immediately earned points with me. Would she be a friend? Maybe not, but I respected her already.

"Yeah, them?" August asked suddenly, having been a silent observer so far. He'd been so quiet and deep in thought… and of course, all I wanted to know was what that was about.

"Well, yes," Amrys insisted. "You're going, Max is going. You need an elf, so I'm going." She shrugged. "Seems pretty straightforward to me."

"Wait, wait, wait," I said as I put up my hands. "I can't let you—"

"Right, why don't *I* go?" asked Florian. "I'm better suited to travel and protect her, *and* I can be her elven escort. August wouldn't even have to go."

All Amrys said in response was "No."

"And why not?" Florian scoffed.

"It's better if she has an elf that's actually from Emynor, Florian. The last thing we need is to get all the way there and have them reject a knock-off," Amrys quipped back.

I smirked.

Florian opened his mouth to argue, "I'm hardly a knock-off. Max, tell them that I'm from—"

"And August is obviously going," the elven princess added. "Plus, we need you to stay back and be with Danny. No one else here is immune to werewolf bites, so you'll have to keep the medical team safe while they tend to him."

Florian looked like we'd just washed his favorite outfit with the wrong type of laundry detergent. "You want me to *babysit*?" He wrinkled his nose.

"Correct, so now would be a great time to familiarize yourself with those helping him and get settled in for your time at the castle of Barrien. Hope you brought enough hair product to last the week!" She shooed him away rather abruptly, and we were left alone.

I turned to the remainder of the group, feeling a sense of relief now that Florian was out of earshot. He was an exhausting creature to be around, even if he had his uses. "As much as I appreciate your kindness—and your ability to politely tell Florian to go fuck himself—I can't let you endanger yourselves like this for me."

Amrys offered me a warm smile, but August was still miles away. "Any friend of August's is a friend of mine," the elf said honestly, her tone genuine and her bright green eyes communicating a message I couldn't quite make out. "If it helps at all, tell yourself we're doing it for Danny. Besides, I could use some time away from this stuffy castle." When she turned her attention from me to August, she reached out as if to pat him on the shoulder but then withdrew her hand before touching him. What was that about? "I'm going to go pack. I imagine we'll need to leave as soon as possible."

"Right, of course." August gave me an uneasy half smile before walking over to one end of the sitting room, where two double glass doors led out onto a balcony, if my memory served me correctly. He opened them, and a rush of frigid air assaulted the room.

"Need some air?"

He laughed. It was halfhearted, soft, but it was still his laugh… and it brought me more comfort than I imagined a single sound could. "Not exactly." The sound of wings beating soon filled the air, and then a creature landed on the patio before crawling inside of the sitting room. It was large, perhaps the size of a big dog, the kind you might see running around the street market begging for scraps, and jet-black, with a silvery sheen to the scales on its wings; this was the dragon I had seen overhead the night before.

Before I could ask what I was looking at, August reached down to pet the creature's head as if it were a puppy. "Magnus," he addressed the dragon, scratching under its chin when it tilted its head up to respond to its name. "Surely you remember Max?"

I gasped as I looked the creature over. "*This* is the *micro* dragon?"

"Not quite so micro anymore," August corrected, smiling down at the animal.

I crouched down so that I was eye level with it, keeping my distance. Sure, we'd gotten along months ago, when the creature was the size of a rat and easy to put in my pocket, but I didn't expect it to like me now. "He's stunning," I mused, putting my hand out toward him. The dragon sniffed the air curiously before crawling forward, its head bowed as it inspected me. I stayed the course, allowing him space to leave if he wanted, but he eventually closed the gap between us to smell my hand, then butt his forehead against it. He was just like a big kitten. "Nice to see you, Magnus," I said softly. Moments later, he was resting at my feet.

Amrys packed, I took what little I had remaining in my saddlebags, and we geared up to go. Florian begged us to change the plan up until the second we were out the door. I liked leaving him whiny and irritated.

Wraith had rested and fed the night before, so thankfully she was in better spirits than when we had arrived. August and Amrys also took their own horses; Heckle, who wasn't quite as personable as Wraith but still a friendly face, and Merrick, a stunning white Emynorian steed that had moved to Barrien with its elven owner. Magnus would follow as far as he could and be used to deliver messages between our group and Florian so that I could stay apprised of my brother's condition.

Before we left the castle, however, I went up to his room to see him. The medical staff, the best in the continent according to August, had cleared out at least briefly, and Danny lay in his bed, sweat slicked from fever, but in clean clothing. They were keeping him as cool and comfortable as possible, but I knew that the werewolf venom must be making its way through his veins slowly and painfully. I sat on the edge of his bed and took his cool, clammy hand in mind, then pressed the back of it to my lips. "I'm sorry," I said against his skin. "I'm sorry I let this happen to you. It's my job to protect you, and I failed."

I closed my eyes and fought back a shuddering sob as I sat there with him. *I* was supposed to take the pain, the misery, the sacrifice with a smile on my face, not put him through it. "I promise I'll make this right," I told him. A form shifted in the open doorway. "And if Florian does anything to bother you," I said, a little louder this time, "I'll kick his ass."

"Very cute," Florian remarked, leaning against the doorframe so that he was blocking it. After I had tucked Danny's hand back into the covers and kissed his forehead, I got up to face the elf.

"Thank you for staying with him."

Florian's gaze narrowed as he stared into the room, not looking at me. "Just be careful out there."

"Always am," I murmured, approaching him so that I could be let out of the bedroom. He didn't budge.

When he looked at me again, he added, "I mean with August and Amrys. They're happy, little menace. Don't go messing that up." I was about to leave when he caught my arm and stopped me again.

"What?"

"If he turns before you get back," Florian said, no longer in a teasing mood, "then what?"

I knew he was itching for a plan that involved him getting to take down a werewolf and had little consideration for the fact that the werewolf in question would be my brother, but it was an important question. Surely, he was wondering if I expected him to let a werewolf run rampant in Barrien just because it was related to me. I swallowed hard, unable to look Florian in the eye, and shook my arm loose from his grasp. "Then you keep him contained until I return."

"Then what, Max?"

"Then I'll handle it from there," I told him seriously, through gritted teeth. "He's *my* brother." *If someone needs to watch the light drain from his eyes, it'll be me.*

NEXT STOP, Dalcester Street Market, where I was sure to be greeted with open arms by my favorite shopkeepers and townspeople! What could go wrong?

"You've got a hell of a lot of nerve showing up in here, Max the

Menace, after what you pulled!" Beatrice scolded me as she came around the counter and grabbed me by the ear. "*And* what you did to that poor man, do you know what you did to him?" she whispered harshly in my ear.

"I know, I know, I'm sorry I didn't tell you that I was—"

August cleared his throat nearby. "I'm sure Max would love to explain why she's back, but we are in a bit of a hurry, unfortunately." He tossed a bag of crystals onto the counter. "We'll be waiting outside, Max," he told me before heading back out. "I think you've got the list of everything we'll need."

"He bought up all my damn patchouli," Beatrice told me as she rummaged through her shelves to fulfill my purchase list.

"What?"

"The patchouli, you know, that I put in your perfume. Every time we get it in stock he's in here asking for another order," Beatrice complained as she plucked bottle after bottle of potion from the shelves. "Can't imagine you ever really wore it that much, since you smell like dirty horse and ass every time you come in here."

"Uh huh… horse ass, that's me…" As I stood there, I glanced over to the curtain dividing the back room and recalled the day that August and I had visited. It had been both a day that made me question my belonging and easily the most riveting sexual encounter I'd ever had. My breath hitched in my throat as I recalled the way August had begged and moaned for me. I bit my lip to drive the thought from my mind. It was wrong for me to let my mind wander like that. First of all, we were on a mission to save my brother, and second, August was standing outside with his fiancée! My stomach turned at the reminder… did they have those moments together? Had they gone to the back room? Did he have a sweet nickname, like Nightshade, for Amrys? Did he utter it through breathless moans when he was coming?

"And he shows up here before we're even open," Morgan stated plainly, then popped up from behind the counter like they usually did.

"Hi, Morgan."

"Hi." Morgan put up a hand in an awkward wave, then diverted their gaze again. We were both people of few words.

"I'm sorry to have caused such a mess, but I really appreciate—"

"Just be nice to that boy, okay?" Beatrice piped up again. She pulled her glasses off to rub the bridge of her nose, as if my presence was headache-inducing. Meanwhile, Morgan had picked up the spectacles, sprayed them with some concoction from a glass bottle, and was polishing them dutifully while their partner scolded me some more. "We all know you're afraid of commitment, but sometimes you gotta get over those fears for the right—"

"Darling, they're engaged, remember? Amrys and August," Morgan reminded Beatrice.

She scoffed, then waved her partner off. "Yeah, yeah, engaged, whatever."

My head spun.

"Alright, that should be everything," Morgan told me as they packed up the remainder of my order into a canvas drawstring bag. "A lot more than your usual order."

"Yeah, well, it's a unique situation," I told her. "Speaking of, I need something else from both of you… a few things, actually."

"Ooh, you're pushing it," Morgan commented before disappearing behind the counter. What they did behind there all day, I had no clue. They reached up once to place Beatrice's clean glasses on the countertop.

"Bye, Morgan… I'm sorry, I'm sorry, but it's for Danny." I rubbed my face in frustration. Really, it was for me. What would I do if Danny died? And whose fault was it that he was on the brink? Right. "I'll do anything you want once I get back, I promise! I'll organize your potions alphabetically."

"Hey!" Morgan argued without coming up again. "That's my job!"

Beatrice glared daggers at me, but I knew she wouldn't be mad forever. I'd have to make it up to her somehow, when all of this was over. When I left her shop, I had the ingredients and recipe for a potion with a very unsavory name as well as the whereabouts for the ingredient needed to reverse a werewolf bite… and a growing debt to multiple people: August, Amrys, Florian, the kingdom of Barrien in general, Beatrice, Morgan. Oh, and Magnus. Probably Wraith, too. Definitely Danny.

I tucked the potions and parchment into my saddlebag, and we were off before I could piss off anyone else or set another shop on fire.

The clock was ticking.

THE SOULMATE SPECIAL

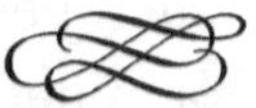

MAX

e had traveled most of the day in resolute silence, but as the sun began to set and the chill of late winter evening settled in, so did exhaustion. Adrenaline had carried me through several days of panicked travel and a night of sleeplessness, but my body was finally fighting back. I yawned as we passed tree after tree after tree. Under different circumstances, I might've been more inclined to observe the scenery and pocket the information for my mental map, but I could barely keep my eyes open. I yawned again.

"Me, too," Amrys commented absentmindedly. "I know we're in a hurry, but perhaps we should stop for a bit. We'll be no use if we're struggling to stay awake."

August gave a grunt of agreement, and I nodded a little, knowing that she was right. I didn't want to stop, but we would soon have no choice.

"Do you see anything on the map?" I asked as the scenery continued to blur together.

Amrys was squinting at the wrinkled parchment in her lap through the dying evening light. "No... nothing close..." she murmured as her horse kept perfectly steady and straight with zero guidance from her.

I shook my head as if that would wake me up a bit and tried to survey our surroundings a bit closer. Wraith snorted. "There's a sign ahead," I noted aloud, fighting back another yawn. "A tavern maybe?" It was the first sign we'd seen in hours. Before I could take a closer look at it, August and Heckle pulled past me to get a closer look, and I breathed an inadvertent sigh of relief. It had been nerve-wracking having him behind me, even though we'd spent weeks on the road together before with him immediately against my back.

"It just has two cups on it," August called back to us. "And an arrow." His profile in the dimming light nearly knocked me on my ass, and I instantly regretted letting him go ahead. If Wraith hadn't known to keep following, we would've probably stopped dead in our tracks to stare. Every time I caught sight of him, my chest ached. My arms ached too, like they wanted to reach for him… my entire being was fighting against the distance between us—the distance that I had put between us—and the fight was almost as tiring as the rest of this expedition. I stared for longer than I should have and admired the way his back, broad and strong, looked from behind, and the click of his cane, which he'd strapped against one of his saddlebags, against the saddle.

"Max?" Amrys had pulled up and stopped next to me, trying to get my attention while she folded the map. "What do you think?"

"Sure," I told her with a nod once I was able to tear my gaze away. I hoped she didn't notice how unintentionally disrespectful I was being; I knew he was engaged, knew that they were together, and above all that, knew that my wandering eyes had no place on our current outing. "Lead the way." I stifled a sigh of relief when they both pulled ahead of myself and Wraith. Somewhere above, Magnus swooped by, keeping a distant eye on us. I wondered if he was still ticklish or had better control of his fire magic by now.

The sign took us down a road off the main path, the dirt of which eventually became overgrown with moss and small white flowers. Still, we followed until we were in a lush clearing, the greenery of which did not fit with the time of year, and I realized that the spaces around us glittered with magic; we were out of our element. The stopping point before us was a petite wooden shop, the front of which was open with a rustic counter that looked out onto a seating area, and the patrons of which were all enjoying hot cups of tea and coffee as if they weren't in the middle of the woods in winter. Some looked more seasoned than others—tired, beaten-up travelers like us—while others looked as though they were attending their weekly royal tea party and chatted with their friends easily, comfortably, in the plush setting. The sign at the front of the shop read "Mounds N' Grounds," the meaning of which I hadn't quite digested upon our arrival.

We left our horses at the entrance to the clearing, then made our way toward the counter. "I've got it," I told our group before looking back at them. "What'll it be?"

"Coffee," August said with a thankful nod.

"Peppermint tea for me, please," Amrys added. *Elves.*

I turned toward the counter just in time to come face-to-face with the individual working there and found that all air had left my lungs. Before me fluttered a sprite[1], which wasn't necessarily a new encounter for me, but she was almost naked, just tiny white flowers covering her groin and nipples, the breasts of which were shockingly massive for a creature so small. "Welcome!" the creature said brightly, hovering over the counter so that she could greet me. Her hair, a rainbow of colors, seemed to float around her tiny, doll-like face. "Would you like to hear about today's coffee specials?"

"Uhhh…" Words escaped me, so I turned toward my traveling partners in shock.

Amrys had a hand over her mouth and was attempting to stifle an onslaught of giggles while August mouthed: *"It's a boobie bar."*

As much as I tried to swallow my embarrassment, my cheeks

burned with heat as I turned back to the counter and attempted to avert my gaze from the sprite's gigantic knockers. "Um, yes, two of… whatever the special is and a peppermint tea, please." I plunked a few crystals on the counter and gestured to an empty table in the clearing. "We'll be… over there."

"Your change!" the sprite called after me as I hurried away, the laughter of my companions following me.

"It's a tip!"

August and Amrys managed to hold it together until we were seated, then proceeded to laugh directly in my face. If they hadn't literally been the kindest people on the continent for offering to help me save my brother, I would've hated them, but instead, I laughed too. "Shut up!" I told them between giggles.

"Didn't you see the sign?" Amrys asked, still trying to cover her mouth while she laughed. August was blushing almost as hard as I was.

"I guess, but I'm tired! I didn't realize what it meant until I was face-to-face with…" I made a gesture as if I were holding two giant breasts in front of me. "Those!"

Our own amusement entertained us until another sprite, similarly dressed, delivered our beverages. Her strength to carry a tray with three cups the size of her entire body was impressive, but she didn't spill a single drop and set each steaming hot mug down in front of each of us with flair. While Amrys sipped her tea—the peppermint of which was strong enough for me to smell across the table—quietly, I took a big sip of my own beverage with a silent prayer that it would give me energy. The flavor was rich, deep with varying layers that took me a moment to identify; the coffee itself was smooth, enveloped in vanilla, caramel, and perhaps the blue lavender that Yeast to West Bakery used. It was undoubtedly delicious, and while August casually stirred his as he talked to Amrys, I downed mine in a couple more sips. Sugar. Caffeine. Energy. Some tiny bit of sustenance. I needed it all.

I needed to keep pushing forward. This was only a momentary break, not a roadblock; my exhaustion, the group's exhaustion, couldn't slow us down. I swirled the remaining sip of liquid in my mug as I imagined my brother writhing in pain in his bed, Florian dutifully—but annoyedly—staying beside him. How long did we have before he turned? And what would happen to him if he turned before I was back? My stomach flipped at the thought. I downed the last sip.

My mug had only been empty for a minute when an unexpected warmth began to fill my entire body, and I wondered if I was just thinking about my earlier embarrassment. I must have been red again because August stopped mid-sentence to look at me. "Are you alright? You look…" His voice distorted as he spoke and sounded as deep and smooth as ever, each syllable dripping through my body like lava. "Flushed." I clenched my thighs at the last word and immediately stood up.

"I'm… yeah, I'm fine, just need to get some… air," I managed to say, feeling unsteady on my feet. August was looking up at me from his seat, his almost-full cup still in his hands. "It's… stuffy here, I think…" Oh, hell, his hands… they were so large, so rough for someone who didn't do much manual labor; I recalled that the thickness of each calloused finger was enough to make me feel full, and the light dusting of hair on each knuckle lit something deep inside of me. I stared at them for longer than was natural and found my mouth pooling with saliva before I forced myself to turn and exit the clearing. Had I been drugged?

"Be safe!" Amrys called after me. Her voice didn't sound any different.

I was panting when I finally stumbled past Wraith, who cast me a sideways glance as I made my way into the woods. Why there? I just wanted to be away from everyone else... Whatever was going on with me was not something I wanted other people to witness. The forest surrounding the sprite clearing was lush and dense with greenery and moss and just as humid as the clearing, which caused all varieties of brightly blooming plants to populate the area. Even when I found a tree to lean against and catch my breath, my body still felt alight, and all I could think about was—

"Nightshade, there you are."

I jerked my gaze toward a space between two trees where August suddenly stood. Only, it wasn't August... not really. He was wearing an entirely different outfit than the one I had left him in at the shop. Instead of traveling clothes, he wore my favorite outfit of his: a cream-colored knitted sweater, gray slacks, and worn leather boots. His chest hair was just barely peeking over the top of the sweater, the softness of which I could vividly imagine even from afar. I was hallucinating. I'd clearly been drugged. I was trying to shake myself out of it when would-be-August approached, and I found that I didn't have a single ounce of willpower in my entire body. Every inch he drew closer, my body tightened in anticipation, and I willed myself to stay upright to find out what exactly was going to happen in this delirious August dreamland.

"I've missed you so much," he told me. I closed my eyes and savored those words because they identified a truth within me that I'd kept buried for so long. When I opened them again, he'd closed the gap between us and was standing in front of me.

"I've missed you, too," I confessed, fighting back tears. I wiped my face roughly with the back of my hand.

"I won't see you sad," August said, reaching out a rough hand to stroke my cheek. "Especially not on my account."

I pressed my hand over his and turned my face so that I could kiss his palm, which elicited a deep, rumbling growl from him... and just like that, I was done for. I had completely given myself to this hallucination. I told myself then that Amrys did not exist, that I wasn't pulling him away from her in this fantasy, that he didn't say these things or act this way around her…

"I'm so sorry," I told him. Hadn't I been wanting to say that? But it wasn't like me to apologize or to say how I felt at all… at least I could do it here, in the safety and comfort of my own fantasies. "Will you forgive me?"

"That's enough," August said firmly, reminiscent of the tone with which he'd silenced the entire street market months before. His voice caused a chill to course through my body, which was a welcome reprieve from the unrelenting heat that I had been feeling until then. When I didn't meet his gaze, he tilted my chin up, but not with his hand; instead, the hard wooden handle of his cane nudged my face up toward his, and I was rendered speechless. My fingers tangled in the collar of his sweater, and I told myself that Amrys had never seen him in—or out of—it. It was my sweater, just like he was my August, at least for a moment. "No apologies," he told me finally, his molten honey gaze searching mine for something I couldn't quite decipher.

All I managed was a halfhearted "okay."

"That's my girl."

It was a wonder my knees didn't buckle beneath me at his words. Then he was kissing me. He tasted like coffee. Vanilla. Caramel. Blue lavender… and every little memory I had left of his unique flavor. He tasted like… the warmth of a roaring fire, the tenderness of a massage on sore muscles. He tasted like protection and comfort and… I fell into him like I'd been longing to for months. He caught me. "I've got you," he said against my lips before kissing me again, this time more harshly, like he intended to punish me with sensation. When his nimble fingers found the front of my blouse, I let him undo the buttons until my chest was on display. If that was what he wanted, then he could have it. My submission felt like an apology, but it wasn't enough.

I snaked my hands beneath the fabric of his sweater, my sweater, and traced the ridges of his abdomen before I found the edge of his pants. I hesitated there, worried that if I moved too quickly, my time with August would be over. The thought alone sent a spike of panic through my body. Instead, I focused on his belt buckle, the sensation of the smooth metal between my fingers, and the way his pants caught on the heft of his erection even when they were fully undone. I settled on my knees on the soft forest floor, not caring how dirty my clothing got in the process, and pulled his slacks down his legs while looking up at him. He was beautiful from every angle, but from here I admired the mountainous size of his chest, and the peaks of his upper lip. There had been a time when those lips had been mine to kiss alone and that chest had been my nightly pillow. At that moment, I forgot what I'd given it all up for… probably something really, really stupid, like the perceived importance of my identity as a scummy, broke mercenary or my independence, both of which were proving to have very little value.

I pulled my gaze away from his beautiful face only to run my hands down his legs while I nuzzled his cock through the fabric of his boxers. His limbs were strong, thick and furred, and I didn't hesitate as my fingers made their way to the deep, purple scars on his calf. They'd never fully healed, and his gait forever bore the effects of the Umbral attack. I hated that he was in pain, but I loved the scars because they were a trait of *my person.*

"Max, don't—"

I halted my caressing but looked at him with a pleading gaze. "Please?"

"Why would you want to do that?" August scrubbed his face with his fingertips, then ran his hands through his curls as he often did when frustrated.

"It's part of you." When he looked down at me again and dropped his hands to his sides, I sunk down further so that I could trail kisses down his leg, all the way onto each ridged and angry scar. When I worked my way back up, covering as much of his flesh in innocent pecks as I could, I slid my fingers under the fabric of his underwear.

"Ah, Nightshade, what are you doing to me?"

"Loving you," I told him honestly, acknowledging those feelings for the first time aloud. Perhaps this would be the only time I'd ever get to express them. "The only way I know how right now."

When I released him from his clothing, he hissed in defiance. "That's not true, Nightshade," he told me. "What was traveling to the bottom of the Invisible Cliffs if not an act of love? Not to mention—" I cut him off by taking the plush head of his cock between my lips and giving it a firm suck. "Ah, fuck, anything to avoid talking about your real feelings, huh?" He knew me better than I knew myself, I thought, which was surprising given that I was imagining him. I ignored his remark and instead wrapped a hand around his cock, which always felt like it fit perfectly in my palm. He was hard as stone and hot to the touch, and I had missed the way his body jolted at that first contact. I stroked him a little, admiring the softness of his flesh, then dipped my head to nuzzle his balls. He rewarded me with a groan and a dribble of precome that I used to slicken my grip on him.

"Is that so bad?" I asked before running my tongue along the seam of his balls, which tightened in response.

"Ugh, fuck." He let go of his cane, which landed in the brush next to me with a dull thud, and used his newly free hand to pull my hair away from my face. Heat bubbled within me when I realized how intently he was watching me; August was an observer, an appreciator, and didn't often just close his eyes to get lost in feeling. When he didn't reply, I continued my path up the underside of his dick, the head of which matched his shapely lips in shade, before taking him into my mouth. He groaned so loudly I could've sworn the ground beneath us rumbled, and I felt spurred on in my action. "The sight before me is anything but," he said finally before pulling up his sweater to expose his abdomen and chest. "Give me your hand."

I complied, but I would have complied with anything he told me to do. When I offered up my free hand, he pressed it against his belly and dragged it as far up to his chest as I could reach from the ground.

"Hell, Max," August grunted, stroking the back of my hand so lovingly that our interaction almost seemed chaste. "It was torture going this long without you."

I hummed in delight against his flesh, savoring his admission—or the one that my mind had created for him—and closed my eyes as I worked him. I took him far enough into my mouth that I could bury my face in his pubic hair and breathe him in… and each time I adjusted my movements based on his response, his muscles flexed against my hands, and he moaned more deeply. Eventually, he tried to stop me. "Nightshade, that's enough… let me—"

This time I couldn't comply with his request. He wanted to make sure this interaction wasn't just about him, but I needed it to be. It was the only tiny actionable thing I could think to do… I pulled my lips off of him, but didn't stop the steady rhythm of stroking. "No."

"No? Why not?" August's voice was sheer agony now, almost as if it took everything within him not to tip over the edge.

"It's mine." At least in my fantasies.

"What is?" August looked unraveled, his hair a wild mess from his own tugging and his lips parted from panting. He was a work of art.

"Your come," I told him as I pumped him with firm, long strokes. I so desperately wanted to put him back in my mouth, "belongs to me."

"Ah, shit." August groaned, his grip tightening on my hair, before he gave me permission. "You're right, Nightshade. Take what's yours."

When he let me go, I dove for his cock with renewed excitement and took him swiftly into the back of my throat without complaint, using one hand to pump him in unison with my sucking while the other fondled his balls.

"Fuck," he groaned. I could feel his molten gaze on me. "That's it." He reached down to stroke my cheek as I worked for what was mine. "That's my girl. Ah, yessss—" He shifted to grip my hair again instead, not to force me down onto his cock but almost as if he was searching for an anchor to earth. *"Just like that. Drain my balls, Nightshade. Fuck, fuck, fuck!"*

August came in a torrent, nearly drowning me, but I swallowed each drop as if it were a gift before he hoisted me to my feet and kissed me hard. I must've looked surprised because he told me, "You're meant to taste like me," before kissing me again.

"Don't leave me again. Love me like you say you do," August said when he pulled me onto his chest and held me close. But his tone wasn't pleading. Instead it was firm, direct, an instruction. I wanted to comply. I wanted to obey. I held him so tightly I swore nothing—not even my own foolishness—could tear him from my grasp again, but when I opened my eyes to reply, he was gone. I was plunged back into lucidity against my will, and my surroundings shone with bright clarity. Whatever had happened to me, whatever I'd been poisoned with, had run its course, but it had left me filled with longing. I'd be back to this clearing again if it meant that I could see August like that… once Danny was better.

When I wandered back into the clearing, the taste of August's come lingered on my lips. I wiped the corner of my mouth with a finger and licked it clean before anyone else came into sight, then approached the counter with caution. I *needed* to know what I'd ordered, but I wasn't bold enough to approach the sprite at the counter again. I caught sight of a small chalk menu board on the wooden countertop, which read:

<u>The Soulmate Special</u>:

a sweet, smooth latte that takes you on a shared romantic encounter with your one true soulmate.

Notes of vanilla, caramel, and blue lavender.

I swallowed hard and looked around the seating area for our table, which still had Amrys at it. Where had August gone? Shit, I'd ordered him the same thing. I pinched the bridge of my nose and closed my eyes, struggling to steady myself before approaching the group again.

"Is August alright?" I asked when I realized he was nowhere to be found. I guessed that I had inadvertently sent him on some sort of vivid sex dream with Amrys. Great, at least I was bettering their relationship. Had he taken off, too, to have his soulmate hallucination in peace? I shuddered at the thought of him fantasizing about Amrys with the vigor and passion in which I'd thought of him.

"I think so," Amrys mused, setting her empty cup on a tray with ours so it could be returned to the counter. "Seemed like he needed some air, too." She shrugged, then stood to pick up the tray.

I rubbed my face again, certainly feeling awake but also guilty that my own fantasies were delaying our trip. "Sorry… how long was I gone? This place is strange… I feel like I'm losing track of reality."

"Not to worry, it was only a few minutes."

Before I could respond, I spotted August emerging back into the coffee shop area. He was adjusting his belt and hair, both of which looked sufficiently mussed.

---

1. Sprite: a small, faerie-like creature. Sometimes they have giant yabbos.

IT'S JUST A GARDEN

MAX

The Gardens of Wysterum were shockingly close to Dalcester, just over a day's ride, and we felt cautiously optimistic as Amrys tracked landmarks on the map she'd brought along. She was a graceful rider, often riding without looking or without hands, and could use the map while going full-speed on the back of her horse, Merrick. Soon, the terrain turned from city cobblestone and sparse trees to lush greenery, with rolling hills of trees and shrubs that reminded me of some of the paths Wraith, Danny, and I had traveled when we first left Barrien. The air was cool and crisp, and I couldn't help but wonder if our journey was going to lead us through actual flower gardens inhabited by quiet folk and pollinators. I knew better than to believe that wandering thought; in all my years traveling the road, I had never found a place as truly peaceful and innocent as the one I was imagining. Still, the road was clear, the breeze was calm, and the grass was lush and soft. Wraith seemed drawn to it, attempting to graze here and there whenever she spotted a particularly tall patch.

"Focus, Wraith," I muttered to her, steering her back onto the road. "If it seems too good to be true, it probably is."

August raised an eyebrow at this comment and gave Wraith a knowing glance. "I get it. Some things have that pull, girl."

Wraith snorted at him. Were they… agreeing with each other? The king's gaze flicked from my horse's face over to me, where it trailed down my body in a way that I hadn't expected, leaving me feeling flushed. The trip had already gone on too long for my liking. Was I imagining things? Was the look meant for Amrys, who was quite a bit behind me? Not likely, but… I focused my gaze on the road, suddenly feeling the same pull he seemed to be talking about.

As we traveled, I let myself relax a little. It was a garden. Dangerous things didn't happen in gardens… No, flowers grew, people had picnics, bees pollinated plants. All innocent activities. Because it was so beautiful, I decided to hop off of Wraith and walk next to her so that she could have a break from hauling me around.

Magnus soared somewhere overhead. It was still hard to believe the beast soaring above, who was now the size of Wraith when I'd first met her, had once fit in the palm of my hand.

After Amrys had looked at the map for long enough, she joined me and Wraith in our walk, admiring the plants growing on either side of the path. She had planned our trip to the portal down to the minute, and apparently, we had time to kill; the portal didn't open until late at night, and we weren't very far from it.

Much like the clearing in which we'd discovered the coffee stand, the gardens proved to exist in defiance of the natural world; although it was a frigid winter elsewhere, the plants here grew as if they had been soaking up sun and warmth all day. They were bright and full, luscious. I stopped to inspect one closely, wondering what it was that kept them so vibrant, when a small lizard scurried by and caught my eye. It froze in front of me, and I squatted down to get a closer look. Wraith pulled back, yanking the reins from my hand and stepping away from my attempt at discovery when the plant in front of me opened as if it was blooming, then leaned over and devoured the lizard in one bite.

Reptile blood splattered across my face.

The plant righted itself again and returned to its unassuming pose, leaves outstretched.

I wiped my face with my sleeve before standing up myself and looking at Amrys, who had stopped a few steps ahead of me.

"You don't see that every day."

"Let's get a move on," I suggested, the taste of blood lingering on my lips. "I'd hate to see what happens when the plants get a craving for human blood."

Wraith huffed.

"Or worse," I added, turning to her. "Horse. You traitor."

We mounted our horses and decided it might be best to kill some time closer to the portal itself.

"Welcome to the Wyrmhole!" the sign read as we exited the Gardens of Wysterum and approached a massive stone platform overlooking the ocean, the surface of which was getting darker and darker as the sun began to set.

August muttered under his breath, "Who the hell names these places?"

Amrys chuckled to herself. "Wyrm-hole… get it? Because it goes to the Isle of Wyrms." When no one else laughed, she sighed a little and reassured herself, "I think it's funny."

"It opens at midnight," the gatekeeper said, his voice raspy and low. He sat on a rickety chair to the side of the platform, where I assumed the portal would magically appear at the right time. He was tiny and old, maybe as old as my favorite baker in Dalcester, and was bundled in a mountain of blankets and a knitted cap with a pom-pom on top of it. "Only for a few minutes, so you oughta be ready once it does. Otherwise you'll have to wait until tomorrow."

We were about to turn and set up camp for a few hours when he stopped us, rising from his dilapidated chair and pointing his staff, which had been buried in his blanket pile, at my face. He brought it up next to my cheek, pushing my hair away from my ears. "It'll let you through, but there's no telling what they'll do to you on the other side. The only outsiders they allow are elves. No humans, mercenary," he warned me. How the hell did everyone know what I did for a living? Did I have a sign on my forehead? Then he looked at August. "Same for you, pretty boy."

We thanked him for his less than ideal information and pulled aside to figure out a plan of action. "Well, that doesn't help... the only full-blooded elf we have is Amrys, and I don't think it's a good idea for her to go alone," August explained.

"I agree."

Our elven escort piped up. "Hey, don't I get any say in it?"

I rubbed my face with my fingertips, already exhausted by this adventure and unable to focus. "Sure, but... do you have any training with weapons? Or wyrms?"

"Well, no," Amrys admitted.

"Then the only way for all of us to get in is to make sure we *look* like elves. Seems as though that's all the Wyrm... ians? Wyrmites? Wyrm... folks will be looking for."

Amrys looked at me quizzically. "And how do you propose we make that happen? Did you bring some modeling clay with you?"

"Not exactly, and you're not going to like my proposal," I said quickly, rummaging in my pocket for the recipe that Beatrice had begrudgingly scribbled down for me. "I've got steps for a potion here that will temporarily alter our appearances."

"What's it called?" August asked suddenly.

I groaned. "Does it matter?"

August shrugged. "Probably not, but Beatrice always has fun names for these things."

"It's called... *What the Elf?*"

Amrys's eyes widened, and then she let out a laugh that bordered on hysterical.

"See?" August asked, smirking. "Told you, Night—Max." His smirk faded. I wanted him to call me Nightshade. I wished he would. I also wanted to hate Amrys, but damn, she was making it hard.

"Well, go on then, apprentice apothecary," Amrys said finally, still smirking at the name of the potion. I was grateful that Amrys seemed content with giving me space to work on the potion. We had a couple of hours to kill, which was a godsend because I had never attempted to create a potion before, and this one was questionable to say the least. I pulled Wraith over to a patch of grass and let her loose to graze while I unrolled the parchment once more.

"First ingredient," I muttered to myself, rummaging through the saddlebag I had pulled off my horse before freeing her. I pulled out the small vials and pouches of wet and dry ingredients that Beatrice had packed and proceeded to accidentally dump the contents of one of them directly onto the ground. "How does Beatrice do this all day long?" I huffed, picking each piece of phoenix feather up out of the dirt and stuffing it into the tiny vial it had come in. "Oh yeah, she does it in the comfort of her shop, without the imminent threat of death or werewolf brothers looming over her."

When I finally got the hang of what I was doing—or at least didn't keep dropping ingredients instead of placing them into the tiny cauldron I'd purchased from Beatrice—I could see how it might be enjoyable given the right circumstances. I put a few drops of horehound extract from one of the last few vials into my concoction, then looked at the list again:

Flesh of an elf. Can't be hair, that won't do anything.

I pulled the leather cord of elf ears from my pocket and looked down at them, the flesh resting between my fingers. I handled them gently, as if their owners could feel the way I treated them.

"Max," August's voice cut through my internal dialogue in a way only his could. "What are you holding?"

I froze, holding the butchered ears in my hand and unable to look up at him. The mere existence of these trophies had made me sick and sad for so long, and yet, I'd held on to them because I had no idea how to remedy what had been done. Were the elves they belonged to still alive, living in pain and disconnected from their heritage like August was? Or were they buried and gone, still missing parts of themselves even in the afterlife? I swallowed hard, not knowing how to begin to explain my dilemma to August. Time and time again, I broke us... and "us" became more and more separate. Lovers, then acquaintances... Were we enemies around the corner once he realized what I was holding? "Ears..." I said, voice low and remorseful.

"You know," August began, his voice unsteady as he stood above me. I could see his boots and the base of his cane in my periphery. A chill ran through my body; why did I want him, want to be near him, even under circumstances such as this? "Sometime after you left, a soldier returned from Emynor with the body of one of his partners. The story he told the other soldiers about his encounter on the road was... bizarre, to say the least."

"I bet they saw a lot of..." I struggled to find an appropriate descriptor before settling on "interesting things in their travels."

August hummed in agreement. "Yes, interesting. Like a fiery mercenary who killed and butchered his partner once she found out that he'd been keeping elf ears as trophies. Ever heard of something like that?"

I was silent, my throat burning with all of the things I wished I could say. Nothing wanted to come out.

"Why do you think she'd do that, Max?" August crouched in front of me and placed a finger under my chin to tilt it up. I tried to look away, but he wouldn't let me. When our eyes met, he asked me, "Why would you do that?"

"It wasn't right, what they did."

August's voice was even, firm, and he held my jaw in place as he spoke to me. His fingertips were rough against my flesh. "And why was their mistake yours to correct?"

"Because the person I love was hurt in that same way, and I couldn't let those monsters keep walking around like that, proud of what they'd done."

We stayed like that, kneeling in silence, for longer than one might expect. Then August let out a breath as if he couldn't hold it any longer and released me, sighing in frustration. "You can't *say* things like that, Max!" He got to his feet and turned away from me.

"What are you talking about?" I asked, pocketing the ears and standing up as well. "I can't say—you got engaged! Who are you to tell me what I can and cannot say about love?"

August whirled on me, fury in his gaze. It was a quick change from the look I'd seen only moments before. "Don't start with me, Max! I proposed to you, and not only did you reject me, which is… completely your right… but you disappeared! We were making a life together! You were gone for months! And… I followed you for every single one of them to make sure you didn't get your stubborn ass killed!"

I gasped. "You *followed* me?"

"I mean, I had you followed, but I imagine you realized that early on. You can't tell me you didn't see the giant dragon flying overhead everywhere you went!"

I gritted my teeth. "Why would you have me followed?"

August groaned, scrubbing his face with his fingertips as if I was telling him one annoying thing after another. "I just told you. I was trying to make sure you were safe."

I crossed my arms over my chest in defiance. "And if I wasn't? If I got killed, then what was the plan?"

"I don't know, Max." He threw up his hands in frustration.

"Believe me, I spent enough nights thinking about it that I should probably have had a plan in place, but the furthest I'd gotten was making sure Danny was taken care of. Nothing after that would have mattered if you were gone."

"I'd been gone."

"But you were still around. Your heart was still beating. That was enough for me to keep going, okay?"

We stood locked in a stare for longer than I would've imagined. The woods were quiet aside from the pounding of my pulse. Finally, I remembered what he'd initially said, and I felt rage bubble within me yet again. "A life together?" I balked. "I'm not made for royalty, August… not to mention the fact that you've almost been killed multiple times because of me!"

August matched me immediately, his intensity rising as mine did. "Well, I wasn't killed, okay? I can handle myself! How long are you gonna treat me like a spoiled prince? I've kept up with you this whole time!"

"Your leg still hasn't healed! You can't even walk right! I see you grimace every time you look at stairs, August. Or I saw you grimace… Whoever had the idea for the cane and the lift—"

"Amrys," August said plainly.

"Good. She's smart," I told him. "She's good for you."

"Shut up. I'd rather learn to walk without either of my legs than learn to be without you again! I'd rather fucking crawl."

"I've only ever brought you pain, August."

"Don't say my name like that, like you pity me. Don't." The look on his face held none of his jovial lightheartedness, but then again, I hadn't seen that in a long time. Ever since I'd shown back up at the castle, he had looked *different*. Jovial, in a way, around Amrys, which I appreciated, but it felt surface-level, like he was using it to mask his emotional fatigue. "Pain from you is sweeter than pleasure from anyone else. Did you really think I'd scare so easily?" August swallowed hard, as if he needed to catch his breath, and without warning, grabbed my hands. He pulled them up to the sides of his face, where he placed them over the tops of his ears, a spot I'd caressed regularly when we were still together. I had thought I'd never touch them again. "Besides, you've healed me in more ways than one. You've helped me face pain that others inflicted."

I couldn't bring myself to acknowledge his statements. They cut too deep. They were too much, just like he was. He was too much for me, and he deserved someone with the same muchness that he had. "And the royalty thing…"

August growled in irritation, a rumbling emanating from deep in his chest. "You're right. You're a pain in the ass, Max the Menace, and you don't fit seamlessly into my world. But I'd change the world a million times over for you to feel comfortable in it. I don't care where you came from. I just care that you're with me because that's where you belong. What do I have to do to show you that?"

"I…"

"Listen to me. I'm in love with you. I don't know how else to get that into your head. Whatever you want, take it from me… even if it only buys me one last moment with you. It would be worth it. Don't run from me this time." His voice was raspy, pained, as he breathed out his last request. "Please, Max."

"Lovebirds, I hate to interrupt, but the portal is opening soon," Amrys chimed in. "Time to put on your elf costumes."

"She knows?" I gasped, pulling my hands from his ears and looking at Amrys, who had indeed interrupted our moment, even if it was for good reason.

August had the audacity to laugh. "Of course she knows."

Amrys winked. "We really need to go."

I crouched back down next to my makeshift potions station and closed my eyes to steady myself before sliding one of the ear tips into the cauldron. The concoction bubbled, sizzled, and even let out a few crisp pops before it settled into a swirling sage green liquid. We all watched nervously, with very little to reference regarding whether or not I had created the potion correctly; I hadn't given Beatrice enough time to write down anything beyond the recipe itself.

From the distance, the creaky old gatekeeper's voice sounded. *"Ten minutes until the Wyrmhole opens!"*

"Well, no time to dawdle," I declared, pouring the potion messily into two empty vials that had previously held ingredients. "Either this works or we turn into something… ungodly. Beatrice would get a kick out of that, I think." I reached up to hand August one of the vials, actively ignoring his gaze. He made sure that our fingers touched when he retrieved it.

"Bottoms up."

I got to my feet, we clinked the vials unceremoniously, and downed the liquid, which tasted just as grassy as it looked, with haste. It fizzed as it slid down my throat. I suppressed a gag and caught August's gaze just as he grimaced in solidarity. "Sorry, Max, but this tastes pretty awful."

"Yeah, not my best—ow!" I yelped, grabbing my ears as they responded to the potion. They stretched, much like I imagined having your flesh literally pulled in different directions would feel, and my whole body felt tighter for it. I reached up hesitantly to feel for the result and said a silent prayer that the potion hadn't accidentally given me donkey ears. Nope, there they were… perfectly smooth and pointed at the ends. I hesitated before looking back at August; if it had been that uncomfortable for my ears to stretch, I could only imagine the effect of the potion on layers of thick scar tissue.

As if the universe knew how much of a weakness this man was for me, he stood there perfectly composed in the cold moonlight, his restored elf ears peeking through his unkempt chestnut hair. *Well, that's not fair.* We must've stood there in silence, digesting the fact that this was how August was *supposed* to look, for too long because the next thing we knew, a bell was sounding nearby.

"Let's go!" Amrys told us, grabbing my hand to tug me toward our horses in a way that suggested we finally had an understanding between us after so much time of me wanting to hate her but being unable to. How had I even entertained that thought when she had been truly nothing short of a lovely person the entire time?

I turned to follow her, grateful for the interruption. August's admissions, my own, were too much to process in the midst of everything else. But of course he wouldn't let me go so easily. The king caught my arm in a firm hand and pulled me to him to whisper in my ear, "Don't think we're finished here, Nightshade." His voice was low and gravelly, almost threatening, and caused goosebumps to explode across my flesh. "And I like those ears on you."

WHAT THE HELL IS A WYRM?

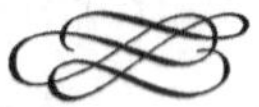

AUGUST

"What *is* a Wyrm anyway?" I asked as we approached the portal, partly out of curiosity and partly as a distraction from what had just happened. I absentmindedly rubbed my new ears.

"Imagine Magnus," Amrys explained, pulling Merrick toward the portal in front of us. "But no legs and no wings."

"Well, that's hardly frightening."

Max cleared her throat with a skeptical laugh. "No legs, no wings, but add fangs, apparently… and they're a lot bigger. More like a massive snake that breathes fire."

"No horses!" the gatekeeper announced as we approached again.

"And why not?" Max argued. Surely she was wondering how we planned to evade giant, fire-breathing snakes without the speed of our horses.

The gatekeeper shrugged, pulling his knitted cap down further on his head. "Can't say why… the portal just… chops 'em up." The air crackled with electricity, and I winced in response to the intrusive noise as well as the image of three horses being turned to mush by a magical portal. Behind the gatekeeper, the noise increased into an all-consuming whirring, and a spinning wheel materialized, moving so quickly it became impossible to identify the individual spokes, eventually looking like a blur of silver.

With time against us, we relented, and Max pulled the horses aside, tying them up at a nearby post made for that exact reason. Then, we paid and loaded up on the platform.

"Nice ears!" the gatekeeper yelled over the whirring noise of the portal. He stood from his uneven chair, then stepped up behind us as we faced the spinning vortex of wizardry. "Hope they last!" he added. "Portal doesn't open up the other way until midnight, either!"

Before anyone could formulate a response, the old man, surprisingly strong for his frail appearance, went down the line and shoved each of us unceremoniously into the portal.

WYRM WRANGLING

MAX

"How long are those supposed to last?" Amrys asked me as soon as we landed. Well, we didn't really land. Instead, we were spit out of the opposing portal like a rejected meal, sent flying into the dirt of what I assumed was the Isle of Wyrms with little landing cushion. August and Amrys skidded across the ground next to me, and I cringed internally at the pain it must've caused them, but told myself to focus. We were here for Danny. I had no way of knowing his current state at home, nor did I have the time to think about it; I had to get the wyrm fang, no matter the cost, and I needed to do so quickly.

"Not sure," I confessed as I stood, reaching to help Amrys up, then August. He refused assistance, so I dusted my clothing off. "But this is what we have to work with. Better get going." In truth, I doubted that the ears would last a full day. Hell, I didn't even know if we had a few hours; I had absolutely no frame of reference at that point.

The Isle of Wyrms was a land made of moonlight. True, we had arrived after sundown, but the impression of the isle was that the sun didn't exist there. Everything was bathed in starlight-speckled darkness, shades of cerulean and sapphire. The buildings were dark, too, aside from the windows which sported their own twinkling lights. I paused to gather my wits and found that I had to squint to adjust to the lack of light. Whatever lived here, wyrms included, must have had immaculate vision.

August popped up by my side, clearly taken aback by our surroundings as well. "Not very welcoming, huh?"

"No, but there's an armorer here that makes the best griffin leather pieces…" I mused aloud. I patted my chest plate, a piece that had been with me for many, many years and showed no sign of the beatings it had endured.

He glanced down toward me, brows knitted in confusion. "How'd you manage to get your hands on armor from all the way over here?"

"I've been here before," I told him with a shrug. "There *might* be a warrant out for my capture." I dropped the comment so casually that it took me a moment to notice August's concerned expression. I couldn't help but laugh. "This is Florian's homeland," I explained. "But the last time we were here, I might've caused a bit of trouble." We didn't have time to talk more about my adventures in the moonlit island because we were soon approached by the Isle of Wyrms welcoming committee—a single, heavily armed soldier who towered over all of us, even August. He was slender, the hands he used to point his weapons at us thin and smooth. Despite the glittering armor the man wore, his broad and angular bone structure was clear, especially in the razor-sharp jawline that peeked out from beneath his helmet. But the biggest identifier was his complexion; his flesh was a light gray that almost glowed in the moonlight, and his stark, white hair looked like it was made of stardust. These were definitely Florian's people. "Halt!" the soldier commanded. "What business do you have in the Isle of Wyrms?"

Amrys put on her most diplomatic smile. "Just visiting!"

"Just visiting with a human? Surely someone who thought to plan a 'visit' to the isle knows enough about it to know that's forbidden. We don't take kindly to humans here."

I didn't risk a glance at my traveling partners, but I knew they were hiding their wide-eyed surprise just like I was. A human? Ah, shit. I reached up the side of my face as if to scratch it and found that my hair was tucked behind my ear, which had returned to its normal shape already. My elf disguise had only lasted me a few minutes. Because the soldier hadn't been looking at August when he spoke, I assumed his ears remained; perhaps something about his own elven blood helped them stick.

Amrys was a pillar of confidence and quick thinking. "Neither do we, clearly," she said. "We're here to dispose of this one. Nothing would please me more than feeding her to a wyrm as punishment for her crimes."

The soldier sneered, his gaze shifting from me to the elven royalty behind me. I felt like a child stuck between bickering parents. "And who, exactly, *are* you?"

Amrys bristled next to me, her annoyance radiating off of her. "Princess Amrys of Emynor." I pictured her standing with her arms folded over her chest.

Most other soldiers would have buckled at the idea of disrespecting their ally's leadership, but this one didn't care. "Who is he?" the soldier asked, pointing his staff at August as if he were also a "prisoner."

Amrys didn't miss a beat. "My guard."

The soldier gave August a once-over, lingering on his cane before turning to address Amrys again. "Your guard uses a cane?" he asked in disbelief.

My hackles raised, and my shoulders tensed, but August's grip on one of them tightened in response as if to temper my rage. "*Stand down, Nightshade.*"

"Yes, he's quite skilled with it, actually. Perhaps we'll give you a demonstration before we leave. However, at this moment, our priority is… disposing of this ingrate."

"You're aware that your prisoner is fully armed, I assume?" His gaze trailed over my body again, assessing the arsenal of weapons I kept on me at all times. I didn't look much like a prisoner. My heart pounded against my chest as I wondered how Amrys would explain this one away, and time continued to slip by, the cure for my brother's ailment seeming less and less reachable by the minute.

Amrys tilted her chin up in defiance. "Of course we're aware! How foolish do you think the ruler of your ally city is? She's been… magically incapacitated, if you must know, and I thank you to cease the incessant questioning before I report you to your own ruler!"

Even under his thick helmet, I could tell that the soldier was rolling his eyes. "Yeah, yeah, don't get your royal garments in a bunch. I take it you remember the way to the Wyrm Pit?"

The princess waved him off as she gestured to August. "This way, *guard*."

Much to my surprise, August grabbed me by the wrist to escort me as if I were his prisoner, and heat coursed through my veins as if we weren't on a life-and-death mission.

"And make sure you strip her of all that armor before you throw her in!" the soldier called after us. "The wyrms can't digest metal!"

"How did you know the way to the Wyrm Pit?" I asked once we were clear of the soldier. I used my free hand to adjust my hair so that it covered my ears. August didn't let go of my other wrist for some time.

"It was a lucky guess. Besides, how hard can it be to find a pit of legless, fire-breathing dragons? The isle isn't that big."

Not much later, we were peering over the edge of a pit into a swarming, slithering pile of wyrms; they looked like giant, poisonous noodles. They came in an array of colors, and their scales shimmered in the bright moonlight.

"Does it have to be a pit?" I asked no one in particular, biding myself some time before I had to face the fact that it was a pit, had to be a pit, and of course the pit was full of poison noodles. "Why can't they put dangerous creatures on the top of a mountain or something? Pits are so hard to get out of." I turned back toward the rest of the group. "You're going to have to lower me down."

"The hell we are!" Amrys argued. "August, tell her she can't go down there!"

August's gaze was pleading, but resigned. He knew better than to argue with me. His knuckles were white as he gripped his cane. "Max, there has to be a better way to go about this."

"Do you have another idea? I'm the only one who knows enough to put up a fight with one of those things, especially if any of the locals see us. If they find a human lowering an elf into there, we're done; they'll kick me over on principle. I need some time to kill one or incapacitate it long enough to get the fang. Then you can pull me back up as soon as I'm done." Knowing the size of the wyrms now, it was clear that a single, well-placed bite could kill me. But if that meant that I'd come up to the surface with a fang embedded in my side, then that would still be one way of getting the job done.

"Max, please don't—"

I looked at August, really looked at him, for a moment. Even with all he'd been through, he had remained a truly good man. While the rest of us had been hardened by our trials, he was kind, gentle, and passionate. I knew then that having the chance to exist beside him, to love him, no matter the outcome, was a gift in and of itself. "I have to… for Danny," I told him. "It's my fault he's hurt. Just promise me that you'll get the fang back to Barrien for him if I don't make it… and take care of my baby brother, okay?"

"Nightshade—"

"I love you, you big idiot," I told him finally. I smiled a little, recalling the first time he'd told me that exact phrase. "Don't worry. You don't need to say it back."

Magnus flew somewhere overhead, almost imperceptible except for the way he temporarily blocked some of the moonlight with his dark body. I left August in his unresponsive stupor and tugged on the rope I had fastened around my waist, then started to back my way down the side of the pit. I probably should've left Amrys with some parting wisdom or gratitude, but there wasn't enough time. Hopefully she knew that I appreciated her more than I had expected to.

The wyrms were loud. Not unicorn or karuga screech loud, but surprisingly loud anyway. They growled and hissed as if I were entering a pit full of feral cats, and some of them leaped toward me as I descended; they were hungry. One even positioned itself directly below me with its mouth open. I halted my descent, completely at a loss for how I was going to get one separated from the group without being ambushed. "Getting it alone isn't even the hard part," I muttered to myself. "How the fuck am I going to pry its mouth open and pull out a fang?" It felt impossible, even for me.

August must've sensed my hesitation somehow. "Max!" he called from above, leaning over the edge of the pit to look down at me. I met his gaze, then followed his cane, which he was using to point down into the pit. "That one."

"What about it?"

"It's moving slower than the others. If you can separate it from the group, it might be an easy target."

I squinted through the dark and realized that something was indeed causing one of the wyrms to move slower. It was smaller, too. As far as I knew, it didn't matter what quality of wyrm the fang came from, so I zeroed in on it. Sorry, slow wyrm. You're mine. "Maybe, if I can figure out how to get the rest away," I thought aloud as I continued my descent. I was close enough now to the group that they were making unsuccessful but dangerously close leaps toward me.

When I found a safe spot to pause, I took inventory of my weaponry: blades might help with taking down my target wyrm, but they'd do nothing to fend off an entire group. Perhaps bringing bows and arrows for August and Amrys would've been helpful, but I had no clue if either could operate them. My belt only had a few potions on it because I hadn't been sure of what to pack; one of them had been a suggestion from Beatrice, however. After unhooking it, I gave it a firm shake, and the bottle began to glow a bright yellow; the wyrms immediately beneath me began to hiss as the light shone on them. "Pocketful of Sunshine[1], indeed," I told myself. They hated sunlight. I wondered how Florian had acclimated away from the isle. I pushed my feet into the side of the pit, effectively projecting me out farther into the group of wyrms as I swung on the rope, then chucked the bottle toward the middle of the swath, as close to the slow wyrm as possible.

As soon as the group scattered, scrambling over each other to escape the explosion of sunshine streaming from the shattered bottle, I loosened my rope so that I could lower to the ground. I hit the dirt with a thud and hurried toward my target with my dagger drawn. It was scrambling, too, but fell over itself and rolled multiple times as it struggled to get away. Because it was so disoriented by the light, its vision seemed useless, and I was able to climb atop its neck much like I had the unicorn. It thrashed and threw me off, sending me skidding across the base of the pit.

"Come on, Max!" Amrys yelled from above. Normally I hated having an audience, but I was so drained that the encouragement was welcome. I got to my feet again, stifling a groan; it felt like I'd scraped half of the skin off my body. My sad, weak wyrm was still struggling, so I got a running start to mount it again before saying a silent apology to it—like I did for all creatures I had to kill—and plunging my dagger into the center of its head. The blast of light was already fading around me when I pried the beast's massive head open and attempted to dig out its fang with my blade. No luck.

"Hurry!" August chimed in.

"The light!" Amrys hollered.

"Shit, shit, shit." I grunted at the effort I was expending to try to wiggle the fang free. It wasn't budging and instead was just drenching me in goopy, smelly wyrm blood. I sheathed the blade and revised my approach. With one hand, I kept the wyrm's mouth open, then leaped toward it to kick the fang out of its socket. It moved! It took several more attempts before the tissue connecting the fang to the creature's skull separated with a sick tearing crunch, and the tooth plopped onto the ground next to its previous owner. Then, the light was gone.

I dove in the dark for the fang, shoving it into my pocket and praying that I wouldn't pierce my own leg with it. The remaining wyrms hissed and barked, but the sound was less of a complaint now and more of a warning. I tugged on the rope, willing my partners to pull me back up as quickly as possible, and started moving for just a moment before something knocked me loose, severing my connection to the rope and sending me back down to the base of the pit.

---

1. Pocketful of Sunshine: a potion that creates a blast of sunshine. Can be used to blind wyrms.

HOW MANY TIMES CAN I LOSE YOU?

AUGUST

*M*ax hit the ground at the base of the pit and once again, I saw my reason for living begin to slip through my fingers.

"Max!" I yelled, hoping that she would stir. I had seen this woman get knocked around and kicked off of every type of creature on the continent, and she *always* got back up. She had to. Max the Menace couldn't be taken down by a herd of wyrms; that wasn't how her story ended - hell, that wasn't how *our* story ended. "Fuck, she's not moving! I need to go down!"

I was already rummaging through Max's extra pack for an additional rope when Amrys came up next to me. I could see her reach out to touch me briefly before stopping herself and telling me, "Stop! If it was difficult for Max, it'll be impossible for one of us. There has to be another way."

I scrubbed my face with my fingertips, willing some Max-level idea to come to me. Anything. Then the moonlight vanished for a brief second once more, and I remembered who had been following us. I cupped a hand around my mouth to magnify my voice, not caring if it drew the attention of the entire isle, before yelling, "Magnus! We need you!"

The creature clocked me immediately, letting out a roar that rattled my teeth in my head before diving down toward us. Somehow he was bigger still than the last time I had stood next to him, which had only been a few days prior. His head came up to my shoulders, and he landed in a way that caused all of our supplies to scatter from the impact of his wings. "Magnus," I addressed him, pulling his massive head toward mine so that our foreheads touched. "I need you to get Max." Magnus chittered, some sort of commentary I hadn't fully learned to translate, but I tried my best to fill in the blanks. "She's down there, in the pit. Pick her up and bring her—"

"Wait, they won't let her back through the portal like that!" Amrys chimed in. I looked from her back to the dragon.

"Bring her to Wraith, okay? We'll meet you there." I thought about the fang in her pocket. "Don't let her drop anything. Go get my girl, okay?"

Magnus made another sound that reminded me of a massive bird, then crawled to the edge overlooking the cliff before diving down. The wyrms were immediately on high alert, and at a distance, it was difficult to tell if they'd see Magnus as one of their own or a threat. As he made his way into the base of the pit, landing his massive body over Max's to protect her, they all began to attack. Magnus hissed, shoving wyrms away from Max left and right until he managed to gingerly grip her in his claws and pull her limp body out of the pit.

We watched the dragon carry her off, and I forgot to breathe until the two were completely out of sight. Magnus had grown at an alarming rate and was stronger than I'd expected, but carrying an adult human—no matter how petite Max was—back to the mainland was no small feat. It was a long trip, even with wings, and he would need to stop and rest. My heart sank at the thought of Magnus fending off predators while he tried to gather enough energy to carry on. Once they were gone, however, there was nothing I could do; Magnus would push forward until his task was complete. I trusted him to do that.

"She'll be okay," Amrys said, finally daring to speak up following the harrowing encounter we'd just faced. The wyrms in the pit below had only just ceased their screeching.

"She has to be," I told the elven princess, unable to look away from the star-speckled sky. "I only just got her back." The continent wouldn't be prepared for the hell I'd unleash if I lost her once and for all.

"Let's go."

"Where?" I asked, finally tearing my gaze away from where Magnus had once been.

"Anywhere. We've got time to kill… the portal doesn't open again until midnight. If we stand here for too long, we'll either be approached by Florian's twin again or you'll get lost in your own head imagining what could go wrong, neither of which we can afford right now."

I grumbled and followed her.

The Isle of Wyrms was pretty, if you could slow down long enough to forget about the soulmate-eating wyrms or the stuck-up night elves. What had first felt like oppressive darkness was actually a deep and multifaceted ocean of blues and purples, all illuminated by glittering starlight. I wanted to appreciate it, but all I could think of was the sight of Max's lifeless body being carried away.

We departed the Wyrm Pit and traveled toward what appeared to be a town square, where several buildings were arranged in a cluster, all shining brightly from the inside. There wasn't a single piece of trash to be seen on the immaculately paved town paths, and the air, filled with the scent of wildflowers, as opposed to that of bodily fluids that graced the streets of Barrien and Dalcester, was fresh and clear. Amrys picked one of the buildings, though none of them had signs that made any sense to us outsiders, and we found ourselves inside of a tavern a few moments later. Did every single town consist of a tavern, a market, and a castle? Sure seemed so. We slid into a table that was just as strangely neat and tidy as the rest of the island.

"Amrys, I'm not really in the mood to drink right—"

"It's a bit early for drinking, don't you think?" A young night elf appeared at the side of our table, notepad in hand. Though her comment might've been lighthearted teasing, the look on her face suggested otherwise; she was scowling, much like the soldier we'd met earlier. It appeared that Florian's attitude was less of a Florian thing and more of a night elf thing.

How did they keep track of time on an island where it was always dark? "Early? I have no fucking clue what ti—"

Amrys kicked me in the shin from under the table, somehow managing to hit my good leg, and cleared her throat. "You're right, it *is* early. Don't mind my friend here. What would you recommend for... this... time... of day?"

Sometime later, we'd been served a meal that resembled nothing I'd ever seen and certainly didn't correlate with a specific time of day in my mind. Amrys picked at it. I pushed it aside immediately. Someone played a harp in a dark corner of the tavern, and the normally calming music made me want to scream; it was maddening to wait there when we didn't know what was happening on the mainland.

"This is torture," I confessed.

"I know, but we need to lie low." She poked the food on her plate again. "Maybe Florian would have been the right elf to bring along."

I scoffed. "Can you imagine?"

Amrys laughed a little. "No, he's exhausting."

W*HEN WE ARRIVED* at the portal, I had lost all sense of time and space. It was still dark. How long had we been there? How long had it taken Max to tackle the wyrm? Much to our surprise, the man on our side of the Wyrmhole was... the same exact man from the side we had entered through. Either that or he had an identical twin with a similar affinity for blankets.

"What can I do for ya?" the portal guard asked. Meanwhile, the elf soldier who had interrogated us earlier was nowhere to be found.

Apparently neither of us had thought to answer the old man, because he asked again, "Well?"

"We need to get back through to the other side. When does the portal open?"

"Oh, any minute now!" the man said cheerfully, twiddling his thumbs over the top of the blanket on his lap.

Amrys and I were full of nervous energy as we stood there, waiting. It was torturous. It seemed the moment of swirling vortex would never come when a voice sounded behind us.

"Halt! You there! Princess of Emynor! Where is the human you brought with you?"

My travel partner cleared her throat and turned around to face the soldier from earlier. "In the Wyrm Pit, of course."

The soldier scowled. "I don't think so. There's a dead wyrm in there... and no body to be found. What have you done? Why are you really here?" He drew his weapon.

The portal guard seemed strangely amused. "Tsk, tsk. You brought a human here? The guard on the other side should've told you that was a bad idea. Oh boy, you're in for it now!"

The whirring of the Wyrmhole suddenly filled the air, the brightness of the spinning tunnel causing the night elf to shield his eyes in shock. "You are not permitted to leave!" he warned. "Cease movement now! You're to be escorted to the royal court of the Isle of Wyrms."

Fully prepared for the legal and war-related ramifications of fleeing the scene of a crime, I grabbed Amrys's hand, tossed the portal guard my last pouch of crystals, and pulled us into the Wyrmhole.

SURROUNDED

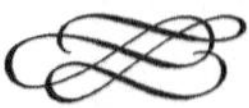

MAX

"Did we get it? Did I get it?" I groaned, my body alight with agonizing pain as I woke. I found myself between August's arms on the front of his saddle. No, *my* saddle; we were riding Wraith. Amrys and Merrick were in front of us. Heckle must've been following in the back. "Did I get the fang?" Wind whipped past us as we rode, and the jostling of Wraith's gait caused my body to ache even more. I let my head loll back against August's chest.

"You got it, Nightshade," he told me, his voice low and deep against my ear. "We're going home. Stay with me."

Then, for the first time in my life, I confessed: "It hurts." A heaving sob wracked my body. This felt like the culmination of all of the abuse I'd put my body and heart through, and I didn't know how much more I could take. We were so close to getting back to Danny, but I hurt. I ached. I wanted to cry and scream and surrender.

August's voice was pained when he responded, "I know. I've got you. Just hold on."

We didn't talk much for the rest of the trip. Amrys and August rode hard, pushing our horses to their limits to get back to Barrien as quickly as possible. It would all be for naught if we didn't make it to Danny in time, and they knew that. I let myself rest against my lover's chest and tried to focus on my breathing, focus on the end in sight. Here and there, August reassured me: "I've got you, baby."

WHEN WE ARRIVED at the castle of Barrien, our home, it was surrounded by chanting cultists who sported torches. You would've thought we were hiding a creature made of reanimated corpse parts in the castle.

"Repent now or you're gonna howl!" the group shouted in unison, most members looking rather proud at what they felt was clever phrasing. The group walked in a circle in front of the building. Meanwhile, Barrien guards held steady against them, blocking the entrance to the castle with an array of weaponry. Magnus's wings beat loudly above us, drawing the attention of the ground. Despite the distraction, they didn't cease their chanting. *"Repent now or you're gonna howl!"*

We approached on horseback, just as we'd left, only this time we were much less energetic and hopeful. Perhaps we'd made it in time, perhaps not. All we knew was that the cure was in my pocket, burning a hole through it, and the clock continued to tick… counting against us. We attempted to break through the crowd, but they stood in our way confidently, ready to be trampled as long as they could get their message across. Normally such a confrontation would've given me a second wind, but my fatigued body was barely hanging on.

"Get back!" August shouted above me, urging Wraith forward. "Step on them, Wraith," he told her.

"There's a werewolf being kept in this castle!"

"Is that the king's secret weapon?"

"Is the king a werewolf? This is punishment for his crimes, his sins against Emynor, against the people of Barrien!"

"Sinners repent! The end is near! The wolves are coming for us, it's your fault!"

In the distance, the lighting of the castle bedrooms flickered in the dark. As we approached the front gate of the castle, I realized just who was guarding the entrance.

"Max!" Sidney cried, immediately rushing to Wraith's side. "What's going on?"

"We need to get in. We need to get to Danny," I told her.

August called out to the guards at the gate, "Thorne, Aldric, let us in! Keep these fools back!"

FANG SOUP

MAX

We slipped into the castle despite the best efforts of the Covenant, who proceeded to bang violently on the castle door once we were inside. They were relentless, and soon, the chanting ceased and was replaced by belligerent accusations and at times, unintelligible shouting. Amrys scaled the staircase while August and I scrambled into the elevator. It was necessary—climbing the stairs was now near impossible for both of us—but the speed of the lift felt like agony, especially with the sounds of chaos unfolding outside of the castle.

Once on the floor of our chambers, I rushed to Danny's room and half expected to find Florian fighting a full-fledged werewolf. Even with the recent explosion in their presence, so little was known about them aside from how the infection spread and how to dispatch them. There were theories, sure, about moonlight and transformation, but none had been fully proven. Before I even reached the door, however, commotion from outside sounded through the windows in the hall.

"Stand down!" one of the Barrien soldiers, whom I'd recently learned was named Aldric, shouted.

When the ruckus continued, the mob clearly not intimidated by weaponry, another voice chimed in.

"Magnus!" Sidney called. The dragon gave a roar in response. *"Let 'er rip, babe!"* Then the windows were alight with an orange glow, and I realized that Magnus had breathed fire at the entire group down below. I had no clue what sort of damage he'd done, but the flames had certainly elicited some yelling from the Covenant.

I turned to August. "We'll need Sidney," I told him. "I don't know what to do with the fang." It was such a wonder we'd gotten that far at all that I clearly hadn't planned much further ahead.

He nodded. "On it."

We parted ways, though I hated to be away from him again, and I forced myself to Danny's room. Florian sat by his bedside dutifully, just like I'd told him to… but they both looked awful. Danny was pale, thinner than the last time I'd seen him, which was saying a lot because he'd always been a scrawny little boy… Despite what I'm sure were the doctor's and attendants' best efforts, his clothing was soaked through with sweat. Callahan hadn't looked quite so bad when we'd caught him pre-transition, but maybe Danny's young body simply couldn't put up the same fight. Florian, meanwhile, looked as though he hadn't left my brother's side since we set out for the Isle of Wyrms. It had only been a couple of days, but for someone who survived solely for himself, I was shocked to see his devotion. I'd have to talk to him about what appeared to be a silver-bladed cleaver sitting on the nightstand, however.

My mouth was dry as I entered the room, unsure of where to begin. Shouting of all sorts echoed through the halls. "Florian," I addressed the elf, leaning at the foot of the bed to keep myself upright. "Thank you. You can go."

I replaced him at Danny's bedside and took his hand, grimacing at the way it felt small and almost lifeless in mine. He was cold and clammy. I used my free hand to place the wyrm fang on his bedside table, then pressed my head to the back of his hand. "I'm so sorry," I told him in the sudden silence of his room. Would this be where my brother died? I thought back to my mother's death, the one I'd painfully witnessed while little baby Danny played cheerfully on the other side of her bedroom door, and realized that I'd seen enough death and loss for anyone's lifetime. It had always felt like I was being punished for a crime—or for my sins, as I'm sure the Covenant would insist—but I'd never been able to deduce what that crime actually was? Was it sheer existence that made me feel like I would be in repentance forever, made me feel like I didn't deserve the good things that attempted to wiggle their way into my life?

As bustling filled the hall behind me, I realized that perhaps I had gotten it all wrong. My eyes snapped open, and I leaned forward to brush a stray onyx hair from my brother's tired face. All along, I had thought that the awful things in my life had been punishment for some unidentifiable wrongdoing, when in reality, all of the help I had along the way, navigating what sometimes felt like a bleak existence, was actually a reward. My friends had banded together—friends that I didn't even know I'd had until recently—to help me: Florian, Amrys, August, Sidney, Beatrice… They'd all rallied, all risked their lives and safety to help me save my brother. August had done nothing but poured all of his love and resources into supporting me, no matter how vehemently I had pushed him away just because I believed I was undeserving. I *had* been given a home, a safe place to call my own, surrounded by people who loved me… all I needed to do was let myself accept that and the gifts that I had been given. I didn't need to suffer or repent. I just needed to exist. It was enough.

"Max!"

I perked up as Sidney and August entered the room. Their presence alone sent a pang of vulnerability through my heart. August stood in the doorway, leaning heavily on the frame, and gave me a reassuring nod.

Sidney's floating bag—still a sight to behold even though I knew what it was—followed in behind her, and she immediately began rummaging through it.

"What do we do? How long before he turns?"

"We're cutting it close, my mercenary darling. We need to make the fang into a liquid… a fang soup, if you will… and get him to drink some of it, all within the next few minutes." She pulled out a mortar and pestle, then shoved them into my hands while she dug around in her bag for vials of ingredients that I had no familiarity with. "Break off the end of the fang and start crushing!"

I did as I was told, removing the fang from the nightstand, and found that it was nearly impossible to snap apart with my bare hands. I searched my body for my weapons, but they were nowhere to be found. "August…" I nearly whined, hurrying over to him by the door. If anything, his hands were stronger than mine, even though we were both fatigued from our journey.

"Got it." Somehow he still found the time to give me a swift wink before grabbing the fang with his hands, which I marveled at even under the pressure of the moment, and snapping the end off for me.

"Thanks."

"Pleasure," he added, then looked to Sidney. "What can I do?"

The witch wasted no time in shoving an empty glass jar into his hand. "Water."

Meanwhile, I ground the fang tip with the mortar and pestle as if someone's life depended on it because, well, it did.

When August returned, his brows were knitted in concern. We hurried to mix the water and a few other ingredients in with the crushed wyrm fang, which unfortunately had only been ground down to a chunky powder, before I attempted to feed it to Danny.

If he wouldn't open his mouth, I had no clue how he would swallow… and of course, he wouldn't open his mouth.

A streak of moonlight shone through the window of Danny's room.

"Come on!" August was by my side in a flash and placed a gentle hand under Danny's chin, tilting it back so that he could open the boy's mouth. His lips were parted just barely enough to tip the end of the mortar into it. I was shaky as I tried, dribbling some of the liquid down his chin.

"Steady, it's okay. Keep going."

I tried. I tried to focus. Danny's chest rumbled with an inhuman sound as I worked to get drop after drop of the liquid into him. The moonlight shifted so that he was directly in the beam and as a result, his body began to writhe in a way that made it look like something was dying to break loose. "Hold him down!" I pleaded.

August and Sidney secured his body, which was suddenly shockingly strong with the power of transformation, and I dropped the soup down his throat as much as I was able. It should've been a moment of relief when I saw his neck move with a swallow, but I couldn't breathe. He thrashed wildly, his skin stretching and straining, and then suddenly went limp.

Panic struck me, and I dropped the mortar. The sound shattered the uncomfortable silence that had filled the room in Danny's stillness. My friends backed away from the bed a little, as if they were already preparing to give me space to process my brother's death. But I stayed glued to his side. I watched closely for the rise and fall of his chest, but when he didn't move, I told myself, "It can't end like this. It doesn't end like this. I'm not being punished. We're home. Danny has a home to enjoy. We have adventures to go on." I turned to August in tearful desperation, and he placed a firm hand on my shoulder in solidarity before I turned back to Danny.

The futile war between Barrien's protectors and the Covenant continued to wage outside as we looked on with bated breath, willing my brother to come alive.

HOME IS A PERSON

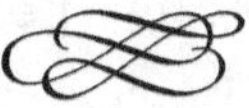

AUGUST

And then there was life again, sudden, like a crack of lightning, and just as jarring. Danny gasped and sputtered, and Max slipped from my grasp to comfort him.

"I'm here, I've got you. It's okay," she told him as she smoothed his hair back away from his sweat-slicked forehead. I stood by silently and swallowed down all of the fears that had been bubbling up in my throat and threatening to burst forward when Danny had stopped moving. He looked around the room with those dark eyes, identical to his sister's, and I was reminded that this boy and his sister were my home.

Max was quick to pour her brother some water and held him gently while she dropped the liquid between his parched lips, then tucked him back in to rest. He was quiet and frail, but the way the bold and bright full moon shone on him with no effect reassured all of us.

Sometime later, Sidney—who had stepped out to give us privacy—reappeared. Meanwhile, I was determined to never leave Max's side. "We need to get rid of these Covenant assholes," Sidney announced. "I don't think they're going to leave without proof that we're not harboring a werewolf…"

I scrubbed my face with my free hand, the other one holding tightly on to Max's. "The fact that everyone in the castle is still alive should be proof enough." I looked from Sidney to Max, who I knew was feeling protective of her baby brother.

"Send them in… I want this all to be over."

"Just one," I told Sidney. "They can pick one person to come in and see that there's nothing dangerous here. Then they need to be on their way, or we'll remove them by force."

"Try it again."

"Max, seriously, we don't need to do this. I'll tell the whole kingdom to fuck off, for all I care. If I had any siblings, I'd pass off ruling to them and be on the road with you full time. You have to know that."

Max the Menace grabbed the sides of my face, stroking the edges of my ears, which had long since gone back to their scarred and butchered state. "Stop that, you big idiot," she told me, a soft smile playing on her lips. "You are a good and just ruler. Barrien needs you; you're making it better each and every day." She pressed her forehead to mine, and I closed my eyes to bask in her presence. Gods, I'd missed her so much. "This is your home… and nothing was stopping it from being mine, too, except for my own fears."

"We can make it the perfect home for you, whatever you need," I told her earnestly when my gaze met hers again.

"It already is."

"Anywhere you go, Nightshade, that's home to me." I released her hands for a moment so that I could undo the cord around my neck and pulled off the engagement ring I'd had made for her.

"You kept it. And my tooth."

I smiled, then used my cane to help lower myself onto one knee in front of her. "Marry me, Nightshade. Marry me and be my home forever."

"Yes."

A COURT OF GARTERS AND POCKET KNIVES

MAX

As soon as winter took its final frigid breath and the hesitant warmth of spring crept into Barrien, we were wed. I found myself grateful for our engagement period because it allowed us to plan not only for the wedding, but for our partnership with Emynor, which had once again been put into question when August announced that he would not be marrying Amrys. The princess was thankfully willing to vouch for his commitment to preserving their newfound alliance. She and I spent ample time together as we devised our plans, and I learned more and more why I'd been so inclined to like her even from the start of our relationship. Our friendship reminded me once again how fortunate I was to be surrounded by so many goodhearted people.

Despite my reserved nature, I agreed to marry on the castle grounds and make the wedding public. In fact, it was my idea. I would've rather been married in an intimate ceremony in the woods or without a formal ceremony at all, but I understood that part of being married to the king of Barrien meant that I had obligations to its people. That day, the grounds were bustling with attendees ranging from other royalty to the common people of Barrien and its surrounding cities. The people needed a union to rely on, so why not let them be part of the creation of ours?

I wore a cream-colored gown with a lengthy train, the fit and brightness of which felt just as foreign to me as my masquerade ball gown had almost two years prior. And August… August was the picture of kingliness as he stood at the altar, dressed in black and silver with a matching cane made especially for the occasion. Magnus, who had nearly doubled in size over the previous months, sat upright on one side of him. Next to the dragon was my kid brother, alive and well aside from a small scar from the werewolf attack, which he showed anyone who would give him a moment's attention. The king was beautiful, as always, and he smiled immediately upon seeing me.

We exchanged vows, August's intense and emotional, mine reserved but deep and honest. August promised to spend the rest of his days exploring the deepest parts of my soul, while I promised to adventure to the ends of the earth with him by my side. And once our union was official, the audience cheered, including all of our friends, some of whom had traveled across the continent to join us. Juniper gave me an approving smile as we passed her on our walk back down the aisle together. Sidney, too, watched with joyful glee; at her side was her own dragon, a reddish beast she'd named Cinder. Beatrice and Morgan had forgiven me for my prior transgressions and arrived to show support. I even spotted Ermaline and her children, as well as a few very busty but well-dressed sprites hovering in the audience. But we didn't run off together and begin our newlywed journey immediately. Once we reached the end of the aisle as a married couple, we turned to address the group, the size of which was staggering.

"Friends, family, loved ones… people of Barrien…" August addressed the crowd, then turned to one side of the aisle, where a group of Emynorian royalty, led by Amrys, had dutifully gathered.

"Our brethren from Emynor. We thank you from the bottom of our hearts for joining us to celebrate this union. The new queen of Barrien, however, has insisted that we also prioritize the union between Barrien and Emynor on this day and would like to present the elves with a gift."

We invited the group to follow us to a clearing on the castle grounds, and once we arrived, Sidney and Cinder joined us at the head of the group. "Sidney, if you please," I said to her, still feeling alien in my new role and my outlandish outfit. Nevertheless, she raised her arms toward the clearing and, after only moments of whispered incantation, tore a hole in the atmosphere, which turned into a swirling, glistening vortex much like the Wyrmhole.

"This," I told the group, steeling my nerves so that I could project my voice across the crowd, "is the Emyrien Portal. It will allow the people of Barrien and Emynor alike to travel between our lands. Our hope is that this will lead to further growth, sharing of resources, and allyship between the two kingdoms. However, as a show of good faith, the portal will be manned by Emynorians on both ends, so that they may determine who can and cannot utilize this passageway."

∽

AFTER THE CEREMONY, we visited Callianthe's grave and left my wedding bouquet there.

∽

"WELL, MY WIFE, QUEEN OF BARRIEN," August addressed me once we were back in our chambers. "Is this," he asked as he took my hand in his, inspecting the wedding ring on my finger, "enough to keep you from running off again?"

I used my free hand to stroke my chin in mock pondering. "Hmmm, I'm not sure. I suppose you could always… tie me up."

August's expression was unreadable when he said, "I could."

"But you won't?" I almost protested. There was something freeing about the idea of being immobilized, about not having to consider what to do.

"I don't think I need to," August told me, running a hand along the side of my neck before pressing a benevolent kiss to my lips. He littered a few more across my cheek before he spoke into my ear, his voice low and gravelly, *"I think I can say, 'on the bed, wife,' and you'll listen. Am I right?"*

I was breathless when I nodded in agreement. "Uh huh."

"And you'll do as you're told, you'll take me however I want you to, because—"

"Because that's how much I love you."

"Mmm." August kissed my neck, suppressing a groan against my flesh. "I'm going to need to hear that a few more times before the night is over, Nightshade."

I would tell him a million times if he wanted.

When August had me on the bed, the flowing fabric of my wedding gown billowing around me, he hiked up the skirt around my waist. His tone switched from that of a ravenous predator to his usual, lighthearted self when he noticed the small blade strapped to my thigh. I hadn't forgotten the details, though; I'd swapped out my leather holster for white lace instead.

"Who brings a knife to a wedding?"

"Your wife."

August smiled and heat spread between my thighs; I was certain he'd always have that effect on me. "Let's put it to good use then, shall we?" All I could muster was an obedient nod. "Good." When he sat upright again, he used the blade to cut my wedding dress straight down the middle, then pulled it apart to expose my bare chest and abdomen. He licked his lips as he raked his gaze over me, then ran the blade ever so lightly between my breasts, down to the waistband of my panties. "These need to go, too, don't you think?"

My voice was barely a whisper. *"Yes."*

Seconds later, my undergarments were in shreds. The king of Barrien spent the rest of the night between my thighs.

BEAST BRIGADE

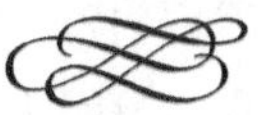

AUGUST

After all that we had been through, I felt a strong connection to those who had supported me and Max in saving Danny's life. With that came a dizzying sadness at the thought of them leaving Barrien; sure, they all had lives to live, paths to follow, but we had become so close that we felt like a family. With the resources that the kingdom had, it was tempting to ask them all to stay, but for what? Just like I couldn't ask Max again to abandon her ways and stay in the castle all day long, I couldn't ask Sidney to live a tame, magic-free life, or Amrys to abandon her need to help Emynor... nor would I have wanted to. I knew that each of them needed to follow their passion, their purpose, just like I did.

We had been discussing the group's plan to disband and go their separate ways, unsure of what that might mean for Amrys, who had offered up her entire life for the sake of peace between the kingdoms, when Florian flounced into the sitting room.

"Emynor calls for aid."

We all turned to him in surprise. "Good evening to you as well," Max addressed him.

"This is no joking matter, little menace."

"Well, spit it out, Florian," Amrys chimed in. "What's happening to my people?"

"Centaurs have crossed the water and are invading the city." Florian flopped a map of the continent down on the drawing table in the room, and we gathered around, watching as he indicated the path of the centaurs. "They're arriving from here," Florian explained, drawing a path with his finger. "And they're ruthless in their attack." I'd never seen one in my life, but in stories they were a vicious beast.

I looked over to Max, who was watching the map intently. I looked at every single member of the group in the sitting room.

"Tell them we're coming," I instructed. The way Max beamed at me was confirmation enough that it was the right decision.

We were about to dive directly into planning when Danny's voice caused us all to look toward the entrance of the room. "I'm coming, too!"

"Like hell you are," Max said immediately, glowering at the boy from across the room.

"Oh, come on," Danny protested. He looked like he was fighting the urge to actually stomp his feet into the floor. "I survived a were-wolf bite. Doesn't that count for somethin'? How am I supposed to relate to my rich classmates now anyhow?"

I scoffed. Max rolled her eyes. Sidney chuckled to herself. Then, Amrys commented, "Better get to work finding some extra-small armor, then."

GLOSSARY OF CREATURES AND POTIONS

CREATURES

KARUGA: a giant, pit-dwelling monster with a mouth that resembles a butthole. It has an affinity for anything living and produces babies through the ends of its tentacles, which contain buds that grow them. The karuga's tentacles also have hooked claws within each sucker.

MICRO/MINIATURE DRAGON: a dragon, but miniature. Comes in a variety of colors. Very fashionable!

SPRITE: a small, faerie-like creature. Sometimes they have giant yabbos.

TOOTH FAERIE: cat-sized spider-like creatures which feast on teeth and are typically drawn into a home by those left under children's pillows. Once they identify a target, however, they won't rest until they have extracted all of their teeth. They make a tinkling sound when they move as a result of all of the teeth inside of them clinking together.

UMBRAL: a giant wolf with two sets of eyes, huge claws and teeth, and toxic saliva. Their saliva is deadly to humans and many other races; elves can recover from an Umbral bite, but the pain of the wound itself is agonizing. Only spotted in the Grimmaker Woods, possibly extinct.

WYRM: basically a dragon, but no wings or legs and giant fangs. They come from the Isle of Wyrms.

POTIONS, ALCOHOL AND OTHER LIQUIDS

BLOOB: blueberry-flavored lube. Made with local blueberries!

HIPPITY HOPS: beer made with frog legs. Causes loud belching that sounds like a frog croaking.

POCKETFUL OF SUNSHINE: a potion that creates a blast of sunshine. Can be used to blind wyrms.

WYSTERUM: sparkling wine from the Wysterum region of the continent.

SAVERS SALVE: general first aid, used for cuts, scrapes, and other minor injuries. Can disinfect serious wounds like an Umbral bite, but cannot heal them.

SOULMATE SPECIAL: a coffee drink made by the sprites of Mounds N' Grounds. Has notes of vanilla, caramel, and blue lavender. It is said to produce a shared daydream between true soulmates.

MISCELLANEOUS

GROIN GOBLINS: slang for pubic lice.

SOUL SPHERE: a tool used by witches that involves splitting one's soul into a glass sphere.

CALCINITE (also known as the NEON SHACKLE): a neon green gem mined from the Invisible Cliffs. It is harmless to most beings, but depletes the magical abilities of elves and for that reason was weaponized by the kingdom of Barrien during their war with Emynor. The gem is no longer mined, sold, or utilized.

ABOUT THE AUTHOR

Francesca Crispo is a fantasy romance author living near Seattle, WA. She received her B.A. in English Literature from Arizona State University in 2016 and her M.Ed. from Arizona State University in 2018. When she isn't writing or running a business full-time, she enjoys spending time with her family and dogs!

facebook.com/francesca.crispo.author

instagram.com/francesca.crispo.author

tiktok.com/@francesca.crispo.author

Rabbit Heart: Book 1 of the Terrafolk Trilogy

Seaborne: Book 2 of the Terrafolk Trilogy

Woman King: Book 3 of the Terrafolk Trilogy

Beholden